"Victori

Sandy Forre
ear, trying to hea ....ppeu ner
bags just inside the hotel room door. She was out of
breath. Traffic leaving Denver was hectic, but she'd
made it in time for the wedding festivities at Eustis
Park's historic Preston Hotel. "Dennis, is that you?"

"Yeah, but Victoria is in danger." He coughed.

"What kind of danger?" Sandy grabbed the
doorjamb to steady herself while her eyes rested on the
pad and pen on the end table next to the bed. Carefully
stepping over her bags, she grabbed the writing tools.
"Did you hear me? What kind of danger?" Her voice
rose an octave.

No answer.

"Dennis, are you all right?"

"No. I need help." His raspy voice was barely
audible.

"Where are you?"

"At the hotel, in the spa. Please come. Warn
Victoria."

"What's wrong?" The line went dead. *What's
going on here? Victoria couldn't have prosecuted the
wrong man. I saw him. I worked that case. That man
was pure evil, but we put him away. How can Victoria
be in danger? From whom? An accomplice?*

Sandy scribbled one word and checked her watch.
2:17 p.m. The rehearsal dinner was at 6:00.

She tried to steady her hands while dialing
Victoria. "You have reached Victoria. Please leave a
message. Beep."

Praise for Karen Van Den Heuvel

"From its chilling first scene to the final resolution, *HIDDEN BLOODLINES* is a story that will linger in readers' memories. Karen Van Den Heuvel has deftly woven historical tidbits into a tale of the struggle between good and evil to create a memorable debut novel, one that left me anxious to read her next book."

~Amanda Cabot, bestselling author

~*~

"Karen Van Den Heuvel has achieved an almost impossible feat—combining faith, suspense, and romance into one seamlessly written novel. With a chilling opening, the story continues at breakneck speed to an ending you never saw coming. Pick up her debut book *HIDDEN BLOODLINES* for a read that you can't put down."

~Jane Choate, author of 34 novels

For Diana,
Thank you!
Karen Van Den Heuvel

Hidden Bloodlines

by

Karen Van Den Heuvel

The J.C. Classified Series

Hidden Bloodlines

Cover Art by *Debbie Taylor*

The Wild Rose Press, Inc.
PO Box 708
Adams Basin, NY 14410-0708
Visit us at www.thewildrosepress.com

Publishing History
First Crimson Rose Edition, 2016
Print ISBN 978-1-5092-0878-4
Digital ISBN 978-1-5092-0879-1

The J.C. Classified Series
Published in the United States of America

Dedication

This book is dedicated to my loving family,
whose support and encouragement kept me going.
I love you!

Chapter 1

"Victoria prosecuted the wrong man."

Sandy Forrester pressed the cell phone closer to her ear, trying to hear the strained voice as she dropped her bags just inside the hotel room door. She was out of breath. Traffic leaving Denver was hectic, but she'd made it in time for the wedding festivities at Eustis Park's historic Preston Hotel. "Dennis, is that you?"

"Yeah, but Victoria is in danger." He coughed.

"What kind of danger?" Sandy grabbed the doorjamb to steady herself while her eyes rested on the pad and pen on the end table next to the bed. Carefully stepping over her bags, she grabbed the writing tools. "Did you hear me? What kind of danger?" Her voice rose an octave.

No answer.

"Dennis, are you all right?"

"No. I need help." His raspy voice was barely audible.

"Where are you?"

"At the hotel, in the spa. Please come. Warn Victoria."

"What's wrong?" The line went dead. *What's going on here? Victoria couldn't have prosecuted the wrong man. I saw him. I worked that case. That man was pure evil, but we put him away. How can Victoria be in danger? From whom? An accomplice?*

Sandy scribbled one word and checked her watch. 2:17 p.m. The rehearsal dinner was at 6:00.

She tried to steady her hands while dialing Victoria. "You have reached Victoria. Please leave a message. Beep."

"It's Sandy. You must be at the bridal tea party. Call me. It's urgent."

I have to get to Dennis. He's not one to cry wolf, and he needs help. But what is wrong with him? He sounds injured, but why contact me? Why not just dial 911? Unless Victoria is in imminent danger...Victoria please call me! Sandy called the front desk. "I believe one of our wedding guests may be hurt at the spa. Can someone meet me there?"

"Absolutely, ma'am. I'll send our wedding coordinator over right away. She's a medic." The voice of the gentleman at the front desk radiated concern.

"Thank you."

Running out the door, she dialed Peter. Voice mail again. "Hey. Was hoping I didn't get your voice mail. I just received a strange call from Dennis. He's at the spa." Sandy paused, contemplating the worst. "And I think he's hurt. Call me as soon as you get this."

Sandy grabbed the purse she'd dropped to the floor and jumped into the elevator she left minutes ago. *I was just admiring this Otis elevator. Now I wish I could get this old thing to move faster.* She dug through her purse hoping to locate her pepper spray while the elevator made its slow descent. She found the spray and let out a sigh of relief. Dennis's call scared her. *Thankfully, I have some protection.*

Remembering that the spa was on the ground floor of the Manor House, adjacent to the main building just on the other side of a courtyard, Sandy turned left out of the elevator. Finger on the trigger, she kept her pepper spray poised to shoot. As she passed the tour office, from the corner of her eye, she saw the historic display case. Something looked wrong, but now was not the time to worry about that. When in town, she always made it a point to stop by to admire it.

Sandy was aware of every sound, the footsteps of people on the floors above her as well as the creaks and other strange sounds familiar to old hotels. She had the feeling that she was being followed.

A quick look around the breezeway confirmed she was alone. Sandy walked through the Dreamer's Coffee Shop glancing in all directions and opened the exterior door. She shivered as the cold gust of air hit her. It was noticeably colder than it had been when she first arrived. The cold front was moving in fast. The fancy jacket she'd worn in anticipation of the rehearsal dinner wouldn't keep her warm no matter how hard she held it together. It was useless in these temperatures. Come to think of it, so were her silk skirt and pumps. How she longed for her down ranch coat and jeans.

Sandy hurried out the door and turned left, trying to limit her time outside in the howling wind. The covered walkway offered little protection. Icy rain combined with snow stung her cheeks, her lashes weighing down her lids with the weight of the mix. As she approached the entrance to the spa, new sounds assailed her—the hissing, clinking, squealing, and shuddering of the boiler room attached to the spa. Far from comforting, the noise did nothing to calm her already frayed nerves.

She peered into the front window, but she saw only

darkness. *This isn't right. What is Dennis doing here, and why is it dark? This is creepy.* Sandy looked around for the woman who was supposed to be meeting her there. *I hope she gets here soon.* She double-checked her pepper spray to make sure it was ready to shoot and patted the outer pocket of her purse for her cell phone. It was there. She took a deep breath and reached for the door handle. Before she had the chance to turn the knob, the door creaked open.

"Dennis?"

No answer.

Stepping forward, Sandy tripped and fell over something large. Arms flailing, she managed to catch herself before her face hit the ground and pushed herself up, standing shakily. She grabbed her phone and pressed a button to shine the light on the object she tripped over. She sucked in her breath.

"Dennis?" She bent over and shook him. Frightened by his failure to respond, she started to punch in 911, but never made it beyond the 9. Someone grabbed her arm so hard she could feel the welts start to rise.

"I wouldn't do that if I were you."

Sandy froze. There was something familiar about the voice. "Who are you?"

Her breath caught as the attacker stabbed her in the arm with a hypodermic needle. The burning sensation spread as the drug surged through her bloodstream.

All her life, Sandy had been the strong one. Abandoned by her mother as a toddler, she rode on the back of her father's horse before she learned to walk. She worked the ranch with her dad and was stronger than most, but it wasn't enough this time. She could not break free. The pepper spray had fallen to the ground and was totally useless. She twisted around but only saw a ski mask. Panic engulfed her.

The drug took effect quickly. She went limp, and as she fell to the floor, she felt like a rag doll on a roller coaster, a helpless, hopeless rag doll.

Unable to move, Sandy watched as the man with the ski mask stepped over Dennis and taped her eyes open with duct tape. *Why is he doing this to me? What is he forcing me to watch? Isn't anyone there to help me? Dennis, wake up! Help me please!* The masked man lifted her seemingly lifeless body; hysteria bubbled up inside her. He carried her into the boiler room where the walls and ceiling were covered in plastic. It reminded her of the time the painter prepared her living room before he sprayed the doors. But there was no paint or any brushes for that matter, so why the plastic, unless…In the center of the room, Sandy noticed a gurney. But this wasn't a hospital. And why was that black tool box sitting on the table next to it? It was like…

Eyes held wide open by duct tape exuded panic. Sandy tried to scream, but the drug made that impossible. She could not move a muscle. Even if she could scream, not a soul would hear her over the deafening noise from the machinery. He had chosen this spot carefully. In that split second, Sandy knew who had drugged her…the Raven.

The man who had killed at least fourteen women. And now she was to be his next victim. She had been given his drug of choice—pancuronium bromide. It paralyzed the body, while leaving the senses fully aware. How could this be happening? Victoria had just successfully prosecuted the Raven. Charles Ramsey was behind bars. Who was this? Sandy's heart sank as she remembered Dennis's call. He said Victoria had prosecuted the wrong man.

Frantic, Sandy started through her mind's case files. *I saw the photos of Ramsey's basement—the "operating" table, black tool box, spattered blood, jars of hearts from countless victims, and plenty of adrenaline and pancuronium bromide for who knows how many more victims. There were witnesses who put him with the victims. Did he have an accomplice?* Sandy's mind raced, but she came up empty. Her thoughts went from the horrors of the case to precious memories of her beloved father. There was no doubt, she'd be with him shortly. *Please, Lord, protect Victoria, give her wisdom, and give me the strength for what is next.*

"I always like my victims to experience the full effect of my work." Out came another hypodermic needle and a large fishing hook. "A little adrenaline should make sure you stay awake." The man hummed as he injected her again, pulled out the needle, and lifted the hook. "This is to make sure you don't swallow your tongue. Don't want any complications, do we?" He pulled her tongue out and secured it to her chin with the hook.

Lord, help me. Dull my pain. Take me into your arms quickly.

"And now for the unveiling. Ta da...." He pulled the mask from his face and grinned.

How can it be? It isn't possible. Not you! Sandy's mind shouted silently. *How many hours did we spend together? Does it add up to days? Weeks? Months?*

How could you! He opened his black metal toolbox and she could hear him hum above the machinery. Her eyes felt so dry. She needed to blink desperately.

Carefully, he laid the tools on the table as he broke into song. Sandy recognized the song. It was his favorite, the theme from *The Titanic*. He had played it so often, she had caught herself more times than she could count, singing it herself. It had gotten to the point where there were times she couldn't get it out of her mind. Now it would be the last song she heard.

He smiled as he turned first with the scissors. She tried desperately to move, to run away, but all she could do was watch helplessly as he cut off her fancy jacket and favorite silk blouse. He continued to sing.

Sandy watched as he placed the scissors into the toolbox and picked up the mini saw from the table. He brought it over to her with that lopsided grin, revved it up, and turned it off.

Sandy had read enough case files to know what was next. Horrified, she realized how much he enjoyed torturing his victims. *I never so much had a glimmer of this man's true character. How could that be after I spent so much time in his presence? His preparations seem almost like an act of worship. How could I not have sensed such evil?*

He put on a full-face dentist's mask and turned on the saw. Sandy screamed silently as he cut her chest open, slowly, precisely.

Chapter 2

Slowly, precisely, Victoria Bailey raised the knife, positioned it over the beautifully decorated cake, and cut the first piece. Others might hack, but she was determined that everything would be perfect today. Her best friend, Elizabeth, deserved no less. After all, it wasn't everyday you had a bridal tea party.

Victoria looked up to see Elizabeth watching her. The bride-to-be smiled at her maid of honor, and turned to look at each of her friends. "I just wanted to thank you ladies for sharing the most important day of my life with a cake and tea."

Victoria grinned. "And you picked my favorite— vanilla cake with chocolate icing."

Elizabeth checked her watch. "That's because this is not just a thank you for sharing my special day, it's also a celebration of the last day of your trial. Ladies, a special news report is supposed to start now." She nodded at the hostess. "Can you please turn it on?"

"Yes, ma'am."

The large screen television came to life.

"We find the defendant, Charles Ramsey, guilty in the first degree for the murders of…"

During the trial, Victoria had carefully avoided watching the television coverage and had been successful, until now. It's not that she thought watching it would jinx her, but it drained her physically, emotionally, and spiritually. Watching the news was not the best way to get replenished. But how was her friend to know? The deed was done.

She gave the television her full attention now, and saw her diminutive frame standing next to her five foot eleven second chair, Sandy. She had never realized how dramatic the visual contrast was between them. The weight of the world seemed to rest on her shoulders; standing, she supported herself with her hands pressed against the prosecution's table. *At least I didn't fiddle with my hair the way I normally do when I'm nervous.*

Victoria turned inward as her mind drifted back to the trial and to Sandy, who was an absolute godsend. Although Sandy worked for Brian's firm and Victoria's partnership officially started upon the trial's conclusion, Sandy was assigned to her as an incentive for Victoria to come aboard. Without her incredible computer genius and organizational skills, the trial wouldn't have gone as smoothly as it did. There's no doubt, she would have won her verdict, but it might have taken longer.

"Victoria." Her attention snapped back to the TV with the cruel pronunciation of her name.

"The Raven will stop at nothing until he owns you—heart, soul, and body. Remember me when you belong to him. I'll see you in hell." Chuck Ramsey's hideous laughter faded as the officer dragged his large, barrel-chested frame from the courtroom.

The drama she earlier experienced pierced her soul. Once again, Victoria felt the fear claw at her stomach while this last vision of Ramsey's flaming red, Einstein-like hair and cruel laughter echoed in her mind. *Regardless of Sandy's fears of an accomplice, there's no doubt in my mind he worked alone.*

"Are you all right? You look pale," Elizabeth asked with raised brows. "Maybe this wasn't one of my better ideas." She caught the hostess's attention and nodded toward the television. "Please turn it off."

Victoria looked at her best friend. "It's okay. I'll be fine. I'm just glad this role as special prosecutor is coming to a close—only the sentencing hearing left." She gave her a forced smile. "Just a little longer. Let's focus on you, not me. This is your weekend."

Elizabeth held her in a comforting embrace. "I'm sorry, my friend. I guess the physical and emotional toll this must have taken on you never occurred to me. I've been watching the news, and you were so amazingly strong and brilliant."

Pulling back, she put on a smile. "Don't worry about it. Let's enjoy this delicious cake before we have to leave for the rehearsal. I know, let's replace Ramsey's hideous laughter with a little music."

"Anything in mind?"

Victoria tapped her chin as she thought. "How about a little Josh Brogan?"

"You got it."

The soothing music filled the air. Victoria was not present emotionally, just physically. The horrors of the trial of such an evil man drained her. The photos were bad enough, but the day she visited the crime scene, her nightmares began. Although she should be joyful, she felt like an interloper listening to the excited chatter of the ladies discussing their version of what life would be like for Elizabeth after she said, "I do."

She gazed out the window. The sun disappeared right before her eyes, and the wind started to pick up. "Ladies, I think we should head over to the chapel for the rehearsal. The weatherman might be right on this one."

Elizabeth took a deep sigh. "Maybe not. We still can hope the front will pass us by without hitting us head on. You never know in the mountains. Ladies, why don't you grab your coats and anything else you may need and let's meet at the chapel. Victoria, why don't you ride with me?"

"You go on ahead. I'll be right behind you." She tried to check her phone for messages, but it was dead. She sighed and shook her head. *I must have forgotten to plug it in with all the commotion. Well, maybe it's for the best.*

****

Victoria pulled into the parking lot of the Chapel on the Rock and glanced at her watch. *Ah, a few minutes to catch my breath.* She stood at the base of the stone steps and let her eyes take in the beauty of the chapel. Its small size and carefully placed stonework gave it such a quaint, welcoming feeling. She could tell that the builders took pride in their work. She remembered Elizabeth's excitement over securing this chapel. The fact that Pope John Paul II and other dignitaries had attended mass there was a bonus. Not exactly the place she would expect her best friend to marry, but beautiful nonetheless. Glancing at her watch, Victoria realized she'd better get going.

She ran up the stairs and rested to catch a deep breath of fresh mountain air. The altitude was rough and the on-again, off-again mixture of rain, sleet, and snow was getting worse. She smoothed her suit, brushing off the wet flakes, and walked through the door into the chapel.

The rustic architecture of the stone interior made her feel as if she stepped back in time. She breathed deeply; vanilla and rose fragrances assailed her senses. A plain altar consisting of a raised stone slab adorned the front of the chapel. Its simplicity was breathtakingly beautiful. Victoria lingered at the door trying to absorb all this little chapel seemed to offer her. She could see why Elizabeth had chosen it.

Victoria made her way up the short aisle to the front, where Elizabeth, Brian, and the rest of the bridal party were waiting.

Elizabeth smiled. "All here but the priest and one groomsman. I hope they'll make it before it gets worse out there."

A gust of wind hit the group as the chapel door opened and they turned. Victoria watched the two men racing in from the cold with their heads tipped down. Both tall, there was something familiar about the way one of them moved. Hair covered in snow and moisture, he brushed at it, looked up, and smiled. "Sorry we're late. Brian, great to see you."

That smile. That voice. It couldn't be. Victoria felt like an observer from another dimension, unable to move, unable even to breathe. It was the man she had hoped she'd never see again.

"You too, David." While they shook hands, David's broad, warm smile met Elizabeth's. "Ah, our beautiful bride." He covered her hand in his. "I'd give you a hug, but I don't want to get you wet." As he dropped her hand, he removed his coat and draped it over the pew.

Elizabeth smiled. "Father David, glad you got here. I'd like to introduce you to the wedding party." She placed her hand on Victoria's back. "My maid of honor, you know."

Victoria's heart raced as the priest turned in her direction and their eyes met. His expression was one of pleasant surprise as he leaned over to give her a warm embrace. She remained stiff, unforgiving. *You think you can treat me as if nothing ever happened! I think not!*

He pulled away, "It's so good to see you. You remember my brother, Christian?"

Her gaze moved to Christian whose broad smile relaxed her stiffened demeanor. Although David was tall, he was even taller, making her tip her head back a little more. He grabbed her hand and held it with a warm firm grip, a little longer than necessary. "Hello, Victoria. Nice seeing you again. It's been a while."

Captured by his eyes, dark pools of green she could easily get lost in, her heart skipped a beat. "Yes. I believe you became a Navy SEAL candidate right after we met, didn't you?" It felt like she was in a time warp. Strange, how a seemingly innocent brief meeting could create such an intense attraction that would be vividly remembered years later. And, just as clearly, she recalled her disappointment when she learned that he joined up with the SEALs.

"That's right. I have my own company now."

She couldn't concentrate on the rehearsal. Her mind was filled with thoughts of two brothers, so similar and yet so different. She hadn't seen David since the day he graduated Notre Dame. He had done it. He'd actually become a priest. And then there was his all too handsome brother. They shared the same chiseled features, dimpled chin, high cheekbones, dark hair. Christian was taller, bulkier with extra muscle.

The eyes were a different color, Christian's emerald to David's blue, but both as penetrating. He took her breath away the first time she met him, but she quickly dismissed it as an aberration since she was in love with David. Seeing him, though, brought back memories as the minutes sped by, and then the rehearsal was over.

Elizabeth looped her arm through Victoria's as they left the chapel. "When Brian told me he'd already asked Father David to marry us, I didn't give it another thought. It's been so long, it never occurred to me that you might care until I saw your face when he came through the chapel door."

Victoria thought back to the night of David's graduation and how eager she'd been to spend the rest of her life with him. That was the night she expected him to pop the question. But the question never escaped his lips. Instead, he told her of his decision to become a priest. After all the time they spent sharing their mutual hopes and dreams, he never mentioned the priesthood, not even once. David was supposed to be her life mate, but he had left her. She smiled, "Of course, but it would have been nice to have a heads-up. You know I've never been into surprises."

Elizabeth walked her friend to the door. "And when was I supposed to give that to you? You were in the midst of the trial when I found out. You aren't upset, are you?"

"Of course not."

"Okay. How about that brother of his? I'd go so far as to consider him eye candy. I never met him until now, but if I had, he would have definitely given Brian a run for his money." She arched her one eyebrow and gave her a half smile. "Well, I need to speak to Father

14

David before we leave. I'll see you back at the Preston for the rehearsal dinner. The banquet hall is called the Gregory Room."

****

Victoria, still unsettled by the brothers' appearance at the rehearsal, used the fifteen-minute drive to the hotel to regroup. The white hotel up on the hill always made her stop and wonder. Its beautiful southern architecture seemed out of place in the Rocky Mountains. Although she had never stayed there before, she was fascinated by its history and was looking forward to the next couple of days. Parking, she went up to room 222 where she would share the first night with Elizabeth before moving to another room.

This was the room where all the dignitaries stayed. She looked around and shrugged. Nothing special as far as she was concerned. Standard size room, king size bed, dresser, desk, chair, and a television mounted in front of the bed. To the right was the bathroom. *Ah, just where I need to go to freshen up.*

This is an original, including the hotel's only bear-clawed tub. There was not even a regular shower, only one of those hand-held ordeals. She would look forward to a relaxing bath after the tough day she just experienced.

Victoria glanced into the mirror above the sink and did a double take. Her pallor gave an almost ghost-like appearance. A little lipstick, a little rouge, a hairbrush, and some spray ought to do the trick. She fussed a bit and gave herself a smile. It was amazing what a bit of makeup could hide.

****

Victoria couldn't believe how calm she was. After

all, the man had broken her heart, and thanks to him, she'd shied away from relationships with other men. Her mind returned to what had once been painful memories, but her heart didn't seem to hurt. Maybe it was because of Christian. She couldn't deny the attraction she felt for him today. Before she moved to the next event, the actual rehearsal dinner, she needed to do something to help settle herself down. The trial certainly hadn't helped. The stress of it was enough to knock anyone's emotional stability for a loop. *Why did my heart flutter when I saw Christian? Is there something there? The presence of both brothers complicates things...it's hard to think clearly, without any emotion...*Victoria sighed.

She stopped in front of the banquet hall Elizabeth had referred to as the Gregory Room for the rehearsal dinner. On each side of the door was a very large portrait. Maybe if she studied them the way her uncle taught her, she'd be able to get her turbulent thoughts under control.

She first studied the one on the left. It was Eli Preston, the man behind the hotel. *He has the same nose shared by the Van der Kruis men. Why did I let my anger about the way David left eat at me for so long? I expected to be filled with hate when I saw him, but I wasn't. And Christian—what were those strange sensations I felt? They weren't new. Does that mean they were wrong because I was with David the first time I felt them?*

Victoria shook her head to clear her thoughts and moved to the portrait on the right side of the door. The stone-faced man in the formal attire of the mid nineteenth century seemed to stare her down. The caption read "The Honorable Windham James, the Fourth Earl of Macraven." *Macraven. Ravens are the farthest thing I want to think about now.*

She closed her eyes tightly, focused on her breathing, and made the decision to take control of her emotions. She could do this. It would be no more difficult than facing a hostile jury. After taking ten slow, even, deep breaths, she opened her eyes. It was time.

Victoria entered the Gregory Room and was once again struck by the beauty of the hotel. This was what she needed—to think about the room, not the man she could never have or the one that might have gotten away. The deep richness of the dark wood held a sharp contrast to the white and pink roses that decorated the room. She took another deep breath, focusing on her sense of smell. What a heartwarming combination of scents. Elizabeth loved roses, so it was no surprise that this room was also filled with them. The smell of roses mixed with the surf and turf emanating from the kitchen reminded Victoria of the time she had spent with Elizabeth's family. This was good. She would think about her best friend and all they had shared, not about…

The harpist played soothing music from some of the great composers. She'd just completed a piece by Bach, and was starting another by Mozart. The atmosphere should have warmed not only the body, but the soul. However, Victoria's soul was met with the unfinished business of years past.

She sighed deeply as Elizabeth came up beside her, looped their arms together, and propelled her to her seat. "I thought you'd enjoy sitting with three handsome men. Father David you definitely know, his brother Christian who you met before, and Brian's best man and law firm partner, Peter Mack, now your new partner."

Since Victoria had not met Peter Mack before the rehearsal, let alone before hiring in, she focused her attention on him. What she saw was a man who visually was the opposite of the Van der Kruis men. Where David and Christian had dark hair, Peter's was ash blond. Peter's eyes were light gray compared to David's dark blue and Christian's emerald green. Peter was of medium height with a wiry build as opposed to David and Christian's tall, lean, but muscular frames. Although you could tell David and Christian were brothers, Christian was a little taller and his muscles more defined. Must be the SEALs training. *Enough! Stop comparing every man you meet with the Van der Kruis men!*

Peter stood and shook Victoria's hand with a gracious smile. "Hello. We didn't really get to speak at the rehearsal. Sorry I missed meeting you earlier while our firm courted you, but I was out of the country on business. I did give you my vote though."

Victoria forced a smile. *Just where I wanted to sit, at a table with David, Christian, and one of the firm's named partners. Great. Even though the bride and groom are across from us, this evening could go from bad to worse…Attitude is everything in a situation like this.* She struggled to put on her best face.

Christian also stood and held out the chair for her. Their legs brushed as she took her seat, the sensation electrifying. A contrast of emotions coursed through her veins. She felt an anticipated excitement and fear of the unknown.

Victoria noticed Elizabeth lean in close to her fiancé and whisper something. They laughed together, and then she hit his arm. Brian winked as he stood.

"We want to thank you all for joining us in celebration of one of the happiest events of our lives. We thought it was appropriate to enjoy the rehearsal dinner in the room named after my great-great-great-great-grandfather. How many 'greats' was that?" He laughed. "I never can keep it straight. Well, anyway, thank you for coming and sharing in this momentous event." The clinking of the glasses started as Brian sat and gave his bride-to-be a kiss with a smile. "I can get used to this. Cheers everyone."

"I saw you on the news," Father David said to Victoria. "Scary stuff. Are all your days that unsettling?"

"No, but let's say I'm rarely bored." She looked at him sideways with a raised brow. "Forgive my confusion on what to call you. Do you prefer Dave, David, or Father?"

"You can call me by whatever name makes you most comfortable."

She nodded and looked down at her hands. "Father David it is then." *That would help me keep my distance and remind me of the choice he'd made.*

Christian leaned over. "I understand you were selected as special prosecutor for the Ramsey case. Will you continue with criminal law?"

Her heart sped up. She knew it wasn't the question, but had to be her close proximity to Christian. "I'll do some, but I'm not sure if it will constitute the bulk of my work at this point. I just joined Brian's firm and one of my areas will be the criminal cases existing clients find themselves embroiled in. I'll also handle high profile class action cases and whatever comes my way."

"Why did you choose criminal law, say over business or family law?"

Victoria looked hard at him, wondering why he was so interested in her career, and she shrugged. "I guess it's because the first job I was offered was as a prosecutor, and it seemed exciting to me. Kind of like the roll of the dice when I look back on it. Law school gives you a general understanding of every area of law without the specifics on how to practice unless you take certain clinics. I kind of landed here." She looked from one brother to the other. With David, she saw a more mature man, with intense deep blue eyes that had seen more than most. On the other hand, Christian's dark green eyes flickered with amusement and something else. What was that something else? What was the source of his amusement? "How did you both meet Brian?"

"In Poland on one of our daily hikes."

"And what were you guys doing in Poland?"

Father David answered. "I was at a retreat and Christian was working on a job-related project. We were able to meet up."

At her other side, Peter cleared his throat. "So, Victoria, I bet you're relieved that the trial is over. Will you take a few deserved days of rest in the mountains?"

Victoria's gaze pulled away from the brothers. "I was planning to stay just till after the champagne breakfast, the day after tomorrow."

"You may want to think about taking a few days. You're allowed, you know." He smiled.

Victoria took a better look at Peter. He smiled easily, revealing perfect white teeth. *Were they natural, or did he whiten them?* "I'm thinking about it, but as I'm sure you're aware, work forever calls."

"You can work too much, you know."

"That's what I've been told."

When the band kicked up with a fast dance, it was a little too loud to continue her conversation with Peter. Victoria watched Elizabeth and Brian open up the dance floor. Someone shouted, "We ought to get this on YouTube!"

Peter turned to her. "I think the best man and maid of honor should join the bride and groom."

"I think you're right."

Gliding to the dance floor, Victoria let herself feel the music as Peter brought her into his lead. She felt eyes on her, flashed Peter a bright smile and said, "You move surprisingly well for such a high-powered attorney."

He spun her. "Look who's talking. Where did you learn to dance?"

"I danced competitively for years before college."

The music ended, Peter bowed over her hand and kissed it. *The last person who kissed my hand was a French statesman.* "Are you this gallant with all the ladies?"

"My mother taught me well." Her hand tucked in his arm, he escorted Victoria back to the table where Christian was standing there with his arm extended, hand open to take hers.

"May I have this dance?"

Smiling, she let him take her into his arms where their movements flowed in unison, fitting together like two parts of a whole. She felt his strength, his resolve, his anticipated interest, and she was flushed with excitement. It was something Victoria could not remember experiencing in a long time. She tilted her head back, gazed into his eyes, and wondered, what now?

****

While Elizabeth danced with Brian, she kept her eyes glued on Victoria and Christian. "Brian, I never gave Victoria a heads-up. Maybe I should have, but when I look at the way she and Christian have reacted to each other, I think surprises might have been what she needed!"

He smiled and leaned his head closer to hers. "I love surprises, both ways, as the recipient and the giver."

Elizabeth giggled. "Yeah, maybe surprises are good even if you think you don't like them."

"Sometimes when you let sleeping dogs lie, you're in for a better surprise."

"Speaking of dogs, your associate Sandy has not only assisted Victoria on the trial, but she's been working hard on my pooch business. I told Victoria under no uncertain terms was Sandy to work through the dinner and party after. Have you seen her?"

He cocked his head. "No, I haven't. I haven't seen Dennis either. I thought they were coming together since neither had a date."

"They were."

He took out his phone. "I'll try her cell phone."

While Brian tried to reach Sandy, Elizabeth saw Victoria make her way over and gave her a raised eyebrow while her foot tapping sped up.

"Elizabeth, you look more like a mother whose kids aren't home by curfew rather than a bride-to-be."

"Sandy's still not here yet. You didn't send her back to the office did you?"

"Absolutely not. I told her to do nothing more than lock up the files and head on up. I expected her here quite a while ago, and I've been watching for her."

Brian hit the "end" button on his phone and then tried Dennis. "There was no answer on either phone, so I just left a voice mail to call me when they got this message and that we were expecting them to relax a little tonight with us."

Elizabeth sighed. "Can you try the office and see if either of them left yet?"

Brian dialed. "Hello, Ruth. Can you tell me if Sandy and Dennis are still there? Okay. Thanks."

With a smile, he answered their unspoken question. "Dennis left yesterday morning, and Sandy left shortly after you did, Victoria. Maybe they decided not to come for whatever reason. They know the schedule."

Elizabeth sighed. "Okay, I'll stop fretting. It's almost like I'm looking for something to worry about."

The ladies returned to their dinner, but Victoria noticed the men went over to the side to talk. Elizabeth looked at Victoria's plate. "Don't you like the steak and lobster?"

She moved the food around her plate. "It's delicious. I'm just not too hungry with the type of week I've had."

Elizabeth swallowed a piece of steak. "I'm glad I can enjoy it." She smiled. "Delicious."

Peter took the mike. "Okay, everyone. It's time for the guys and gals to go their separate ways. After all, it is the night before the big day. Guys can head toward the Billiard Room. Gals, just go next door to the Carson Room. Dessert and entertainment await you."

****

While the guests filed out, Victoria made her way in the opposite direction toward the exterior door. Dinner had been overwhelming. Maybe a little fresh air would help.

She pulled open the door, stepped outside, and was hit by a bitter cold wind. She shivered. The small shelter over the steps kept the worst of the snow away, but she tilted her head up and let the swirling wet snow that fought its way in wash over her face. Perhaps the cold would freeze her emotions and allow her to get through the next couple of days. David had broken her heart once, and she had been careful not to let it happen again. Christian awakened emotions she had long closed off. *Clearly Christian has cracked open the door to my heart and jammed his toe inside. Do I want to let more of him in and risk another broken heart?*

Her respite ended abruptly when she sensed someone close in on her space.

Chapter 3

There was no sound, only a whisper of warm air. She felt his presence before he wrapped his jacket around her. Engulfed in its warmth, the pressure of his hands gave comfort, and his scent took her to another place and time…a warmer, happier time, a time of innocence.

She leaned into him, allowing herself to get caught up in the moment. *Ah Christian, you feel so good, and I am so tired. That trial…*

His fingers lifted her head up, their eyes searching, questioning. He leaned down, and she felt his breath on her face. Closing her eyes, the familiar taste of mint that came with his tender kiss released dormant butterflies in her belly, creating a welcome heat. The sensation shimmered throughout her system before it engulfed her brain in fog. Heart racing, her heart controlled her mind. *I need more, much more.*

Slowly she opened her eyes and pulled back. Her breath caught. "What have I done?"

A grin spread across his face, eyes twinkling. "More than expected, better than imagined."

I need to backpedal. Gain back my control. "It was the cold, the stress of the trial, the unexpected. I didn't intend to kiss you. That thought was farthest from my mind."

"Was it?" Head tipped to the side as he studied her

face, he reached up and gently brushed the hair away from her eyes. "You know that you want me."

Removing his jacket, she shoved it into his chest. "You don't know what I want." She lifted her eyebrow. "Your scent reminded me of David. I don't know how much you know about my relationship with him and how it ended."

"Not much. Why don't you enlighten me?"

"In a nutshell, the night I thought he was proposing, was the night he broke up with me to enter the seminary. Needless to say, what happened with David has made it difficult for me to open my heart again to another."

He took her by the shoulders and searched her eyes. "I'm not David, and it is my intention to prove that to you."

His eyes searched so deeply. *If he could read my mind...* "So why did you come out here? Was it to just take advantage of me?" She smiled.

"Hmmm." He lifted his brow. "First, let's go back to your comment about smelling like David. We were raised on the same soap and we enjoy the same mints." He smiled. "Now, to answer your question, Elizabeth was looking for you."

"Ah, and you just offered to find me?"

"Something like that. It's cold...here." He rewrapped his jacket around her, held it in place with his arm, and walked her back silently into the room, now devoid of all but the servers.

****

The Carson Room resonated with laughter and chatter. Samantha's shrill voice was easily heard above the others. Victoria scoped out the attendees and spotted her Shirley Temple type blond curls bob as she giggled incessantly.

Elizabeth made her way over to Victoria. "There you are. We thought we lost you there for a moment."

Victoria shrugged her shoulders. "I just needed a little fresh air." *And got more than I bargained for.* Nodding in Samantha's direction, she added, "How you've kept this friendship going from childhood is totally beyond me." She shook her head in dismay. "I guess patience is not one of my virtues."

"No, but you have other virtues. Besides, if everyone were like you or me, this world would be a boring place. Samantha adds an innocence that'll always remind us of our youth. That's one of the reasons I asked her to be a bridesmaid."

"Maybe your youth, but not mine."

Approaching their table, Samantha jumped up to greet them. "Hey," she squealed with delight as she pecked the air beside Elizabeth's cheek and then Victoria's. "I gotta ask you something very important, Elizabeth. How in the world did you find such a cute priest? What a waste though." Her brows knit together. She sighed and slowly shook her head. "All these unavailable men leaves slim pickings for us singles."

Victoria caught Elizabeth's glance and rolled her eyes.

As they sat, Victoria looked around the table of bridesmaids, amazed at the unusual group of friends Elizabeth had accumulated. Her gaze settled on Jacqueline, Samantha's polar opposite and another close friend. She had pin-straight chestnut brown hair that barely moved as she nodded in agreement with Samantha. Instead of trendy glasses, she wore tortoiseshell glasses that were a permanent fixture on her face. Victoria fought the urge to do a makeover on her. She had beautiful large green eyes hidden by ugly frames, and with just a little makeup, she knew she could do wonders with Jacqueline's pretty features.

Samantha interrupted her thoughts. "Since you're the maid of honor, Elizabeth wouldn't let us open our gifts until you came." She picked up her gift and pointed to Victoria's. "I see you have two, being the maid of honor and all. Let's open them!"

Victoria watched the ladies open their presents, then picked up the gift wrapped in the same type of box as the others. Slowly she lifted the tape from the edges, removed the paper, and then the top.

Samantha grinned. "I love it! We all have the same Swarovski crystal and sterling bracelets, but different dogs. And look, the color is a reflective clear so it accents whatever clothing we wear! How smart is that! Plus, what a cute reminder of your business."

Victoria lifted the bracelet from the box. "It's beautiful. I have a poodle." She smiled at Elizabeth. "Thank you."

"You're welcome. Why don't you open your other box?"

She always loved to open presents slowly. Carefully she removed the paper and raised the top. "This is exquisite." She lifted up a locket. On the outside was a poodle with sapphire eyes wearing a diamond collar. Inside, was a college photo of the two of them at Notre Dame, the dome in the distance on the left side, and a watch on the right. "I will cherish this."

Elizabeth smiled and winked, "In more ways than one."

Jacqueline, usually the quiet one, had something to say. "Samantha, I was just thinking about what you said about the cute priest decreasing the supply of available men." She shook her head. "All is not lost. Take my date for instance. I met him just last month, and the best part is I didn't even have to make the first move."

That earned her a pop on the arm. "You never make the first move. You just sit quietly and wait."

"Well, this time it paid off." She grinned from ear to ear. "He came up to me and introduced himself." She puffed out her chest with a smile so big it looked like it might crack her face.

Samantha giggled. "That's promising."

"It is, and he's such a gentleman. We talked for a long time and one thing led to another, and I just asked him if he'd like to escort me to your wedding, Elizabeth."

"He's here, so he obviously said yes."

"He said more than yes." Sighing, she continued, "He said he'd love to and didn't even have to check his calendar." She had a far off look in her eyes.

Victoria shook her head gently from side to side and turned inward. The conversation continued as just a buzz in her ear. She had mastered the art of appearing to listen, while delving deep into her own thoughts. It bothered her that she felt so confused and found it quite unsettling that she was so easily comforted, warmed, and stirred by Christian. *Stirring doesn't seem to be the right word. He opened Pandora's box.* She shivered.

Independent for so long, she relied on no one but herself. Ever since David left her, she was bound and determined to depend on no man. She would not let another get close enough to risk another broken heart.

Her mind raced. *What is going on!* A tidal wave of emotions was awakening. She felt a longing she didn't want to feel. She thought she had mastered the ability to control her mind and body. *I can't lose control.* Her fists tightened in her lap.

Elizabeth watched her best friend. "You care to talk?"

"No." Victoria put on her perky face. "It's been a big day all the way around. I just need to catch my breath." She released her hands and rubbed the chill out of her arms. "I'm just regrouping here. Thanks for asking."

"Tell that to the others."

****

The bachelor party was on a roll, and watching from the sidelines with his brother, Christian felt like a fly on the wall. A pool tournament was in progress before the scheduled ghost tour and the guys were having a great time.

Christian leaned on the wall opposite the door to watch and listen. His mind whirled. He hadn't planned to kiss her…although there was no doubt that he wanted to. *Some may think I'm hunting in my brother's pasture, but he made his choice, I'm making mine…No regrets. Besides, there's something between us and I intend to find out exactly what…*

He thought back to the time he first met Victoria at the Hammes Bookstore at Notre Dame. When they had reached for the same book, her smile captured his heart. He asked for her number to meet for coffee. She hesitated in response, then turned him down. He didn't realize who she was at the time, until his brother brought her home to meet the family. *No wonder she turned me down. Although there was no way she knew we were brothers, in her mind she was taken. But when David introduced us, I saw something in her eyes…I couldn't stay.*

The beer loosened up a few lips. Peter just missed getting the choice ball into the hole.

Austin, Elizabeth's carrot-topped, tall, geekish first cousin who was more like a brother than a cousin, said, "Whoa, Peter. Not like you to miss that shot!"

"I'm having trouble keeping my mind on the ball."

"That's totally not like you. You're a master at the art of concentration."

"Yeah, but it's not every day you come face to face with the woman of your dreams." He shot the others a lopsided grin.

"And who might that be?" Austin first wrinkled his brow, than opened his eyes wide. "Don't tell me, Victoria."

Peter opened his arms, cue stick in one hand, chalk in the other. "The one and only."

Austin chalked his cue. "Let me give you a bit of advice. Don't hold your breath, Peter. No man has ever been able to capture her heart. It's made of ice. I was at Notre Dame with Elizabeth and Victoria. They were seniors; I was an incoming freshman. The seniors in my dorm let us all know those two were ice queens."

Brian cleared his throat.

"You know, I mean no disrespect to your lovely bride, Brian. After all, she is my favorite cousin, but they were the killer team. Any guy who got too close risked a broken heart. I have to tell you, I was shocked you won over Elizabeth, but I must say, Victoria was always the more heartless of the two."

Christian watched his brother. Clearly, he was listening intently and pondering. Knowing his brother, the slight changes in his facial expressions made it apparent that he did not like what he heard. Christian knew that Austin's description did not sound like Victoria. She loved life. Her laughter was music that kept on playing. She was not only full of love and life, but her sweet disposition drew people to her like a magnet. His attraction to Victoria never diminished, only now his fate was sealed with that kiss. *Victoria, I don't know who you became, but I still want you as I've never wanted anything in my life. This time, I won't let you go.*

He continued to watch. Peter's comments annoyed him, and his brother's furrowed brows pulled at him. *Ah Victoria, what is your magic?*

Brian rubbed his jaw. "Yeah, well I think the fact that we knew each other when we were children helped open a door, and we just hit it off. The chemistry was right."

Austin hit another in. "You know, this has been such a whirlwind, I never even asked Elizabeth how you two reunited. I know you played together as young children right here at the Preston, but Elizabeth hasn't been up this way in years."

"Peter was instrumental." Brian raised his brow to Peter and grinned. "Weren't you?"

Peter placed his left hand behind him and took a deep bow. "Absolutely."

Brian turned toward Austin. "You already know that Elizabeth was interested in launching a new division of her family's company that focused on pooch products."

"Oh, yeah."

"Well, her research indicated that Colorado was the most dog-friendly state in the country, with owners interested in anything related to dogs. She was referred to our firm and when she called, initially she spoke to Peter."

Peter said, "That's right. But I was the wrong man for the job, while Brian was the firm guru for setting up and launching this type of company. I arranged their first meeting."

Brian nodded. "Before we came face to face, neither of us put two and two together. It had been a while. Then she walked into my office." He got a far away look in his eyes. "It was the same beautiful face but more mature, on a taller, statuesque body. Her complexion was still perfect with those gorgeous, big blue eyes. The child was long gone, and in her place was an incredible woman who took my breath away."

Christian thought of Victoria, beautiful with raven hair and large deep brown eyes that were easy to get lost in. She was still petite with a presence that turned heads when she entered a room. *What would my brother's life have been like if he had chosen a different path with Victoria? I would have no chance, but do I now? I'm only unattached because I lost my heart to Victoria when we met. My heart still belongs to her.*

Brian's voice pulled him back. "She recognized me immediately, but for different reasons. She remembered me as the funny guy who got her in trouble." He scratched his head. "Can't imagine why?"

Austin laughed. "How long did it take you to convince her you'd do right by her?"

"Fortunately, not long. The more time we spent

together getting this new division off the ground, the more time we wanted to spend together. After the division was announced, we decided to do our own celebration and the rest is history."

While waiting his turn to take another shot, Peter asked, "How did Victoria and Elizabeth get so close?"

Christian watched Peter stand with his legs apart and the cue balanced in both hands. *His interest in Victoria bothers me. Is it just jealousy or something more?*

Austin checked out the remaining balls. Clearly, he was on a roll. "They were college roommates, paired together from the first day in the dorm, and still best friends to this day. I didn't mean to come off negative about Victoria. Regardless of her reputation as an ice queen when it comes to men, she's done amazing things. She's a great lady, very professional, brilliant, an incredible attorney."

Peter cleared his throat and shifted his weight to his right leg. "Now you're preaching to the choir. Professionally, I know who she is. After all, she had my vote to join the firm."

Austin asked, "Do you know the extent she's given back to the community? She works tirelessly protecting the rights of victims and helping the underdog."

Christian watched David let out his breath. He had been holding it, but with Austin's last comment, it is obvious that was more like the Victoria they all knew.

Peter nodded his approval. "I know it's extensive. It's one of the reasons they chose her as special prosecutor for the Raven case. It was a political move, what with all the media attention this case has generated." Peter looked at Brian. "In spite of her reputation as ice queen, is she seeing anyone?"

Brian chalked his cue. "Looks like my turn is coming up quick." He shot Peter a smile. "Elizabeth did let me know that Victoria isn't hooked up with anyone now. But you have to tread lightly here. After all, she's joining our firm, and we don't need to make her feel uncomfortable."

Peter shrugged. "I'm a big boy. She's a big girl. I know the rules. I'm sure she does too."

Austin got the eight ball in. "Yes!" He made a fist and pulled his arm down. He turned to Father David. "Father, you and Victoria seemed to know each other."

"Yes. We go way back."

Peter raised his brow and asked, "How far back?"

Father David shrugged. "Notre Dame. Before you got there, Austin."

"What was she like?"

"Well, the Victoria I knew was sweet and loved life."

Austin looked at Brian and smiled. "You're up." Straightening, he glanced at David and moved to let Brian in. "She's a great lady, but I would never describe her as sweet, at least when it comes to men."

Christian saw David finger the rosary ring he wore. "That's all I know."

****

The wind sounded like the rumbling of a roller coaster as the storm intensified; lights flickered and went out. All chatter ceased in that moment, then, the clock chimed twelve times. Back-up generators illuminated the exit signs while candle light released its warm glow.

Victoria pulled her jacket closer together as the

temperature steadily dropped. She felt more like an interloper while Samantha prodded Elizabeth and broke the silence. "We kind of got side-tracked before you told us how you found such a dish for a priest!"

"He was Brian's choice. Brian and Peter had gone to Poland on client business with a couple of their associates. This was before he and I hooked up. Brian stayed a few extra days for a little sightseeing and hiking. While on one of his hikes, he fell into a pit."

Samantha interrupted. "Brian doesn't seem to be the type that'll just fall into a pit."

Elizabeth shrugged. "He did because the pit was hidden by branches."

"Why would someone cover a pit with branches? That's dangerous."

"That it is, and we never did find out why it was there, but anyway, Brian broke his ankle and was stuck. He started calling for help, hoping someone would find him, and someone did."

Samantha, eyes wide, asked, "Father David?"

Victoria's attention snapped back.

"Yes, and his brother, Christian. They had been out on a hike when they heard Brian calling."

Samantha interrupted again. "Hmm. The brother."

"Yes. Fortunately, their backpacks contained a few more supplies than Brian's did, and they pulled him from the pit. Christian had some emergency medical training and temporarily set Brian's ankle. They brought him out of the backcountry and to a doctor. The three of them kept in touch through the years."

Victoria let out her breath. She didn't realize she had been holding it. Typical of the Van der Kruis brothers to be the first to jump in and help someone.

That had always been their way.

Samantha slammed her hand on the table and the others jumped to attention. "Now, how about this brother of his? I saw him at the rehearsal. No doubt he is as gorgeous as Father David is, but in a different way, a little tougher looking. Is he available?"

Victoria smiled to herself and thought of that kiss. *What could have possibly gotten into me? It was as if I had an out of brain experience...No doubt my body was there and responding quite well on its own. If I used my brain, that would have never happened...and I would never have released what I so carefully locked up inside.*

Elizabeth grinned. "He's not a priest, but I don't know anything about his love life, so I don't know if he's available." She had a twinkle in her eye.

"Ooh, now this is getting interesting. Ladies, we may have another hopeful," Samantha announced with a smile. She turned back to Elizabeth. "Tell us more."

"That's about all I know. When I asked Father David about him, he didn't say much."

Victoria had enough. She placed both hands on the table and stood up. "Ladies, it's getting late, and the temperature is steadily dropping so I'm going to turn in. Tomorrow is going to be a big day, and we all need our beauty sleep!"

"I agree," Elizabeth said, grabbing the candle in front of her place setting. "Ladies, don't forget your candles."

Victoria, candle in hand walked out with Elizabeth. When they were out of earshot with the other ladies, Elizabeth stopped. "Sandy never showed."

"I know; I've kept my eyes open for her. Let's see

if she checked in."

They left the Carson Room, and as they approached the Gregory Room, Victoria looked up at the painting of Lord Macraven and hesitated. It appeared as though the portrait winked at her. A chill passed through her body, and goose bumps rose on her skin. She felt colder than during her brief reprieve outside in the snow and wind. Victoria rubbed her arms and made an abrupt turn to the left, catching up with Elizabeth just on the other side of the fireplace and sitting area. She was at the registration desk.

"One of our guests should have checked in by now, but we haven't seen her. I need to know if she made it before the storm. Her name is Sandy Forrester."

The clerk smiled and asked, "Are you having a nice party, Ms. Harrington?"

"Yes, I am, but right now I'm a little concerned over Sandy."

Victoria added, "She should have arrived quite a while ago."

"Let's see. Here we are. She checked in at 2:10. Normally, I could check the room's recorded phone log, but with the electricity out, I don't have access to it. There's a hand written notation where she left word not to disturb her. She's fending off a migraine."

Elizabeth frowned. "That doesn't sound like Sandy."

Victoria nodded, "Yeah, but this has been a very tough week for her so I'm not surprised."

"Okay then. At least I know she made it." Elizabeth turned back to the clerk. "And how about Dennis Ryder? Has he checked in yet?"

"Yes, ma'am. He checked in yesterday."

"Hmm. I wonder why he didn't come to dinner."

Victoria shrugged. "He's a guy, and you mentioned he was escorting Sandy. If she couldn't go, I doubt he would have wanted to go alone. And, being a guy, he was probably happy for the excuse."

"Makes sense."

The clerk smiled. "Ladies, why don't you take these two flashlights? That candle may not be enough, even with the emergency lighting."

Victoria turned her head back toward Lord Macraven. It was too dark to see the portrait, but she still felt the chill.

Elizabeth tipped her head to the right, "Victoria, are you okay?"

The front door blew open.

"That door has just started giving me trouble." The clerk ran out from behind the registration desk and fought it closed. "Sorry, ladies. For some reason, this latch isn't holding. I called maintenance and thought they fixed it." He shook his head.

"No problem," Victoria said. "It just startled us." She looked at Elizabeth. "How about we head up? Tomorrow is a big day."

Chapter 4

The wind howled. Crash! Christian watched Austin jump, and turned toward the window in time to see a large branch thrash against it.

"You okay, Austin?" Father David asked.

He flinched, as if deflecting a punch, his face getting paler by the moment. "Yeah. That's some storm heating up. Is it always like this in March?"

Brian shrugged. "Not always, but you never know what's going to happen in the mountains. There's a saying among the residents of Colorado—if you don't like the weather, wait five minutes."

The lights went out.

"Ooooooooooooo." One of the guys did his best at trying to make ghostly sounds.

Christian wasn't impressed. "Okay, anyone have a flashlight?"

The lights flickered. Christian heard Austin gasp and followed the direction of his shaking finger pointed at the wall.

QUOTH THE RAVEN, "NEVERMORE." appeared in dripping red letters.

"Funny, guys." Brian laughed. "I know this is a bachelor party and all, but how did you anticipate the storm?"

Brian walked toward Father David and stopped short in front of him. "Okay, I might expect this from one of the others, but not you!"

"Excuse me?" Father David asked.

"There are a couple spots of red on your sleeve. What kind of paint did you use?"

"None. I had nothing to do with the writing on the wall. I don't know how it got on me." Frowning, he took out his hanky.

When Christian saw what he was about to do, he caught his wrist. With his lips pressed together, he examined his sleeve. "Don't touch it. We may need to examine it further."

"Fess up, guys!" Brian prodded.

No answer.

Just then, their tour guide showed up in a heavy black dress, with layered white lace petticoats and a lace hat in the style the maids wore in the early nineteen hundreds. Smiling, she said, "Good evening, gentlemen. My name is Renie, and I will be your hostess for this evening's tour."

Christian was intrigued by her appearance, almost luminous in her historic attire. "This is a perfect night for a ghost tour. The Preston Hotel is registered as one of the most haunted hotels in the United States. Let's start on the fourth floor."

Father David rolled up his sleeve. "Guys, this is where I bow out."

Christian nodded. "All right, but when you take off the shirt, preserve the red marks. Put it in the plastic laundry bag in the closet, but don't leave it for pick up."

"Will do."

Renie approached the brothers with a glint in her eye. "Father, I've never had the honor of a priest on the tour. You'd add a special dimension. Won't you reconsider and join us?"

David turned his gaze from Renie to the writing on the wall. "Excuse us, Renie." Christian signaled David with his head to step aside to talk.

"What's on your mind?"

"This is more than a prank. I can feel something sinister, almost like an unseen presence in the room. Do you want me to come?"

"I hear you, but I don't need you there. Go back to your room and pray. If there is something sinister, we can use the prayers."

Renie approached them. "Will you join us, Father?"

"Not tonight. Good night all. Enjoy the tour."

****

David made his way to his fourth floor room using the side staircase closest to it, alert to any sounds or movements.

He saw no one.

The old stairs creaked as he made his way up, taking them two at a time.

Just a few steps from the fourth floor, he felt the hair stand up on the back of his neck. He had the uncomfortable feeling that someone was watching. Stopping at the top of the stairs, he listened for any unusual sounds.

Straining his ears, he heard only the sounds of the storm—the whistling of the wind, tapping of branches against the windows, debris banging against downspouts.

He looked around, saw nothing, but felt a presence. He hoped he wouldn't have to use his special training as an exorcist.

Someone was watching.

"I know you're there. Let's talk."

Nothing.

"Do you need help?"

Nothing.

"My name is Father David. Why don't you come out where I can see you?"

Nothing.

He carefully searched the area.

Nothing.

David pivoted left and walked down the hall to Room 402, his room. He opened his door, stepped over the threshold, and looked around. He was alone.

He heard the floor creak in the hall, stepped back out, and quickly turned around. He saw nothing.

He stood with his head tipped, straining to hear for a sound other than the raging storm.

Nothing.

David turned back and walked into his room. He had to get the shirt off and protect any useful evidence that might be there. Carefully, he unbuttoned the shirt, took it off, placed it in the clean laundry bag, and set it on the floor of the closet for safe keeping.

He needed to spend time with God. After putting on a long-sleeved black T-shirt, he knelt at the foot of his bed, bowed his head over folded hands, and began to pray.

As he touched his forehead, he began, "In the name of the Father…" He touched his heart. "And of the Son…" He touched the left side of his chest. "And of the Holy Spirit…" Then the right. "Amen. You never cease to amaze me, Lord. We think we have it figured out, and we learn we still don't. Thank you for reminding me that only through you, can I find strength. Only through you, can I overcome. Only through you, can I find peace."

A heavy branch crashed against the window. He looked up, and then placed his forehead on his folded hands.

"My yoke is heavy, Lord, but you can make it light. I have a tidal wave of emotions tearing me apart. I never stopped loving her, although I love her with the type of love you have for all your children, an agape love. What happened to her? Am I the reason she became cold toward men? I was so happy to see her, but clearly, she is still angry. She never forgave me. Heal her heart, Lord. Let her find forgiveness so that she can move on in her life."

David started sobbing; pent up tears fell on the bed covers. His shoulders were wracked with deep sobs, the likes of which he hadn't experienced in years.

He wiped his eyes on his sleeve. "Help me help her, Lord. The Victoria of today is not the one I knew. Where is that fun loving girl? What have I done to her?" He took out his hanky and blew his nose. "If I ruined her chance at love, please help me fix it. Please give our breakup closure with peace. Closure so she can move on." He breathed in deep, held his breath, and let it out slowly, shaking. "Lord, I trust in you with all my heart. I cannot lean on my own understanding, for I am just a foolish man. In all my ways, I acknowledge you. Only you can make my path straight. Thank you, Lord."

The floor creaked outside his door.

****

As the group started up the dark staircase one floor at a time, Christian watched Austin squirm and chatter.

44

"You know, guys, I've never been into horror movies for a reason. I like to sleep, and I have to tell you, it's awfully dark and creepy at this hour."

Brian laughed. "Austin, that's the point. We wanted a bachelor party with a twist."

Austin mumbled, "You got one. I suppose you ordered up the storm then?"

"No, but it sure works to give the effect."

"Yeah, well, it's definitely got the effect for me."

One of the guys laughed.

Renie opened the door to the first room. "This is the former ladies' lounge, room 419. I need to tell you the story of Lord Macraven, the ladies' man who haunts this hotel and the fourth floor in particular."

The men filed in, Brian closest to the end table, Christian near the door where he could observe the others. While Renie spoke, Brian, ever the prankster, hit the television controls to turn it on and off. Simultaneously, the wind started up and the closet door opened. The group gasped, and Renie took advantage of the fear that spread throughout the group. Peter, standing next to Brian, laughed. He sidled up to Brian and whispered something in his ear. Brian smiled.

"Let's continue on to room 412, the most haunted room in the hotel." Renie smiled a half smile while her right eyebrow lifted. "This is where the children stayed."

Christian stood off to the side and waited for Brian. "Nice touch."

Brian grinned. "The television was my thing, but I had nothing to do with the closet. I think the wind played into our hands."

Entering the room, a couple of the guys got hit on

the back of the head with balls. "What the…?"

Renie's half smile returned. "Ah yes, the children at play. This was their room after all. Many died here and the balls you feel…well, let's just say they are not to be forgotten."

The wind started getting stronger, the rattling got louder, and it felt as though the floor moved under them. "This floor is not weatherproofed as you all can feel. Please follow me out." Passing through the door, Renie gracefully pointed to the left. "The stairs here on the left go to the bell tower. There have been numerous photographic sightings of a male ghost on these stairs."

A loud crack of thunder made the men jump. The lights went out.

Christian stilled in a fight-ready pose and waited, his senses on heightened alert.

"I'll have the flashlight on in just a minute. No need to be concerned."

The whistling and rattling from the wind continued as Renie's flashlight illuminated the hallway. "Okay, this is just going to make it more interesting. Let's head off to the second floor and take a look at Room 222, one of the most popular rooms to visit, after all." Renie placed the flashlight angled to her own face and smiled an eerie smile. "The ghost of Mrs. Wilcox will keep your clothes nice and tidy."

Austin mumbled. "I'll take my clothes wrinkled, thank you very much."

The group descended a different set of staircases winding their way down two floors. The men stayed close.

Renie stopped outside the door to Room 222. "When this room is occupied, we normally cannot show it." Renie smiled. "We don't like disturbing our guests, but in this case, Ms. Harrington was gracious enough to allow you to enter so that you would not miss out on any portion of the tour."

Renie knocked. When there was no answer, she opened the door with her key. "In the daytime, this room has a beautiful view of the mountains up front and the ridge to the side. Mr. Gregory, this will be your bridal suite tomorrow night."

No response.

"Mr. Gregory?"

Renie placed the flashlight beam on each person's face. "Mr. Gregory, where are you?"

The guys all looked around.

No Brian.

"When was the last time anyone saw Mr. Gregory?"

Mumbling spread throughout the group. "Don't know." But one lone voice said, "I think the fourth floor by the stairs going to the bell tower."

Christian noticed the level of mumbling rise and get more frantic. Trying to calm things down, he said, "Guys, I'm sure there's a reasonable explanation."

Peter added, "Yeah. You know what a prankster he is. By the way, he caused the television to go on and off in that room, and I bet he's pulling another one of his pranks. As a matter of fact, he's probably laughing at us right now."

Austin nodded in agreement. "That sounds like something Brian would do. After all, who but Brian would want a spooky bachelor party to start with?"

Christian doubted Brian would take it that far, but he asked, "Is there a secret passageway around here where he could be hiding?"

Renie ran her tongue over her teeth. "Not to my knowledge, but Mr. Gregory probably knows this hotel even better than I do."

Peter answered. "I think the best thing would be for all of us to go back to our rooms. If Brian is watching us right now, he'll know that's what we're doing. If he's not, he's probably on his way back now. The emergency generators have all the stairs lit. No one will go on the elevator; it's not working anyway without electricity. I'm rooming with Brian, so if he doesn't show up, I'll know about it."

Renie nodded. "I'll retrace our steps."

Christian hesitated while everyone filed out and returned to their rooms. Renie stopped at the door and half smiled. "Don't worry; I'm sure he's fine."

Using the emergency lighting, Christian slowly and cautiously made his way back to the room he shared with his brother. Sensitive to any sounds, movements, and changes, he was on high alert. Christian was always the cautious type, and the SEALs training only served to enhance his awareness.

He stood outside his room and waited. He sensed something.

Chapter 5

The storm shook the windows as the old hotel creaked. Snow-burdened branches banged. The howling was so loud, it was doubtful that the wild animals could sleep.

"Victoria, are you awake? I can't sleep." Elizabeth groaned.

"I can't sleep either." *But not for the same reasons. That kiss…how dare he take that kiss…he had no right…but why did it feel so right?*

Elizabeth sat and propped herself up with her arms behind her. "By the way, the locket I gave you was specially designed with a GPS."

"Ah, part of the 007 collection you started for me."

"Yeah. I feel better knowing you have some protection with what you do."

"I love the stuff you've dreamed up for me."

"Good…I never imagined a whiteout like this in March." She sighed deeply. "This sure puts a kink in my plans."

"I've never known you to let something like a storm put a damper on things." Victoria rolled to her side and supported herself with her arm.

"You think? Remember that storm our first week at Notre Dame…?"

While Elizabeth talked, Victoria's mind wondered back to Christian. His touch, it was electrifying. And that smile, that warm embracing smile that made you feel you were the only one in the world. Those lips…tender, probing, sensing her needs, and responding with a fervor that matched hers, taking her higher. She attended a Van der Kruis family dinner shortly after he left for the SEAL candidate program and remembered a story his mother shared about him as a baby. He needed minor surgery, but it required anesthesia. The doctor told his mother that Christian was the first baby who smiled on his way out, and greeted them with a smile when he woke up. *What happened to that baby? Did active duty change him?* She let out a deep sigh and played with the hair in front of her ear.

"Earth to Victoria! Have you heard anything I've said?"

"Sure. I'm just tired, that's all. Sorry."

"Not to worry. You'll make up for it in this mess. Hey, suppose we can't get to the chapel for the wedding?" Elizabeth moaned and fell back.

"Well, it's a good thing then that everyone you need for the wedding is right here."

Elizabeth rolled onto her side to face her best friend. "You're right. Even Father David is here. By the way, how about that brother of his? He couldn't keep his eyes off you!" She raised her eyebrow questioningly.

Victoria let out another deep sigh and shook her head as she studied her friend. "You are imagining things, my friend. You know I've written off relationships. Guys are all the same—they'll break your heart if you let them. And this one's the brother of the guy that led me to that conclusion, so they share the same genes and that makes him even more suspect!"

"I know that breakup with David left a bad taste in your mouth, but if you let that anger stay pent up inside you, the only one you hurt is yourself. You gotta let it out, and now is as good a time as any. I saw something today when you looked at Christian. At a minimum, it was a twinkle. Tell me I'm wrong."

Victoria studied her friend. *If only she knew...She won't let up. I know her.* "All right then." She pushed herself up, swung her legs off the bed, and stood. The banging of the branch caught Victoria's attention again, and she walked over to the window. Standing straight, she took in a deep breath of air, and let out an ear-piercing scream to the beat of the thrashing branch.

Startled, Elizabeth jumped and fell out of bed. "What was that?"

She smiled innocently. "You said it wasn't healthy to leave things pent up inside. I just let it out."

"That's not exactly what I meant."

Victoria helped her friend up. "This weekend is all about you, not me."

"About that tea today. I'm really sorry my surprise flopped. I guess I missed the earlier news brief, or I wouldn't have turned it on. His threat as they dragged him from the courtroom was not exactly what I expected."

Victoria shrugged. "What's he going to do to me from prison?"

"I don't know. It's still frightening."

"Yeah, but it's cases like these that launched my career. It's rough, though. That's why I'm not surprised Sandy needed downtime. She's great, but not used to working on cases like this."

"Great is an understatement. She's absolutely amazing. I don't know what I would have done without her hard work on my new company."

"Speaking of your new company, I'm proud of you for not just joining your family business; you launched an entire new division in your family's empire. I've been so out of touch with everything but the Raven's case, I forgot to ask. How's the purchase of that new high rise in downtown Denver going?"

"Peter and Dennis, his paralegal, are handling the real estate portion. We thought it would be in the company's best interest if this new division had a physical presence in Colorado. We closed on it this past week. While we're on our honeymoon, the staff will move us in."

"What made you think about pooch products? You've never been excited about pets of any sort, let alone dogs." Victoria plopped back down on the bed and turned over onto her stomach, propping her chin in her hands.

"We wanted to diversify, and my dad laid it on my lap." Imitating her father, she lowered her voice an octave. "'Elizabeth,' he said, 'as the future CEO, I charge you with finding that special niche for diversification.' I wanted a relatively new area that hadn't been oversaturated, and my research confirmed my observations."

"And that would be?"

"People who are passionate about their pets tend to go overboard. They will spend more on their pets than they will on themselves. They will do more for their pets than some will do for their own children."

"I can't even imagine that. How sad."

"Yeah. It is. But it seems to be the state of our country. Just look at the people who go over the top for the environment. They're willing to save a whale, but not a baby. Psychological studies show that most of these people prefer animals to people. And that group is growing."

"I think I read something about that."

"I'm sure you have. I wanted to start with one particular target, and that was dog lovers. Colorado is ranked one of the top states for dog enthusiasts. So my initial focus is on dog products, cute, different, organic, and wholesome, manufactured right here in the U.S. of A., not China."

"Do you even own a dog?" Victoria couldn't resist asking.

"I do now. While I was preparing to pitch my idea to the board, I realized I would probably have more credibility if I owned a dog, and not just any dog. I adopted one from Poodle Rescue."

"Smart. This way you appeal to all dog lovers, and it is a relatively hypoallergenic dog without the mess of shedding. Do you carry a photo like most dog lovers do?"

"Of course. It's on my key chain." Elizabeth grabbed her keys off the end table and thrust it at Victoria. "Have a look."

Victoria pushed herself up to sitting position as she looked at the picture. "Are you sure this is a poodle? It has hairless ears and bright blue eyes!"

"Oh yes, it is a poodle. The breeder dumped him because he has a mutant gene called color mutant alopecia. His color is off, he has hairless ears, and he's missing the thick hair for which poodles are known.

He's going to be our cover dog. He's so different, he's adorable, and no one will be able to snag our brand. He's definitely one of a kind. And the best part is he's smart and potty trained himself."

"Leave it to you to use your business sense even to adopt a dog."

"Enough about what I've been up to. It's your turn. Let's start with men. I hate to say this, but as your best friend…Maybe you can hide things from other people, and maybe even from yourself, but what I witnessed today was a double dose of unfinished business."

"Nonsense."

"Don't give me that. First, I saw you stiffen when Father David hugged you. The anger just below the surface could be as clearly seen as the tropical fish swimming in the Florida Keys. The second dose was your reaction to Christian. I could feel the current between you. As a matter of fact, I might have been electrocuted if I crossed your space! You need to move on from the emotional scars you carry from David, so you can explore new beginnings."

"Please. I have moved on, or haven't you noticed."

"I haven't noticed, because you haven't moved on in that area. Career moves don't count."

"In my book that's all that counts."

"Before Brian, I might have agreed with you, but not now."

"That's only 'cause you're blinded by love, girlfriend."

"Maybe, but I'm proof—the evidence so to speak—that a great guy is worth having. Well, I didn't mean to get all preachy with you, but as my best friend, I want you to have what I have."

Victoria shrugged. "I'm happy enough. I don't need a guy to make me happy."

"Speaking of guys, I wonder how Brian's holding up after his bachelor party." A loud banging on the door interrupted their talk. When the intruder identified himself as Peter, Victoria opened the door. He was standing there, trying to peer into the room.

"What's going on?"

"Is Brian here?"

Karen Van Den Heuvel

Chapter 6

"Why would Brian be here?" Victoria let Peter in. "You should know he's not supposed to see the bride until she walks down the aisle."

"He never returned to our room."

Elizabeth frowned. "How can you not know where he is? You were with him."

"Yes, but he disappeared during the tour. The plan was to play a couple of rounds of pool and then start the ghost tour so that the clock would strike at midnight during the tour."

"Did you finish the tour?" Victoria asked.

"Not quite. As you know, after the tour started, we lost electricity at intervals. The last anyone saw Brian was on the fourth floor. But the lights went out for good then."

"So he never left the fourth floor with you?" Elizabeth asked.

"We're not sure. We didn't realize that Brian was gone until we came here, to your room, and the tour guide addressed him. When there was no answer, we realized he was missing. We're just not sure when he disappeared."

"Peter, you know Brian loves to pull pranks." Elizabeth had her arms crossed. "If your aim is to rattle me to include me in the prank, I'll not have it."

"I'm not trying to rattle you. At first we all thought

56

it was a prank, you know, the groom pulling a fast one on us after we heard all those ghost stories."

"Did anything unusual happen during the tour?" Victoria leaned back on the desk.

"Some strange things did happen, but we thought it was part of the fun. We all returned to our rooms."

"Isn't Brian staying with you?" Elizabeth started her nervous foot tapping.

"Yes, and I expected him to show up any time, but it didn't happen. Now I'm worried. I thought I'd check here first, thinking he was here. I know it's only 2 a.m., but I didn't think I should wait, especially with this terrible storm."

"We haven't seen him since the rehearsal dinner. Elizabeth and I were just chatting. We couldn't sleep with that loud storm."

"We need to find him," Elizabeth interjected. "It could have started as a prank, but with this wind, he could be trapped or hurt somewhere. He knows this hotel really well. His family has been coming since it was built in the early 1900s so he could be anywhere."

"Peter, round up any of the guys who may want to help us search and meet us in the Aspen Room. Elizabeth and I will be right there."

"On it." Pivoting on his heels, he left.

Victoria saw the anxiety etched across Elizabeth's face and gave her a hug. "It'll be okay."

"Are you sure? I know he's a prankster and all that, but there's no way he'd do this to me on the eve of our wedding."

"We'll find him. Let's get going."

They threw their warm-ups on, grabbed their flashlights, and ran down the grand staircase, stopping briefly on the landing between the second floor where they were staying, and the main floor. Snow and branches beat against the large Palladian window. Elizabeth shivered. "It's not letting up. I hope the electricity comes back on shortly. I don't know how long these batteries will last."

After a brief stop at the registration desk, they entered the Aspen Room. Victoria heard the crackle of a fire and felt its warmth. Drawn to the large keystone fireplace, she stood close while taking in her surroundings. The fire's glow illuminated the dark, heavily masculine room and its occupants. She spotted the Van der Kruis brothers immediately.

Peter stood. "Everyone's here from the bachelor party."

"I didn't realize priests attended such events," Victoria said, clenching her left fist.

Father David shrugged and seemed preoccupied.

Peter paced and stopped abruptly, addressing no one in particular. "Can't we call the local authorities?"

Victoria answered, "First, Brian is an adult with the reputation of a prankster. The authorities, even if we could get a hold of them, which I doubt, wouldn't consider him legally missing yet. Second, phones are down, and the storm is interfering with cell phone reception. We need to handle the initial search on our own."

Christian was watching her as she spoke, but he addressed Peter. "I agree." He glanced at the group. "We need keys and someone who can help us backtrack where Brian's been."

Victoria nodded. "I've already asked the front desk to send someone over."

Feeling Christian's eyes bear down on her, she met his gaze until she heard heavy footsteps and the jingle of keys above the wind. A short, plump woman with mouse brown hair appeared at the doorway with a warm smile. Over her black uniform and white apron, her nameplate read *Maggie*. "Someone needs keys and flashlights?"

Christian welcomed her. "That's right, Maggie. We also need a tour guide. We're missing Mr. Gregory and need to retrace our steps through the tour. Our guide's name was Renie. Perhaps she's available to take us?"

"I was the only one around. Don't know where Renie is, but I know all about the ghost tours. I'm the back-up."

"How well do you know this hotel, Maggie?" Victoria asked.

"Quite well, ma'am; you see, I spent many a summer working here."

"Great, Maggie. Would you mind if we borrowed a master key and access card so we can split up to save time? Mr. Gregory could be injured, and the quicker we find him the better."

Maggie's head bobbed up and down. "If Father takes charge of the keys and cards, I won't have a problem with it. They are after all my responsibility."

Father David stepped toward Maggie. "No problem. Since you and Elizabeth are both familiar with the hotel and tour, perhaps you can take Victoria, Christian, and two others with you. I'll need Elizabeth with me and the rest of the guys can help us."

"Fine, Father. May I suggest that your group take the third and fourth floors? We'll take the first two and meet up with you on the ground floor."

"Thank you, Maggie. That's a great plan."

Peter stepped forward. "I've spent quite a bit of time here as well. While you follow the tour, I'd like to check the off-tour places. If this is a prank, Brian may not have followed the tour."

"But I only brought two walkie-talkies that will work during the storm."

"I won't need one. Why don't we meet up on the ground floor in forty-five minutes?"

Christian nodded. "I like that idea."

Maggie gave a walkie-talkie to David and as she was putting the other in her pocket, Victoria held out her hand. "Would you like to hold onto this one, ma'am?"

"If you don't mind, Maggie, I'd appreciate it."

"Sure thing, ma'am." Maggie handed over the other walkie-talkie.

****

Maggie's group started in the Aspen Room. Against the wall was the original mirrored bar cabinet. The room itself had a lot of wood—aspen, pine, cherry, and mahogany. They looked behind anything that would move. "Maggie, are there any secret rooms where Mr. Gregory could be hiding if he were inclined to pull a prank?"

"Not that I know of, ma'am. The hotel has lots of secret tunnels, so I can't guarantee it, especially since this room was for men only in the early years of the hotel. Ladies were not even allowed to step a toe over the threshold."

"I don't think I could have survived at the turn of the century here." Victoria shuddered at the thought.

"Well, ma'am, many a woman did. I'm sure you

60

would have done just fine. Let's check the Billiard Room."

As they walked, Victoria added, "I might have survived, but I would have been a rebel."

Christian grinned. "You definitely would have survived, and I have no doubt you would have been a rebel."

Victoria narrowed her eyes and flipped her hair. "Uh huh, just as I said."

Maggie nodded. "At least this Billiard Room wasn't off limits to ladies. It was a gentleman's recreation room, but women were allowed. They just couldn't play."

Victoria stood at the entrance. "Good thing women have come a long way." She saw the built-in bench along the wall and checked out every inch of the room.

The blood red words, QUOTH THE RAVEN, "NEVERMORE," resonated inside the silent room.

Victoria studied the writing on the wall. "This is a notch above what I would consider a typical prank."

Christian rubbed his jaw line. "Hmm. Brian could have done this as a prank, but I have my doubts."

She walked closer and studied the writing. Chills creeped up her spine as she shivered. "Brian would never go this far. I'm worried about both Brian and Elizabeth at this point. Weddings are stressful when everything goes right, but this…"

"Everything will be all right. I'll make sure of it. I don't know how much you know about what I do, but I specialize in search and rescue. So far I've not lost a soul."

"Good. Let's not make this the first."

Victoria noticed the original balls and sticks

displayed on the wall and walked over to see if there were any traces of the blood red writing, but found nothing.

While rooms were not in use on the other side of the Billiard Room, they inspected those also and found nothing. "The Gregory Room, where you attended the rehearsal dinner is next," Maggie said as she directed her little group out.

They entered a large service room. Victoria liked to take in her surroundings before entering a room, part of her self-defense training, so she hesitated at the entrance. She zeroed in on a rounded stage at one end, with pocket doors that slid into the walls. She looked at Christian who stood next to her mirroring her stance, and spoke to Maggie. "I noticed this stage during dinner. It's where the band played. But has this stage always been a part of the hotel?"

"No, it hasn't been. A movie was filmed in this hotel, and the stage with the pocket doors was built for the time period of the movie. Instead of tearing down the stage, the hotel wanted to keep it. It's very useful for parties, dances, concerts, and of course wedding receptions. There are many ghost stories related to this room, especially stories that happened during New Year's Eve and Halloween."

Victoria reminded the group, "Brian is a Gregory, so if he did pull a prank, he might have returned to this room."

Maggie turned and looked right at Victoria. "That may be part of the problem, ma'am."

"Why would that be a problem?"

"You've never heard the stories?"

"What stories?"

"Well then, this may be important to your investigation. Mr. Alexander Gregory was Eustis Park's first attorney."

"I knew Brian's family had been in Colorado for generations, but I didn't realize he came from a long line of Colorado attorneys. Regardless, I don't see how this would be important to our investigation."

"Yes, ma'am. But Mr. Alexander Gregory made some enemies in his time. Perhaps that's why Master Gregory is now missing."

"Okay then. I'm game, but please be brief."

"Certainly. Let's see. Mr. Alexander Gregory settled here in 1874. He's quite famous for ruining Lord Macraven's plans to buy up thousands of acres in the Eustis Valley. Legend has it that Lord Macraven wanted to turn it into a private hunting preserve for himself and his European friends. This room was named in honor of Mr. Gregory."

"But it's only legend, Maggie."

"Yes, ma'am, but the fact remains that he tried to illegally buy up land and Mr. Gregory stopped him."

"How does this possibly relate?"

"Many stories circulated over the years. One was that Lord Macraven wanted to take revenge on Mr. Gregory, and he haunts the Preston Hotel waiting for the perfect chance. Maybe Lord Macraven's ghost is taking his revenge through your Mr. Gregory."

"That's nonsense, Maggie. Ghosts might be a good marketing tool, but they don't really exist."

"Ma'am, I beg to differ, but I'm just the help. Next we should check out the bar and grill where you had your party for Ms. Harrington, the Carson Room."

****

While Victoria, Christian, and Maggie checked out the first floor, David and Elizabeth were on the fourth. "How about we take a close look at the rooms the ghost tour targeted?" David asked.

"Sounds good. Well, for starters, the fourth floor is considered the most haunted floor, if you believe that stuff. Lord Macraven was a real ladies' man who they say made his money from brothels. Since this is the floor where the nannies resided with the children, as a ladies' man, he supposedly haunts this floor. There are videos and photographs of someone in the window of room 405 by the rail and they claim it's him. In rooms 405 and 419 he grabs breasts." Elizabeth blushed and looked at Father David. He didn't flinch.

"Go on."

Elizabeth cleared her throat. "One lady tried to file a lawsuit against him. Male staff now cleans these rooms. This floor is also not weatherproofed, so in windstorms, the doors rattle, as you have probably figured out by now."

"I suppose it creaks a lot as well?"

"I guess. I haven't thought about the types of sounds you hear."

"That's okay."

"If you can't hear me because of the rattling, let me know and I'll talk louder. As I just mentioned, this floor was for the children and their nannies. Back in the day, children were literally to be seen and not heard."

As they entered Room 419, Elizabeth continued. "Room 419 was the nanny's lounge. The closet door opens, and the latch is broken from the inside out."

They quickly checked the other rooms on their way to room 412. Nothing out of the ordinary.

"Room 412 is supposed to be the most haunted room in the hotel. It was the designated children's playroom. Since they played with balls, some visitors to the hotel claim they were hit with balls as they nodded off to sleep."

"I understand a couple of guys got popped with balls tonight. But why the stories surrounding children?"

"I believe it has something to do with the fact that this hotel had a lot of children die here because of TB. Also, there have been lots of suicides in the hotel." She started wringing her hands. "I hope Brian is all right. I'm really scared."

David gently patted her back. "Trust that we'll find him. Please don't worry."

She started to sob. "The ceremony is only fifteen hours away. Something must be wrong. Brian would *never* do this to me."

He gave her a hug. "Come on. Let's keep at it."

They quickly checked the other rooms. Brian was nowhere to be seen. Before leaving, Elizabeth asked, "Would you mind if we checked on Dennis? He was supposed to be Sandy's date, and we haven't seen either of them yet. Maybe Brian's with him."

"Good idea. Do you know what room he's in?"

"Yeah. Got it from the front desk, 414."

Elizabeth knocked. "Dennis, you in there?"

No answer.

David knocked. "Anyone here?"

No answer.

David used the master key and opened the door. Standing at the entryway, he looked in. "Hm. Dennis's not here now, but he is unpacked." David walked over to the bathroom. "His toiletry kit is open." He turned toward the desk. "His laptop is set up."

"Why would someone leave their laptop out where it could be easily seen?"

"Don't know. Maybe he's with Sandy. If he is, Victoria will find him. Let's check out the third floor."

While they moved onto the third floor, Elizabeth said, "I didn't realize Brian never gave you a heads-up about Victoria."

David stopped and looked at Elizabeth sideways. "Why would he? I don't think he even knew Victoria and I knew each other, let alone dated."

"Good point." She sighed. "Brian, my Brian, where are you?"

The third floor had those guests who made it in before the storm. Elizabeth said, "It may be rude, but I think we should disturb them."

"Agreed. Let's knock and see how they're doing. It'll give us a chance to see who's here, and whether Brian or Dennis is visiting."

David turned to the other two men helping them search. "It'll go faster if you two check out that wing, and we'll check this one. Let's meet on the ground floor."

****

Victoria and Maggie walked up to the second floor with their group. Christian brought up the rear while Maggie continued with a little ghost history.

"Room 222, the wedding suite for Miss Harrington and Mr. Gregory, is haunted by Mrs. Wilcox. She was the chief chambermaid in 1911. On the day the hotel opened for the season, the hydroelectric plant went down. By the way, this hotel was the first hotel to have

66

electricity. Mrs. Wilcox was lighting the gas lamps when she was almost killed. Acetylene was pumped into the rooms, and in room 222, there happened to be a gas leak. When Mrs. Wilcox went into the bathroom, it blew out the front of the hotel. She was blown through the floor into the Gregory Room and survived."

Victoria sighed. "That's pretty amazing, but I'm more interested in what may be relevant to finding Brian."

"Right, ma'am. Perhaps I can quickly finish in case it is relevant. I'm not one to make that decision."

"All right then."

"Thank you. Almost forty years to the day, she died of a heart attack in that room. Mrs. Wilcox's ghost continues on here in this room. She'll even fold and put away your clothes. By the way, four presidents have stayed in this here room."

Victoria smiled. "Maybe Mrs. Wilcox will pick up after me. By the way, Maggie, you're doing a great job. You sound just like a tour guide."

Maggie beamed.

Victoria was having a hard time concentrating on ghost stories that she thought were nonsensical, but she also knew that there might be a clue to finding Brian within them, especially since he went missing during the tour.

"Let's hope we find Mr. Gregory in time for him and Miss Harrington to make use of that bridal suite, shall we?"

"Yes, ma'am."

"Maggie, there's someone I need to see in room 205. I'd like to go there next."

"Okay. We can meet the others at the main stairs."

"Christian, you coming?"

"You go on ahead. I'll be right behind you."

Victoria cocked an eyebrow. Christian nodded.

Maggie led the way. "Just follow me."

They arrived in front of room 205 and knocked.

No answer.

Victoria called through the door, "Sandy, is everything all right?"

No answer.

"Sandy, can you hear me?"

Victoria looked at Maggie. "Please let me in. I don't have a good feeling about this." She turned to see Christian right behind her.

She was the first inside. The bed had no evidence of anyone sleeping in it. Victoria walked over to the side and noticed the hotel pad had one word written on it in Sandy's handwriting. Picking it up, she studied the one word, then tore off the sheet and as she was putting it in her pocket, Christian stopped her.

"Do you mind?"

She handed it to him and after examining it, he returned it. "I'll just keep it in my pocket for safe keeping."

Victoria radioed David. "We just finished the second floor. No, Brian, but I'm in Sandy's room and she's not here either. Her suitcase is here, but unpacked. She left a note on the hotel pad though."

David hit the speak button. "Ten-four. We checked out Dennis's room, and he's not there either. Wonder if they're together. What did the note say?"

"Just one word, *spa*. When I was with Elizabeth, we checked with the front desk, and they told us she left word that she had a migraine."

"Do you think she might have gone to the spa to get it worked out or something?"

"I don't think spas are known as treatment facilities for migraines. And based on my time with Sandy, she didn't seem the spa type. Why would she write that one word?"

"I don't know. Elizabeth is not in earshot. Want me to ask her?"

"No. I don't want to further worry her until we know more. Let's meet at the ground floor in a few."

"Ten-four."

Victoria dropped the walkie-talkie into her pocket.

They met at the base of the stairs on the ground floor. It was dark, with only beams from the flashlights cutting through the blackness. Peter was there already.

Victoria shivered. "This floor is eerie, even though the ghost stories seem to be upstairs."

David, Elizabeth, and the others arrived in time to hear Maggie's response.

"Not necessarily so," Maggie said. "This is the floor with the fifty-foot tunnel dug out by a pickaxe."

Victoria asked, "Can we check out the spa?"

"I don't know if we can get there, ma'am. It's right bad out there now. If there's another way to the spa, I don't know it. Would you like to check out this floor?"

"If we can't get to the spa, we'd better."

"Are we ready?" Christian asked.

Victoria tilted her head toward the tunnel. "As ready as we'll ever be."

Maggie led the way with her high beam flashlight. "Oh my! Oh my!"

"What is it, Maggie?"

"Look!"

Christian and Victoria were the first to get close, followed by David and Elizabeth. Christian crouched down. "It's an antique hunting knife with blood on the blade and a Rockies baseball cap like the one Brian wore in the Billiard Room."

Elizabeth stepped closer. "That's Brian's hat, no doubt. See the heart at the back? I put it there." Cupping her mouth, she shouted, "Brian!"

"Brian, Brian, Brian…" the tunnel echoed in return.

Chapter 7

"No one touch a thing," Victoria told the group. "There may be fingerprints or other pieces of evidence the police will need."

"Let's back out of this tunnel," Father David added as he calmly directed the others out. "Kindly wait at the base of the stairs. I'll be right back."

David, Christian, and Victoria were the only ones left in the tunnel. "There's something disturbing about this place. And I'm not one to have those feelings." Victoria let her eyes take in the closed area.

Father David concurred. "I definitely sense a presence here."

Christian added, "Let's see if there's a blood trail or just this knife."

"That's what I've been looking for, but I don't see anything." Victoria slowly moved her flashlight in a back and forth motion and paused on something dark. "Wait. Are these black scuff marks?" She hunched down to take a closer look directing her flashlight to the darker spots, careful not to disturb the area.

Christian squatted down next to Victoria. "Looks like it, but I don't see any blood." He felt unsettled. Was it his closeness to Victoria, or something else?

Victoria felt a chill go through her body and moved away to inspect further inside the tunnel. She could no longer stand straight up along the sides. "There appears to be an outcropping in the tunnel over here. And there's more blood."

Christian made his way over in a crouched position. "This is pretty cramped, but I see the blood. I wonder if it's Brian's."

"No way to know without access to the CSI lab." Victoria pulled up the turtleneck she threw on earlier closer to her chin and closed the sweatshirt jacket she wore. The hairs on her arms stood on end.

"I have to agree. We need to try to find Brian. If this is his blood, then we know he's injured or worse." He looked back to David, "You okay, bro?"

"Yeah. Just can't shake this sense of foreboding."

Christian turned back to the task at hand and carefully felt the stone walls looking for something, anything.

Victoria shined her flashlight further down the tunnel. "The exit to the tunnel is about fifty feet ahead. Let's check out the rest of the tunnel."

The scampering of feet sent her into Christian's arms. "What was that?" *No doubt, in his arms I feel safe and secure.*

"Probably a little mouse. Not to worry." He smiled and held her tight.

"Sorry, I didn't mean to throw myself at you. If there are two things I cannot tolerate, it's rodents and snakes. Ugh." She shivered as she extricated herself from his arms.

"I gathered as much. Feel free to throw yourself at me any time." Again, he grinned.

"Okay. We better hustle."

Peter called in from the opening of the tunnel. "Any luck yet?"

"We haven't found Brian, but we need to examine the rest of the tunnel. Keep everyone calm," David answered.

Christian led the way. "The exit is supposed to be right up here." He felt along the walls while Victoria beamed the light. "It appears to be blocked off. That's strange. Didn't Maggie tell us before we entered that it would be open?"

Victoria wrinkled her brow. "She did. It's supposed to be open for safety reasons. This is a regular stopping point of the ghost tour. That's why she brought us here in the first place."

"Well, it's not open. Shine the light over the entire area. I want to see if anything unusual strikes us." Christian closely inspected the area, following the pattern of light. "There's something shiny caught in a crack where the door closes."

Victoria reached inside her pocket. "Wait. Let's take a picture of this object before you try to remove it."

"Good call. I didn't know you had a camera with you."

"It's a mini digital Elizabeth gave me last year to add to my 007 collection, as she likes to call it. It comes in quite handy so I never leave home without it." Victoria snapped away.

Christian watched, a bemused expression on his face. "A 007 collection? As in James Bond?"

With her right hand on her cocked hip, she grinned. "As a matter of fact, yes. Elizabeth insists my job is dangerous enough to warrant an array of gadgets in case I need them, just like James Bond, double O seven. Initially, I jokingly accepted them to get her off my back about my work, but I have to tell you, I love what she finds and I have had a use for these gadgets more times than I care to count."

Christian shrugged and smiled. "Works for me." After Victoria took enough angles of the object, he took his handkerchief from his back pocket and carefully removed the object.

"Hmm. It's a gold St. Francis of Assisi medal. Victoria, do you know if Brian had one?"

"Yes, he does. When they launched Elizabeth's new division, she and Brian exchanged St. Francis of Assisi medals to memorialize the event. I haven't seen it, so I don't know if that's his medal, but Elizabeth will know."

****

Elizabeth sniffled. She couldn't hold back her tears as her shoulders racked with sobs. "I'm frightened something horrible has happened to Brian," she said between sobs.

Victoria hugged her and tried to soothe her. "We'll find him."

Christian held the medal in his handkerchief carefully. "I want to show you something, but I don't want you to touch it."

Elizabeth breathed shakily. "Okay. What is it?"

"We found a gold medal of St. Francis of Assisi. Is it Brian's?" He carefully showed her both sides.

"Yes." She reached inside her shirt and pulled out her matching medal. "This was specially made for us. If you look carefully at the animals around St. Francis, you'll see a little dog, just like the one on my medal."

"So it is. Thank you." Christian wrapped the medal carefully in his handkerchief and placed it in his pocket.

Victoria, sensitive to Elizabeth's emotional state asked, "The words *Quoth the Raven, 'Nevermore'* were written in red on the wall of the Billiard Room. Think about what has been happening with Brian. Do you know if there was anything he was working on that could have any association with those words?"

Elizabeth pulled her jacket close and tucked her chin. "Not off the top of my head. I know those words are in Edgar Allen Poe's poem, 'The Raven,' but I don't know how that would relate to Brian. He's such a fun loving, kind person. I don't understand why he's missing."

"None of us do at this point."

Father David rubbed the rosary ring he wore. "The news replayed the verdict and Ramsey's words as he was taken from the courtroom. He mentioned the Raven. Could it relate?"

Victoria brushed her hair out of her face. "I can't see how. Brian had nothing to do with the trial."

Christian looked to Peter. "You were his law partner. Does anything come to mind in your practice?"

"Brian is a business lawyer. I can't even begin to imagine how Poe's famous line could have anything to do with him."

"Okay. Let's check out the roof area where he was last seen."

Austin's old stutter, showed itself. "You you know, I think w-w-w-we should all go back to our rooms and wait out the rest of the st-st-st-storm. When it stops, we can get the p-p-p-police here to handle it all."

Victoria didn't think this group could be helpful. "Austin, you're right. I think you all should go back to your rooms and wait until we get back to you."

"Maggie, can you take the three of us to the rooftop staircase the quickest way possible? Then you'll need to let your supervisor know what's going on. I don't want anyone near that tunnel."

"Yes, ma'am. I'll collect the walkie-talkies now, if you don't mind. But I still say what's going on has to do with the spirits. You should be looking into it, ma'am."

****

They were met with laughter on the fourth floor—deep, eerie laughter.

"It's the spirits. Usually they mean no harm, but I don't remember them sounding this way before. But then again, I've never been around a priest at the same time I've heard the laughter. They usually take hold of Jimmy."

"Who is Jimmy?" Victoria asked.

"Jimmy's the son of our chef, Nate. Been a part of this hotel for years. Jimmy's none too bright, but he usually does like he's asked, except when the spirits got a hold of him."

"What kind of spirits?" Father David asked.

"None that have caused any harm so far, but this sound isn't normal for Jimmy...If it's Jimmy that is. Jimmy, Jimmy!" Maggie called out.

More laughter.

Chapter 8

"Jimmy! Jimmy! This is Father David." He continued to call out, "We'd like to speak to you."

More laughter. "You belong to God. Begone from this place. We'll have nothing to do with you."

"Jimmy, where are you, son?"

Victoria turned to Maggie. "Has he had psychiatric counseling?"

"His pa took him to the doctors, but nothing's worked. Most times he's fine, but then the spirits take hold of him, and they don't let go."

"We need to find him. He might have seen something."

"There's no finding him unless he wants finding. He knows the secret places that I don't even know."

Christian climbed the stairs and tried the door to the roof. "It's locked. Do you have the keys, Maggie?"

"Not to the roof. Management likes to keep it locked for safety reasons."

"Well, if it's been locked the whole time, there's no way Brian would have been able to get up top."

"Unless he's been taken by someone who has access." Victoria thought the talk of spirits was just malarkey. "Maybe Jimmy has access."

"Maybe he does through the spirits." Maggie shuddered.

Victoria huddled into her jacket, tucking her chin

further into her turtleneck. She absently brushed the hair out of her eyes.

"How long do the wind storms typically last?" she asked Maggie.

"Oh, they could be lasting minutes or hours. Never seen them last days."

"That's good. Maybe it'll blow itself out soon." She shivered.

Christian put his jacket over Victoria. "You'll freeze without this."

"You sure?"

"Yes."

Father David turned to Maggie. "I'd really like to meet Jimmy and talk to him."

"He'll come out when he's ready, Father. There's no telling where he's now. He's not even laughing any more. Probably sleeping where he be."

****

Peter accompanied Elizabeth to her room where she paced. Handing her a glass of water he said, "Drink this, it'll help keep you going."

"Thanks." She took a sip and set the glass down. "I'm so worried." She rubbed her temples. *Brian, where are you? Are you hurt? Did this start out as a prank? I can't believe you'd get cold feet. We love each other too much for that. Please come back to me!*

"Yeah, I am too."

Her cell phone rang. She looked at Peter, "It's working! Must be letting up outside for at least the satellite to get through." She didn't recognize the number. "Hello."

"Joe Satori here, Christian's partner."

"Hi! I'm so happy you were able to get through.

78

We've got an awful storm up here."

"Well, sorry to be bothering you at this early hour, but I can't get through to Christian or Brian."

"I'm so glad you called. The storm started close to midnight and during the bachelor party, Brian disappeared. Christian and Victoria are searching for him. We're frantic."

"Okay, take a deep breath. Brian's missing, and Christian and who else did you say is looking for him?

"Victoria Bailey."

"Well, well, this is getting interesting. I didn't know you knew Victoria."

"I not only know her, but she's my maid of honor, but I've never met you. Do you know Brian?"

"Yes. I'm sure you know that Christian and I are partners in J.C. Classified. We've done work for a few of Brian's clients. That's how I met him. Now, you mentioned Brian disappeared during the bachelor party. Are you sure he's not just playing a prank? I understand that he's good for those."

"He is, but we found a bloody knife, his hat, and his St. Francis medal. I know this is not a prank. Brian would never play a prank this extreme at such an important time in our lives. *Never*. He *must* be in trouble." She started crying.

Peter awkwardly patted her back. She tried to smile a thanks, but didn't think she was successful since he looked even more uncomfortable. She closed her eyes.

"All right then, I will get there as soon as I can. Have you called the local police?"

"No. The phones are out. I didn't even know my cell would work."

"Why don't you try now?"

Her voice caught. "I'll try."

"While you try the police, I'll see what I can do from my end."

"Thank you," she said as she sniffled.

Elizabeth tried the emergency lines at Eustis Park's police station. No answer, just the recorded message, "Your call cannot be completed at this time, please try again later." She shut her phone and cried some more.

Shakily she picked up the phone again and dialed Joe. "I can't get through. What now?"

****

Victoria studied the faces of the Van der Kruis brothers. *How can two brothers take such diabolically opposite directions in life? One, giving his life to God; the other to battle. But then, with David's direction toward spiritual battle, maybe there's not such a difference, just the path taken. And then there's me. No doubt, I've been attracted to both. Almost married one. What is their common attraction for me? Having been hurt so badly by one, do I dare risk my heart on the other?*

Christian interrupted her thoughts. "We need to check the roof. Brian may be a practical joker, but I don't believe he'd ever take it to this level, especially the night before his wedding."

"Maggie, can you get the keys from your supervisor?"

"I'll certainly try."

"And while you're at it, Maggie, see if there's a way to get over to the spa without having to brave the elements. I'm worried about Sandy."

"Yes, ma'am," she said and made a hasty retreat back to housekeeping.

80

"We'll wait for you here," Father called after her.

"Guys, you wait here for Maggie, I'm going to check this area out a little more and will be right back." Christian slowly turned and headed down the hall.

"David, I didn't tell Elizabeth about the note. No sense in upsetting her further until we've had a chance to check it out."

"Understood." He gazed into space.

"Penny for your thoughts?"

"Evil surrounds us."

This was the last thing Victoria expected him to say. He piqued her curiosity though. "How long have you had this feeling?"

"Ever since the rehearsal. I can't shake it. It has been gnawing at me, even though I initially tried to dismiss it." He drummed his leg with his fingers, concentrating on something in the distance.

Victoria thought, some things never change. David always drummed his fingers on his leg when he was deep in thought.

"What does it feel like?"

"It's hard to describe." He rubbed his forehead and continued, "A warning filters through my body putting me on alert. I believe it's the Holy Spirit."

"I didn't take you for a hocus-pocus sort of guy," she said with a grin.

David shrugged. "I'm not. This sense is real, and so far, it has never let me down."

Maggie returned just then, and Christian appeared at the same moment. "Here's the key. Don't know if you'll get it open or not because the door opens out. There may be too much snow built up there. My supervisor doesn't know of a way to the spa without going outside, but that doesn't mean there isn't a way, just that we don't know it."

"Thank you. First we'll see if we can get onto that roof." Christian took the key from Maggie's outstretched hand.

He climbed the stairs two at a time knowing there was no time to waste, especially if Brian was on the roof. The latch unlocked, he pressed his shoulder into the door, and began to push. The door opened enough for someone a lot smaller than he to slip out and take a look.

Victoria volunteered. "Let me go, I can get through that space."

"I'm not so sure that's a good idea. The storm's not as fierce as it was earlier, but it's still rough"— Christian hesitated—"and we don't know what's out there."

"I tell you what. I won't go all the way out. I'll just slide my body through the space so I see the immediate area and you can even hold my inside hand. If something's dangerous, you can help get me back in."

Christian knew there was no alternative if he wanted to see if Brian was on the roof. "Okay, but only if I hold onto your hand. I don't want anything to happen to you."

She stared for a minute at him before moving to the top of the stairs. She closed his jacket more securely around her, bracing for the frigid air. The wind whipped at her face, although there was no doubt it had let up. Snow was blowing, but not much was falling. Victoria took the flashlight and started to carefully search the surrounding area. Still hours before dawn, the reflection of the snow enhanced visibility. With Christian's firm grasp of her hand, she felt secure.

"There's a little shelter directly outside this door. It blocked the larger drifts which is why you were able to get the door open at all." She shivered. "Wait a minute. I see something in the snow in the corner of the shelter. I'd like to get it."

Christian held onto her hand harder. "I don't like that idea. What if something happens? I can't get you back in."

"Well, I can't get close enough to see what it is without going out for it." Victoria came back in and crossed her arms. "What's it going to be? It may be an important clue."

"Or it may not be."

Maggie's face lit up. "I have an idea! The maintenance closet is right under these stairs. What if I find some rope you can wrap around her waist so you don't lose her?"

Victoria smiled. "I like that idea. Father David, see if you can help Maggie find the rope. Christian, how about it?"

He sighed. "I don't think there's a better idea. But we need to be quick about it. I don't want you out there that long."

She shivered, "Don't think I want to be out there any more than I absolutely have to."

David handed Christian the rope, and he tied a careful square knot around Victoria's waist. "I want to make sure this doesn't slip out."

She made her way back up the stairs with Christian right behind her.

"Florida it's not, that's for sure," Victoria mumbled. With trepidation, she slowly inched her way toward the corner of the sheltered area. Christian held onto the rope.

"Can you tell what it is yet?"

"No, I need to get closer."

"Be careful and watch your step."

"I'm almost there now." Victoria crouched and stretched her right arm, trying to reach the dark spot while shining the flashlight with her left. "Got it. I'm going to look around while I'm out here. There may be something else."

"Don't take any additional risk."

"If there were tracks up here, they're gone now. Can't see much with the blowing snow. I'm lucky I was even able to find this thing. Fortunately it was in the corner of the sheltered part," she shouted back, not even sure she was heard.

She started back to the door, the rope directing her as Christian gently pulled on it. He grabbed her as she stumbled through the door. "You okay?" he searched her face.

"Maybe a little blue along the edges, but otherwise fine," Victoria said through chattering teeth.

"Let's warm you up and see what we have here." Christian vigorously rubbed her back and arms trying to bring back warmth.

Chapter 9

Victoria looked down at what she held in her hand and slowly turned it. Frowning, she handed it over to Christian. "Looks like one of those smashed souvenir pennies you get out of the machines in Disney World."

"Hmm, it is, but what's it doing in the Rocky Mountains?"

"Don't know. Let's check with Elizabeth and ask her if it could belong to Brian."

"Sounds good." Turning to Maggie he asked, "Are there any other exits or escape routes that could have been used by Mr. Gregory?"

"There are fire escape exits on each floor, supply closets, and out of sight routes for the service personnel so as not to disrupt the guests. There may be other places I don't know about." She rubbed the cross she wore around her neck as she spoke.

"Thank you, Maggie. We're going to Ms. Harrington's room now. Will you be available a little later?"

"Yes." She continued to rub.

Father David touched her shoulder, "I'd like to speak to Jimmy. Do you think you could find him for me? If you have trouble finding him, can you enlist the help of someone he trusts?"

"Yes, Father. I'll do my best." She continued to work the cross.

Victoria watched with fascination, amazed there was anything left of the small silver cross. "Let's get back to Elizabeth." She started toward the staircase.

David came alongside Victoria, while Christian followed, taking his time to carefully scan the area. "Slow down, guys. Jimmy was here, within hearing range, and then he wasn't. Where was he hiding? How did he leave without us seeing him?"

Victoria stopped in her tracks. "You're right. Let's check out this whole area as we go."

A door under the stairs going to the roof led to the maintenance room where Maggie got the rope. Victoria looked to David. "Did you check this room out when Maggie went to find the rope?"

"No, she found it so quickly there was no need."

Christian tried the door. "Maggie must have locked it. Do you have the key, David?"

"Yeah, I haven't returned the master key. I think Maggie was too nervous to remember to ask for it back." He handed it over.

Christian walked into the small space. Pressing against the walls and feeling along the shelves he said, "Nothing special. Just looks like a typical supply closet. There's a guest room next to it though."

Christian knocked first and then unlocked the guest room door and went in. He walked carefully around the walls, touching here, pushing there. "Just another room. Nothing unusual here."

Victoria stared at the supply room, a frown creasing her forehead. "Think about Jimmy's laughter. Was it muffled or clear?"

David closed his eyes. "It was clear."

"So he had to have been hiding in an area with an

open shot to where we stood."

Christian spoke up first. "Yes, but remember, this floor's not weatherproofed, so it's possible he wasn't out in the open, but the sound was still unobstructed."

"Since we're planning on speaking to him, let's get back to Elizabeth and show this souvenir coin to her."

David, usually the optimist, said, "Okay, but it doesn't feel right."

Christian continued to examine the area.

"I thought it was women who relied on their feelings, not men."

"Never make generalizations, Victoria. Not every person or situation will fit them." David smiled as he chided her.

She shrugged.

****

Victoria opened the door to their room and found Elizabeth alone and pacing. "I can't sit still." Elizabeth continued to pace.

"I thought Peter was with you." Victoria scanned the room, seeing no one else.

"He was, but then left. He said he was headed back to his room in case Brian showed up there. He was here though when Joe called."

Victoria's eyes widened. "You made contact with the outside world?"

"You spoke to my partner?"

Victoria looked at Christian.

Elizabeth looked from one to the other. "Yes, twice. I have a satellite phone, and Joe called me when he couldn't get a hold of you or Brian."

"Does he know what's happened here?"

"Yes. I tried to call the police, but couldn't get

through. I called him back."

"What did he say?"

"He's ready to help any way he can; Christian just needs to give him the go-ahead. In the meantime, he's going to try to reach the authorities. I don't know if it was my phone not calling out or the police phone not receiving."

Victoria pulled out the flattened souvenir penny. "Does this look familiar to you?"

Elizabeth picked it up and examined each side. "Yes," she said as she went to her purse, removed her wallet, and brought out an identical flat penny from the side pocket. "We got them this past December at Disney World. Where did you find it?'

"On the roof."

"What? That makes no sense."

Christian cleared his throat. "It does if he was there."

"What would possess him to go out there in this weather? Don't answer that. Where can he be *now*?"

"We are going to find him."

Elizabeth grabbed Victoria's arm, "How about Sandy? When you were on the second floor, did you make sure Sandy was all right?"

Victoria quickly glanced at Christian.

"I caught that look. Is Sandy okay?"

Victoria looked down at her feet before answering. "Umm, we're not sure."

"What do you mean you're not sure? Either she is or she isn't."

"Not quite. She wasn't in her room."

"Well, where would she be then? After all, she left a message at the desk."

"We're not sure about that either. She did check in, her stuff was there, but she left a note with the word *spa*."

"That makes sense to me. Sometimes a good head massage is the best thing for a headache. Do you think she's okay there?"

Christian sent Victoria a look that said *don't say too much.* "Maybe. We can't get there right now and phones don't work. But you may be right. A good head massage can do wonders for a headache. Don't worry, we're also trying to find a way there, but Brian is a priority at this point."

Christian asked, "By the way, I know Sandy helped Victoria second chair that prosecution against the serial murderer and that she helped you on your new venture. Was she doing anything else?"

"That's a pretty full plate if you ask me. I don't think so. Victoria, do you know of anything?"

"Not that I'm aware of."

Elizabeth's phone rang. "Hello." She hit the speaker button. "I have you on speaker."

"It's Joe. I just wanted to touch base. I got through to the Eustis Park captain on his satellite phone. Seems he's known Brian from way back and believes nothing serious is amiss. Said Brian has quite a reputation for pulling pranks, and the captain feels this is something he'd do."

"I beg to differ. The captain doesn't know Brian like I do. He is a prankster, but he would never pull something like this on our wedding."

"I agree. Besides, I don't hold much hope in the locals if they are as trapped as you. Has Christian touched base with you?"

"I'm standing right here." He took the phone the phone off speaker and moved into the hallway as he spoke. "This is what I want you to do...."

Victoria strained to hear more, but couldn't. Elizabeth looked at her and shrugged.

Reentering the room, they heard "Later." He hung up and handed the phone back to Elizabeth.

Victoria raised her brow in question.

"Just making sure resources are available if needed."

A knock sounded at the door.

Chapter 10

David opened the door to Maggie, wringing her apron. "Is everything all right?" He asked in a soothing voice.

"Don't know, Father. I found Jimmy in the Gregory Room rocking back and forth. He wouldn't come with me, but I can take you to him. He's possessed, he is."

Victoria frowned. "What do you mean by possessed?"

"Come see for yourself, ma'am. You'll know when you see."

Three of them followed Maggie out. Elizabeth stayed in her room just in case Brian returned. Electricity was still out, but as they passed the large Palladian window, it was clear the storm had subsided, the wind died down. "Thankfully, the weather won't be working against us anymore," Victoria sighed.

"Not like it had been. Quite a bit of snow was dumped though," David added.

"Without the wind, I can get a chopper here if need be."

"I don't know. Transportation won't be running." Victoria commented.

Christian grinned. "I've got my own resources. Not to worry."

"What type of resources do you have access to?"

"Whatever I need."

"How do you manage that?"

"It's my business."

"Okay, maybe I have not been asking the right questions. I know you've been involved in search and rescue, but these types of resources seem a bit much. What else are you involved in?"

"Ah, let's just say it's handling what others believe is the impossible." He gave her a quirky grin.

Maggie stopped at the door to the Gregory Room and turned to look at Father David. "Father, you'll want to handle him carefully. He's in a strange, delicate way right now. Possessed now, mind you. Maybe you can help him."

Jimmy was on the center of the stage, rocking back and forth, repeating the same phrase over and over again. "The spirit's got him, not her. The spirit's got him, not her. The spirit's got him, not her."

Father David slowly approached Jimmy. "Who does the spirit have, Jimmy?"

"The spirit's got him, not her. The spirit's got him, not her." Jimmy continued to say as he rocked.

"Jimmy, can you stop rocking for me?" Father David asked.

Jimmy continued to rock. "The spirit's got him, not her."

He tried a different approach. He sat down next to Jimmy, crossed his legs in the same manner, and started rocking to Jimmy's beat. "Who does the spirit have, Jimmy?"

Jimmy took a sideways glance and looked forward again. "The spirit's got him, not her."

"Who does the spirit have, Jimmy?"

The rocking continued for a few more minutes and then stopped abruptly. Jimmy slowly turned his head to Father David, who also stopped rocking. The room had an eerie glow from the lit candles surrounding the stage. "Why Alexander, of course." Jimmy continued to rock.

Father David started up again with Jimmy. "Who does the spirit not have Jimmy?"

"The spirit has him, not her."

"Who is the her?"

"She's protected, she is. Protected, protected, protected."

"Who is she protected by?"

"Won't say who. Won't say who."

"Why?"

"Can't say the name. Just can't, just can't."

Maggie gasped as the candles flickered out and reignited with no apparent cause.

Father David was still rocking in time with Jimmy. "Okay, Jimmy. How about Alexander. What is Alexander's last name?"

Jimmy continued to rock. "The spirit's got him. The spirit's got him."

Father David tried a new angle. "What spirit, Jimmy?"

Jimmy continued to rock. "The spirit's got him. *Quoth the Raven, 'Nevermore.'* "

Victoria looked perplexed. "That was written on the wall."

David shot Victoria a glance that made her freeze. He continued to rock with Jimmy. "What do you mean by the raven, Jimmy? Is the raven the spirit?"

Jimmy rocked. "*Quoth the Raven, 'Nevermore.'* "

The candles went out again. When they relit,

Jimmy was gone.

****

"Told you Father," Maggie said as she rubbed her cross, "possessed, he is."

Victoria had seen a lot of strange people, but this was something on the far side of her experiences. "What do you think, David?"

Christian appeared to wait for his response. Obviously, he'd worked with his brother before.

"You have to be careful when diagnosing *demonopathy*."

"I'm assuming that means possession?"

"It includes demon possession, but it's the term for diabolical influence."

"Forgive me if I find this hard to believe. Jimmy looks like a sick boy to me."

"Demonic activity may share some of the symptoms of a mental or physical illness. The main difference is that the illness, or bizarre behavior, is unusually resistant to medical treatment, including prescription drugs. I would need to speak to his father about what medical help was sought, and if anything was effective. You don't want to jump the gun on something like this." As David finished his thoughts, he uncrossed his legs and rose in one graceful motion.

Victoria stood with him, invading his personal space. "What type of symptoms are you referring to?"

"Extraordinary strength, revealing the unknown, and speaking in tongues. Those are just a few. You can read about a clear example in the Bible with the man from Gerasenes in the Gospels."

"Since I don't have my Bible handy here, can you refresh my memory about the story?"

94

"Sure. When Jesus climbed out of the boat in Gerasenes, he was met by a man possessed by demons. This man was naked, homeless, and lived in a cemetery. When he saw Jesus, he shrieked and fell to the ground screaming. He recognized Jesus as the Son of the Most High God. This demon had taken control of this man to the point that he broke the chains he was shackled with and ran into the wilderness."

"But David, that's just a story."

"Victoria, it is not just a story, but the Word of God. The Bible is a key avenue that God uses to communicate with us. Every word is there for a reason."

She crossed her arms looking doubtful.

"Even anthropological excavations and studies have pointed to the Bible's accuracy."

"Well, after what I just witnessed, there may be something to this. So, is this man from Gerasenes a model then of what someone possessed looks and acts like?"

"There really is no cookie cutter model because the symptoms and severity run the gamut. Jimmy's behavior is bizarre, but I need more than just this to make a diagnosis." He turned to Maggie. "I'd like to speak to his father as soon as possible. I believe he's seen something, and if I can speak to his father, we may be able to uncover what he's seen."

"Yes, Father." Maggie continued to rub her cross. "I'll see what I can do."

Maggie bumped into Christian while just about running out the door. "I'm so sorry."

Helping her get her bearings, he said, "You're fine." Looking at the others, "We should get back to

Elizabeth."

"I'm ahead of you on that."

****

As they started back, Victoria wanted to take advantage of the time. "You mentioned you had training in Poland. Can anyone perform an exorcism?"

"No. First of all, the power to deliver people from demons is biblical. Jesus gave us the power and it is still fully effective today. In Mark 16:17 the Gospel tells us 'These signs will accompany those who believe: in my name they will cast out demons.' "

"What are these powers based on?"

"They are based on faith and prayer. In essence, they are prayers of deliverance that anyone can perform. However, just prayers of deliverance are not exorcisms. The Church wanted to guard its people from magicians and charlatans and increase the effectiveness of this power given by Jesus Christ. The safeguard the Church instituted was a specific sacramental called an exorcism. This sacramental may only be administered by bishops and those priests who have received a direct and specific license to exorcise."

Victoria does not even remember a more serious David. "And is it safe for me to assume that you have this specific and direct license to exorcise?"

"Yes, and it's a ministry I take very seriously."

Although Christian walked with them, Victoria noticed he was deep in thought. His silence spoke volumes. She turned her attention back to David.

"Okay. What do you do in an exorcism?"

"As an exorcist I follow the prayers found in the Ritual."

"Where did this Ritual come from?"

"The Ritual was selected in 1614, written by Alcuinus in the ninth and tenth centuries and is governed by Canon Law, Canon 1172 to be specific."

Victoria was fascinated. "How long does an exorcism take?"

"No telling. It can take minutes or hours."

Christian interrupted. "Why don't we check on Peter to see if anything has come up?"

"Great idea."

With only a flashlight and the battery operated Exit signs, they climbed three flights of stairs to the fourth floor and knocked on Room 405. No answer.

"Peter, are you there?" Victoria called out. No answer.

Christian tried the handle and the door opened. "Peter!"

No answer. Christian stepped into the room and abruptly stopped. "This is not the work of someone who's just unorganized, this place looks ransacked."

"Wow. Someone tore this place apart. Drawers are dumped on the floor, suitcases turned upside down, open. There's a foul smell in here."

David sniffed. "You're right. What is that?"

"I don't know, but it smells like something died." Victoria wrinkled her nose and tried to breathe through her jacket to no avail…the pink fleece just wasn't enough.

"Before we jump the gun here, let's see if Peter is with Elizabeth. Maybe he's just a horribly messy person and the stink is old food or shoes or something," David coughed.

Christian moved around the room. "Even this doesn't look like the work of a messy person. Someone searched in here, but whatever they wanted, if it was here, is probably gone."

Through her jacket Victoria said, "I'd rather get Peter to see if he knows what may be missing. Let's head to my room. Maybe you're right and Peter is there comforting her, or better yet, maybe Brian is with them."

They hustled down the stairs.

Victoria quickly unlocked the door and entered first, to a pacing Elizabeth. "Has Peter been here?"

"No."

Chapter 11

There was a knock at the door. Elizabeth grabbed the knob and jerked it open. The disappointment was evident. "Hi, Maggie."

Maggie was out of breadth. "Father David," she called as she peered around Elizabeth. "I spoke to Jimmy's dad, and he's willing to talk to you. He's in the kitchen trying to see what he can do for his guests without electricity. If you'd like to follow me, I'll take you there straight away."

"Thank you, Maggie." David looked to Victoria. "Do you want to wait here with Elizabeth?"

Elizabeth answered for her. "We don't need more than one person to see if Brian shows up. I'd rather the three of you do what you can to expedite things."

Victoria rubbed her friend's upper arm in a soothing gesture. "You know we'll do what we can. While we're gone, I want you to really think hard about your new venture and the role each person had in it. It would be helpful if you sat down at your computer and brainstormed, writing down each person's name, his or her respective roles, and how they interacted. Not only is Brian missing, but since Sandy is not in her room, she may be missing as well. The only thing they really had in common is your new business."

"Will do. I'd rather do something other than wearing out the carpet."

"Thanks."

They hustled after Maggie.

Feeling the warmth of the kitchen as they approached its door, Victoria crossed the threshold; a brief smile flickered across her mouth.

Christian asked, "Care to share?"

"I was just thinking how the glow of the fireplace provides a sense of comfort, even in the midst of the storm."

"I agree."

Maggie's call to Nate interrupted the calm. "I have Father David here and his brother and friend, Miss Bailey."

Nate bent over the stove, fed more wood, and stoked the fire. Wiping his hands on a towel, he grabbed Father David's hand. "Nice to meet you, Father. I understand you wanted to talk to me about Jimmy."

"Yes, that's right."

Nate looked at Victoria and Christian and shook their hands as well. "Nice to meet you. I'm sorry if my son has disturbed you."

Father David took advantage of the opening. "No apologies needed. He may be able to help us, but first, if you could answer a few questions, it would make things a lot easier."

"Anything, fire away."

"How long has your son exhibited this strange behavior?"

Nate tapped his chin thoughtfully, "Quite a while. Since he was about nine years old or so."

"Have you sought medical help for him?"

"Absolutely. After we exhausted the local doctors,

we tried a number of specialists in Denver."

"Did you go outside of Denver?"

"Yes. We even flew him to New York at the suggestion of one of these specialists. No one could help him. They tried all kinds of medicines, even electric shock treatments. He didn't like the electric shock treatments, and when they restrained him, he broke the restraints."

"Had he exhibited that type of strength before this unusual behavior?"

"No. And the doctors told me that they never saw anything like it either. They wanted me to lock him up permanently in one of their facilities, but it was clear to me there was nothing they could do for him. The management here knows that my son is harmless to anyone else, so they let him stay here with me."

"That's awfully nice of them." Victoria brushed the hair out of her face.

"Yes it is, but it also adds to the allure of this hotel. It's in the top five of the most haunted hotels in the country you know."

Father David rubbed his chin. "Yes, we've been told that. This leads me to another question. What do you know about exorcisms?"

Nate shrugged his shoulders. "Not much, why?"

"Since medical treatment has not been effective, it's possible that the source of your son's problems is demonic possession. Has anyone mentioned that possibility to you?"

"No. Some of the staff here, like Maggie"—Nate threw Maggie a smile—"are convinced he's possessed, but no professional's mentioned it. If Jimmy's problem is this demonic possession, can he be helped? I'll try anything for my Jimmy."

"He could be freed through an exorcism, but there are no guarantees." Father David treaded carefully.

"Is this something you can do?"

"Yes," Father David continued, "I am a licensed exorcist, and I may be able to help your son."

"At this point Father, I'll try anything."

Deep laughter ensued, seemingly from the walls. Nate looked to Father David. "Anything to get my Jimmy back. How soon can you start?"

"Now, if possible. Not only do I believe that an exorcism will free Jimmy, but I believe Jimmy may be in possession of information linked to the disappearance of Brian Gregory."

"So you have everything you need?"

"Yes. I've been anticipating this need and I'm prepared."

"Jimmy's favorite hiding place is located in the Gregory Room. Please go there now, and I'll try to ferret Jimmy out," Nate quickly said. "The sooner the better. This may be a hurry up and wait situation though. It may take a while before he shows up."

"That's all right," Victoria offered. They moved quickly, not wanting to dally for a moment, just in case.

****

David slowly opened the door to the Gregory Room. The squeaky hinges caused Victoria to jump, falling against Christian. "Sorry."

He smiled. "Apology accepted, although not needed."

"Normally I'm not this jumpy. I think my prosecution of the Raven combined with what's been going on here has maybe gotten to me more than I thought."

"That's understandable."

David added, "None of this is typical, and experiencing this type of paranormal activity is frightening for anyone."

"Why would you want to work in this field then?" Victoria asked as they entered the Gregory Room.

"I feel it's my calling and my ministry. There's more of a need for this ministry than most people like to admit. It frightens people," David answered with a shrug. "Why don't we sit down and wait. It may be a while before anyone shows up."

Christian stood at the entrance and slowly took in his surroundings. "I tell you what. Why don't you two wait here to see if Jimmy shows up? I'm going to do some exploring on my own." He turned and vanished from their sight.

****

Christian needed time to get grounded both professionally and personally. There was a lot at stake with three missing persons and his reunion with Victoria. He couldn't allow emotion to cloud his judgment. In his line of work, that could be deadly. That being said, he was not going to lose her again, and one of the first things she needed before she could move on was resolution and the ability to forgive. As he continued his own physical search, he thought about how he could make that happen. *Little brother, it has to start with you. You ignited that anger, now you have to squelch it. The first step is the alone time I just gave you. Hopefully it's enough time at least to open the door. Let's see what you do with it.*

****

Uneasy, Victoria sat close to David. "On the one hand the lit candles make it a little more welcoming, but the flicker of light from them creates creepy shadows."

Father David nodded as he looked into the candles' flicker.

Victoria drew on his strength, a strength she remembered much too vividly. Her mind drifted to the past and the last evening she spent with him, the night of his college graduation. He had brought her to their favorite place by the lake, the place where they spent so much time talking about their future together; where they would live, the children they would have. She moved back in time to that very moment. David had looked deep into her eyes and had taken both of her hands in his. Victoria just knew he was about to propose.

He said, "You know I'll always love you."

She remembers almost bursting at the seams as she smiled and said, "Yes."

His next words were like a slap in the face. "I've decided to enter the seminary."

"Excuse me?" was all she could muster as her voice squeaked.

"I have a higher calling."

Victoria recalled her last words. "I thought we had the highest calling possible, together."

"I'm sorry, but I've chosen the priesthood as my life."

Father David interrupted her, bringing her back to the present. "Penny for your thoughts."

She slowly tipped her head up. "You never kissed me good-bye. You just left me. You never gave me any indication you were leaning toward the priesthood. You let me plan our lives together!"

Tears streamed down her cheeks as she clenched her fists. "How could you do that to me? You said you loved me, but you threw me away! How could you!" She pounded his chest.

David gathered her into his arms. "My Victoria, I'm so so sorry I hurt you. I didn't know how to tell you, so I never did until I had no choice. I loved you so much I didn't want to hurt you. I told you I'll always love you, and I always will."

David lifted her chin as she calmed down and looked deep into her eyes, searching. He bent his head and kissed her, ever so gently. It was that tender goodbye kiss he owed her, full of love. "Can you ever forgive me?"

She pulled away and touched his lips with her fingers. "I don't know. I've hated you since that night. I tried to forget you, but the hurt you caused me has always come between me and anyone else. I've kept the door to my heart shut tight so no one could come close to me again."

"Such pain was the last thing I wanted to cause you. Your passion for life was so contagious. You loved hard and laughed hard."

"Don't forget, that passion goes both ways."

"Yes it does, but Victoria, the love and laughter leads to joy for you and others. The anger and hatred only leads to destruction and despair."

The candles flickered, and a deep laughter followed. "Well said, Padre."

Father David stood. "Who speaks?"

More laughter. "You know who we are."

"Show yourself. Who are you?"

"Legion, for we are many." As Jimmy stepped out of the shadows, his cackling laughter seemed inhuman, as if it came from someplace deep within the bowels of the earth.

Nate slipped in as Jimmy appeared and was now at Father David's side. "Father, this is not Jimmy's voice. This is a voice that comes and goes, but it is not my Jimmy."

Father David looked at Jimmy and asked, "Do you know Brian Gregory?"

"Yes. He is the descendant of Alexander Gregory." As Jimmy said his name, he spit. "We hate Alexander Gregory."

"Why?" Father David asked. "You never knew him."

"Oh yes we do. He destroyed my plans! My future for Eustis Park! Happily ever after—not!" Jimmy picked up the solid oak throne in the center of the stage and threw it in anger. "*El cahita utar minome!*"

Nate looked at Father David. "It takes four men to move that throne. It is solid oak and my Jimmy is a little guy. He can't push it, let alone throw it."

"Who are you?" Father David asked again.

Laughter. "Lord Macraven, of course!"

"Lord Macraven is dead and gone," Father David continued. "Who are you?"

"I told you, Lord Macraven. I will exact my revenge on the house of Gregory!"

"Where is Brian Gregory?" Father David demanded in an even louder voice.

A different voice now came out of Jimmy. "Quoth the raven, 'Nevermore.' "

106

"Who am I speaking with?"

"Why the Raven, of course."

Father David continued to press. "Do you know where Brian Gregory is?"

"Follow the vision quests."

"What vision quests?"

"Ask the Ute."

"Who are you talking about?"

"That's for me to know, and you to find out." Peels of laughter faded away. The candle light blinked off and then on. Jimmy was gone.

"It definitely appears he's possessed, and by more than one demon."

Chills ran up and down Victoria's spine. Coldness touched the depths of her being. "How do you know?" she asked, teeth chattering.

"According to the Ritual, there are three signs that are symptomatic of satanic possession, and Jimmy has exhibited all three signs."

Nate piped in, "That superhuman strength has to be one of them."

"Yes it is. As well as speaking in unknown languages and knowing hidden things."

"Well," Victoria asked, "how do you know there's more than one demon?"

David smiled. "Because I just spoke to more than one."

"Other than these three symptoms, what else makes you think he's possessed?"

"The diagnostics are in place." As he spoke, David glanced to the area where he'd last seen Jimmy.

"What are some of the diagnostics?" Victoria asked.

"You always did ask lots of questions." He gave her a lopsided grin. "The fact that medical help was sought and nothing works."

Nate shook his head up and down. "And we've been to the best. Neither medication nor electric shock worked. What other diagnostics are there?"

"Well, it's only through the exorcism itself that we would know. Since we don't know where Jimmy is at the moment, it's important that we look into what we've learned. Nate, do you know anything about the vision quest or the Ute?"

"I don't know what he meant by the vision quest, but the Horse Whisperer is a Ute Indian. Maybe that's the Ute Jimmy referred to?"

"Who is this Horse Whisperer and where can we find him?"

The candles went out.

Chapter 12

Christian appeared to Victoria's right, startling her. He looked down into her eyes and smiled. "No worries," he said in a low voice and turned his attention toward Nate.

"The Horse Whisperer is a Ute Shaman who is magical with animals, especially horses. He's an old man, don't even know how old, but old. We're not sure exactly where he lives, but when the hotel had horses, he took care of them."

"Is he here now?"

"There are horses for Miss Harrington's wedding, so he's here. You'll be able to find the Horse Whisperer with them. The hotel recently renovated the stables and set up pretty nice digs in there for him. Especially during storms, this Ute has a very calming effect on the horses and any other living creature around him. Amazing really."

"Do you think we'll be able to reach the stables with all the snow?" Victoria twirled the hair by her ear.

"There's a little known tunnel off the ground floor that goes from our main building to the stables. I can show it to you, but then I have to get back to the kitchen. Although typically I am not needed this early, with the weather, I'm afraid our guests may need my services."

They hustled to the ground floor where Nate led

them to a small door. "I never noticed this door when we searched this area before." Victoria shook her head. "I wonder what else we missed down here."

"Don't feel too bad, miss. The indoor foliage hides this door. Unless someone knows it's there, it would never be seen."

"I wonder what else we missed," she mumbled.

"Well, I'll leave you here. Just follow the tunnel. It'll lead you to the Horse Whisperer." Nate checked his watch and did an abrupt face.

"Thank God for flashlights," Victoria commented.

"Amen to that. Let's get going." David was the first one in the tunnel.

Victoria felt something brush against her pant leg and she jumped. "Eeeks! What was that?" She pushed back into Christian who was bringing up the rear.

"Don't know. Probably nothing more than a field mouse trying to stay warm."

"What is it with these mice? I hate them. Ugh!" Victoria pulled her collar up and huddled into her jacket.

"Don't think about it. Instead, think about how we should approach the Ute."

"Good idea."

They rounded a corner and came to cement steps. "This is it." David turned and smiled. "Glad it wasn't such a long tunnel."

"Me too. I'd rather be above ground." Victoria followed closely.

David slowly pushed open the heavy wooden door. "Hello! Anybody here?"

A warm glow illuminated the stables. In the stillness that followed, they heard a quiet chant. David put his finger to his lips and held the door for Victoria until Christian caught it. They slowly walked toward the chant, although in hushed tones, it got progressively louder. Victoria was fascinated and moved ahead of David, drawn to the sound and warmth.

In the glow of the candle light, she spotted the Shaman sitting cross-legged in a trance. The horses in his midst looked to the Shaman as their protector. "Amazing…Look at those horses. The way they're transfixed on him, it's almost hypnotic. If this goes on much longer, we may be just as mesmerized by the Horse Whisperer as those horses!"

Victoria turned to look at David when there was no answer. Oh boy, she thought. *Two of them. He looks like he's in his own meditation.* She then checked out Christian who stayed back near the farthest stall to observe. Sighing, she returned her focus to the Horse Whisperer and waited.

The Ute slowly opened his eyes. "Welcome, my brother. I was expecting you." He slowly looked to Victoria, "And you too, Victorious One." He continued to turn slowly toward Christian who was being nuzzled by one of the horses. In response, he gently rubbed his snout while meeting the Ute's gaze. The Ute nodded. "The animals have a way of knowing."

"Why did you refer to David as your brother, and me, Victorious One?"

"I am a Shaman. The man you call David is my brother in the spirits. I see the spirits in my dreams and visions. They talk to me. David also speaks to the spirits. So, he is my brother. They call me the Horse Whisperer. Yes, I commune with the animals, especially the horses, but that is what my name means

111

in my native tongue. Victorious One is what your name means. Names have significance in each person's life."

"How did you know that was my name?"

"It was told to me in my dreams."

David looked to the Ute. "Yes, my brother, we were hoping you could help us. The horses you care for were brought in for the wedding of Brian Gregory and Elizabeth Harrington. Brian has disappeared. An associate of his, Sandy Forrester, is also missing. In our search for him, we came across Nate's son Jimmy, who appears to be possessed by a number of evil spirits. One of those spirits told us to 'follow the vision quests.' When we asked him what this meant, he said 'Ask the Ute.' Are you the Ute he spoke of?"

The Horse Whisperer started to chant. David sat cross-legged across from him, and Victoria followed suit. Christian remained standing in the back.

David appeared to wait patiently in prayer. Victoria shifted her focus from the Ute, to David, and on to the rest of her surroundings. *The peace I feel warms my very being.* She breathed in deep and let the air out slowly. *Peaceful even in the midst of a storm. I don't want to leave this place. I can't even remember my last peaceful moment.* She closed her eyes, trying to capture the essence of her surroundings.

The chanting stopped, and the Horse Whisperer looked to David. "Up above the tree line is a sacred spot. It is where I like to go to commune with the spirits for guidance. They sometimes tell me of things to come, sometimes of things gone by."

"How do the spirits commune with you?"

"This happens mostly in dreams, but I have had visions as well. The visions I have may be small pieces to something bigger. Most of my recent visions have been either warnings or signs of danger. Some of these visions appear to belong in my dreams."

Victoria asked, "Could any of these visions be related to Brian's disappearance?"

"Yes."

Knees bouncing, she asked, "Can you tell us where he is and if he's all right?"

The Horse Whisperer watched the bounce of her knees and slowly brought his gaze up to meet her eyes. "Ah, Victorious One, you have not yet learned patience. In my visions, I saw a raven. It was laughing deep inside a tree. In its claws was a knife. The knife had blood on it. The eagle soared, searching. Darkness was all around."

"Is Brian alive?" David prodded.

"I saw pain, lots of pain, but no death yet. I saw fear, lots of fear, but no death yet. There is an hourglass with the sand almost gone." The Shaman's eyes shifted to Victoria and paused. "Beware of the Raven."

Victoria asked, "How about Sandy? Is she okay?"

He closed his eyes and slowly opened them. "In my visions I saw a woman in white riding a white horse, head thrown back in laughter, a white dove upon her shoulders."

"What does that mean?"

"She is at peace now. She can never come to harm."

"How can she never come to harm?"

The Horse Whisperer closed his eyes and started to chant.

Chapter 13

Victoria jumped up from her seated position. "We've got to go. Time is running out."

Christian held the door and once again brought up the rear. When they got back out through the tunnel and onto the ground floor of the hotel, David stopped and touched Victoria's arm.

"I thought you didn't believe in spirits. Why would you believe the Horse Whisperer?"

Victoria folded her arms and started tapping her foot. "This guy's been communing with something and knew about us. If he says time is running out, I'm inclined to believe him. Before we get back to Elizabeth though, I think we should check out the spa for Sandy."

Christian moved closer. "I agree with you, but I also don't think it's a good idea to leave Elizabeth alone longer than we have to. David, why don't you head back. Victoria and I will go to the spa since we're near the café and the exit to the Manor House. The spa is on the ground floor there."

"All right."

Victoria sighed. "I don't have a good feeling about Sandy."

"I don't either." David moved the notches on his rosary ring. "The Ute said she was at peace. To me that only means one thing."

"Save it, David. Christian, let's go."

114

Victoria led the way through the café and out the door on the side to the Manor House. "Thank God for small blessings. Do you see what I see?"

"Yes. The covering between the buildings is still there and kept out some of the blowing drifts."

"How it remained intact is beyond me. Oh boy, the storm stopped, but it's freezing." Once her teeth started chattering, she couldn't get them to stop. She snuggled into the jacket she never returned to Christian and took a deep breath. *I love his scent.*

"Probably protected by the buildings. Let's move quickly out of the cold." Christian put his arm around her to share his body heat as they raced to the Manor House.

"At least it's not so dark outside. The snow has a way of brightening things up a bit."

Christian reached for the doorknob, but it was locked. He banged on the door, but as expected, there was no answer. He tried the keys he borrowed from David, but they were the wrong ones. "Only one option left. Stand back while I try to break in the door."

"Don't hurt yourself."

"I'm fine; SEAL training prepared me for more than this." He grunted, forcing himself into the door leading with his right side.

The lock broke and the door opened. Cautiously he turned on the flashlight and checked the light switch. "Didn't think there was any electricity here, but thought I'd try."

Victoria stayed close behind him. She shined her flashlight to the opposite sides as Christian called, "Sandy? Can you hear me? Are you all right?"

He tried again. "Sandy, if you can hear us, make a

noise."

Silence.

They walked the entire spa area. "I don't know much about spas"—Christian stood in the center—"but if there was a place to do a massage, wouldn't there be a table? I don't see anything but chairs for hair and manicures."

Victoria took a deep breath, and coughed. "I don't see one either. I smell something odd, don't you?"

He breathed deep. "It smells like incense."

"I don't see any potpourri, or candles, or even incense pots. Where's the smell coming from?"

Christian directed his flashlight along each wall and stopped at the one to the far right. "That looks like a door."

Victoria slowly walked to the door. "Definitely getting stronger."

She reached for the doorknob. "Locked. It's probably their supplies."

"Perhaps. Let me get it open."

"Before you bash in the door, let me check the desk for a key."

She walked over to the desk, opened the top drawer, and felt for tape under the top. "Got a key. I bet it's the one."

"What made you think to look there first?"

She blushed. "It's where I keep my key." She took the key and walked over to the door. It was such a small space, it took only seconds. "Voilà." She smiled as she opened the door.

Her smile vanished. "What the…."

Christian was inside with her. The supply closet led to the boiler room. "There's the smell. Large candles, burned almost to the end, but not quite."

Victoria walked a few feet and stopped. She grabbed Christian's arm and squeezed as if her life depended on it. "Nooooooo! This can't be! Oh no…please no! We got him…"

He put his hand over hers. "Sandy?"

Eyes tearing, a catch in her breath, she nodded. "Her hair…"

"Why don't you wait here?"

She loosened her grip, and Christian moved forward. Victoria waited, terrified. He stopped alongside the table. Her eyes went from Christian's grim expression to his clenching fists; horror welled up inside her. His look said it all. She took one tentative step forward and found Christian back at her side, providing the physical support she needed. She leaned on him, and used his silent strength as she approached the table shaking, her breathing getting more and more shallow.

Victoria's eyes were transfixed by what lay before her. She felt as though she were in a faraway tunnel with Christian's voice in the distance. Lightheaded, stars appeared before her eyes…then darkness.

She first felt a cool dampness on her forehead and a light stroking of her hair. Then his soothing voice…"I'm here, Victoria…so sorry you had to see this…so sorry, baby…"

She slowly opened her eyes and tried to sit up from her reclined position, but she felt as if a boulder lay across her body. "How did I get here?"

"I carried you. You passed out. You're in the spa, in one of the reclining chairs."

She closed her eyes again. The horror of what she

just witnessed flashed across her mind—her dear associate, chest open, eyelids taped, tongue hooked. Lips trembling, voice catching, she whispered, "Sandy, sweet dear Sandy...It was the Raven...He did this to her...I don't understand how...Did I prosecute the wrong man?" Tears poured down the side of her face as her shoulders wracked with painful sobs.

"Shhhh, we'll get him." He softly stroked her hair. "I need to go back into that room to make sure I didn't miss anything. Will you be all right?"

She slowly nodded in response.

The few minutes he was gone seemed like an eternity. Victoria carefully righted herself, as fresh tears poured down her cheeks. Coming by her side, he took her into his arms. With her head on his shoulder, she couldn't close the floodgates of tears. Sobbing, she said, "Perhaps it was an accomplice"—her voice faltered—"just like Sandy feared."

"Tell me about Sandy," he asked as he rubbed her back.

Trembling, she began. "She was such a kind person, dedicated, loving, would do anything for anyone." She breathed haltingly. "She worked so hard, not only at her job, but helping the underprivileged. I think she probably had more projects for the poor going on than anyone I know." She wiped the tears from her eyes with the back of her hands. "And yet, she always found time for God. On and off she prayed all day. I know, because I caught her at it." Victoria breathed in shakily as she thought about her.

"It sounds to me like she was a great example of what it meant to have a relationship with God."

She looked up with a tear-streaked face, sobs

caught in her throat. "Do you think that's what the Horse Whisperer meant when he saw she was at peace?"

"Yes, I do. Sandy is in the presence of our Lord where she will never know pain, only peace."

"But she was so young, and such a painful, horrible way to die. Christian, I know what he did to her."

"I'm sure you do."

She withdrew from Christian's arms and shook her head. "There were some things even too gruesome to put on the news. I guarantee an autopsy will show the murderer gave her a paralytic drug so she could feel everything. Did you see her eyes taped open? That's so she could watch. It's a horrible way to die. No one should die like that." She sobbed anew.

"You're right. No one should die like that."

She pounded the arm of her chair with her fist. "If she had such a great relationship with God, how could He let this happen to her?"

He combed his fingers through his hair. "I've asked my brother that very same question and I will share with you what he told me." He started to pace. "First, understand that you are asking a question that has been asked for thousands of years."

"Figures, there isn't an answer."

He stopped. "I didn't say that. It's just not simple." He closed his eyes and reopened them. "Evil is in this world, and will continue until Jesus comes again and a new world is established."

"So you're telling me that until then, God lets unthinkable things happen to people who have dedicated their lives to Him, like Sandy?"

"Oh boy…I've seen atrocities too, not unlike

what's happened to Sandy. And it's not something I take lightly or can accept. But one thing I have learned, is that when we have a relationship with God, He will lift our burden and direct our path if we let him. But we are not free from the hardships of this world."

"And Sandy?"

"There is no doubt in my mind that Sandy is with our Lord and is at peace. She is in a place where there is only happiness and no pain."

"How do you know?"

"The Bible tells us this, and I have faith it is so. Just as Sandy did."

"You sound like your brother. Don't tell me you get into all that Jesus stuff too."

"Ah, Victoria. Jesus saw me through more terrorizing events than I care to remember. But remember them I do, and I also remember that He never left me nor did He forsake me."

"I don't know what to think now. If I hadn't dismissed Sandy's fear, she might be alive."

"Stop talking like that. You couldn't have done anything. You prosecuted one man who was obviously involved. How were you to know there was another out there? You're not the police. They had no evidence there was another."

"The killer is still out there." Her face whitened further if that was possible. "Oh no, the killer is here…"

"We better get back to Elizabeth and David."

Christian closed the doors the way they found it, although they couldn't lock the outside door. He put his arm around her, as they hurried back to the café. "I'm going to first bring you back to the room, then find the manager. He needs to know about Sandy and make sure the spa is off limits."

At the door to Victoria's room, he stopped, held her by the shoulders, and looked deeply into her eyes. "I don't think we should tell Elizabeth about Sandy yet, but you know her best. What do you think?"

"She's pretty strong, but I don't know. After what happened to Brian…and she did get very close to Sandy. This might just put her over the edge."

"But how about you? How good an actress are you? And what about your puffy eyes?" He raised his right brow and tilted his head.

"Trial lawyers are actresses and actors. But it's easier to act when it's not personal. And this is personal, but I will do my best. Maybe she won't notice my eyes." She took a deep breath.

He kissed the top of her head. "See you real soon."

Chapter 14

Victoria opened the door to her room and caught Elizabeth working hard at her computer, signs of stress clearly evident on her face. It was obvious she was using work as an antidote to thinking about the fact that her wedding may not happen.

She jumped up. "Brian?"

Victoria shook her had.

Plopping back into her chair, she rubbed her temples and stared at the computer screen. "Almost finished. Anything at all that can help us find him?"

"Not yet. Christian went to check on Peter. Has he been by at all?"

"No. I was just finishing up Sandy's role in my new company. Do you at least know where she is?"

Victoria sighed deeply. She didn't want to lie, but Elizabeth was definitely upset enough that she was afraid to add that one last straw. She then looked toward David, who looked to be either praying or meditating, probably both, and turned her attention back to her friend. "No." She came up behind Elizabeth to look at her laptop screen and placed a hand on her shoulder. "I see you've been hard at it. What have you got for us?"

"The list you asked for. I divided it up between the creation of the business and the real estate. It involved two different groups of people, and only a few worked on both. Next to their names I put their job function."

Elizabeth hit print and handed it to Victoria. "Glad I didn't listen to Brian and brought my battery operated travel printer." Her brows came together in frown lines, and she started ringing her hands. "I wish everything was this simple…."

A knock at the door created a moment of hope. Elizabeth quickly got out of her chair and ran to the door. "Brian?"

"No. It's Christian."

Elizabeth opened the door. "Just hoping…I spoke to Joe again."

Christian stepped over the threshold. "Did he leave a message for me?"

Elizabeth looked hopeful. "Yes, he did. He said he's handled your request and is on standby."

"Perfect."

Victoria asked, "How about Peter?"

"Still no sign of him. David? Can you step outside with me? We need to talk.'

Elizabeth frowned. "Why not in front of us?"

"Brother talk, ladies. If you'll excuse us."

Victoria came to Elizabeth's side and hugged her as Elizabeth's tears started again. "There, there…he'll be okay."

"How can you say that?" She looked up at her best friend. "You don't even have a clue where he is. Do you think Peter could be looking for Brian on his own?"

"It's definitely possible, but he hasn't checked in with anyone, so there's no way to know for sure."

The brothers reentered the room, and Victoria noted their grim expressions. "We were just about to run down the list Elizabeth created."

"Good. Let's see what you have."

Victoria skimmed the document. "I'll start with the creation of the business. Brian of course was in charge of the project. Sandy worked under him and was the link between its creation and the real estate."

"That's right. She was the liaison between the two groups to make sure it all came together."

"I noticed you listed some administrative assistants. Ruth is listed for Brian and Sandy. I didn't see her here. Did she come?"

"No. She couldn't make it."

"For marketing, you listed Teddy Whyler, the managing partner of Starlight, Limited. Is he here?"

"He's supposed to be, although I haven't seen him yet."

"Now for the real estate side. We have Peter Mack, his associate Sissy Tram, their paralegal Dennis Ryder, and their administrative assistant, Louise Clarkson. We know Peter and Dennis are here, how about the others?"

"Sissy is supposed to be here, but I haven't seen her either."

"How about Louise?"

"She was invited, but she declined."

"Is this a complete list?"

"As best as I could do. It contains only the people I dealt with. There may be others of course, but they wouldn't be here for the wedding."

Victoria folded the list up and put it in her pocket. "We need your help again." She proceeded to tell her about Jimmy and the Ute. "So, we seem to have some clues, although we don't know how reliable yet. It's a place to start."

"I'm inclined to believe it's a good place to start,"

Christian pointed out. "Elizabeth, you know this hotel better than we do. We need your help in the search."

"All right. But wait, what if Brian comes back here or Peter checks in?"

David volunteered. "I'll stay. You're needed more than I am. I'll continue to meditate on what the Horse Whisperer shared and see if something comes to me."

Christian moved to the door. "That works. Ladies, let's go."

"Be right there. I just want to leave a note in case Brian comes back. It's good to get out of the room. I'll be doing something other than pacing and staring at a computer screen. At this rate, I'll be too skinny for my wedding gown."

Elizabeth scribbled a note, tucked it into the edge of the mirror, and secured it with a piece of tape. "That ought to do it," she said, grabbing her down vest to put over her jacket.

"David, feel free to use my computer."

"Thanks."

Christian with Victoria, pad in hand, were already in the hall when Elizabeth joined them. "We've got to be organized about this. I've been taking notes on my trusty little pad and created a list."

"Then you must have really liked my list."

"Absolutely."

Christian gently closed the door. As he turned around he asked, "Let's have Jimmy's clues."

"His clues included a raven, Lord Macraven, Alexander Gregory tied to revenge, she, spirits, and finally the vision quest and Ute which led us to the Horse Whisperer. I've also noted Edgar Allen Poe only because we've heard a line from his poem a couple of times now, *Quoth the Raven, 'Nevermore.'* It may mean something."

"What about clues from the Horse Whisperer?"

"We have darkness, pain, knife with blood, a raven laughing deep inside a tree, and a soaring eagle searching. We were given a warning about a raven."

"Yes, but the raven piece seemed to be more directed to you."

"Maybe. Ramsey, who I believed was the Raven, did say that the Raven will stop at nothing until he owns me. But the Horse Whisperer could have also been looking at me because he knew I was the note taker." Victoria smiled at that.

"Don't count on it. The killer was referred to as the Raven, and you were the special prosecutor. I believe the Ute's warning was directed to you. Don't take it lightly."

She thought of Sandy and her eyes filled with tears. Visions of her dear associate on that table, strawberry blond hair hanging, chest held open, filled her mind. Softly she said, "Trust me, I won't. We all need to be cautious. Elizabeth, any suggestions about where we should start first?"

"I really don't know. Nothing seems to be too specific. Dark places can mean anywhere. The storm has subsided, but it's not exactly light outside. It's not light inside either for that matter without electricity. We have two rooms that might be a good place to start. Jimmy mentioned Lord Macraven and Alexander Gregory. Since there are two rooms named after them, they're the logical starting points."

"Good idea." Victoria made some notes. "Let's start with the Gregory Room. That seems to be Jimmy's favorite place. Also, he disappeared while we were with him. Now granted, the candles had flickered off so it wasn't exactly light, but I don't believe he exited from the same place where we entered."

"That's right," Christian added. "Does everyone have their flashlights?"

"Yes," they answered in unison.

As they entered the Gregory Room, the hinges squeaked once more, only this time Victoria was ready for it and asked Elizabeth, "Are you aware of any hidden areas in this room?"

"Well, the stage was added for a movie production. It was supposed to be a temporary stage. In order for the performers to come and go inconspicuously, there had to be some places the audience could not see. I'm not quite sure where they are though, but if we look hard enough we should be able to find them." Elizabeth pointed to one area in particular. "I have seen performers come and go from that corner. Let's check it out."

The four of them proceeded to the corner of the stage. Christian was the first there. "Victoria, shine your light while I feel for a door."

"Here we go." She followed Christian's hands and remembered the comfort they provided her just a short time ago.

"Found it."

He managed to open the door, shined his light into the small hall, and found another door. "Ladies, there's something here. Let's go."

They followed close on his heels. Sure enough, there was another door, but it only opened to what appeared to be a small dressing room. The three of them examined the room closely. "I can't find an exit," Victoria said.

"I don't think there is one," Christian acknowledged. "It's possible that Jimmy did come this way, and just stayed here. This might be his hiding place."

"Maybe, but I doubt it. I can't find any evidence he's been here for any prolonged period. We'd see paper wrappers or something."

"Let's check out the rest of the room." Elizabeth already started to back out.

Further examination of the Gregory Room revealed nothing. The threesome was disappointed. While Elizabeth and Christian took the lead and headed for the Macraven Boardroom on the second floor, Victoria paused and studied the entrance to the Gregory Room. Once again, she stopped to study the two portraits, F.O. Preston on the left and Lord Macraven to the right. Something about them beckoned to her.

"Hey guys," Victoria called out, but they were out of earshot, engrossed in conversation.

The portrait of Lord Macraven mesmerized her. "Why do you hold such a prominent place at the entrance to the Gregory Room? What are you hiding?" Chills ran up her spine.

Alone, outside the Gregory Room, Victoria noted the vast reception area had not one, but two fireplaces, one only a few feet from Lord Macraven's portrait. She carefully examined the fireplace, its mantel, and the area surrounding it.

She turned back to Lord Macraven's portrait, captivated by his eyes. She followed the direction in which his eyes appeared to travel. *Could this be likened to the pot of gold at the end of a rainbow?* At the end of this rainbow was a beautiful sculpture of an eagle in flight, searching for its prey.

She took out her notes. The Horse Whisperer mentioned the eagle that searches but does not find. *Could this be the clue revealed by the Horse Whisperer?*

Victoria got as close as she could to the eagle, but she couldn't get close enough. Looking around her, she pushed one of the plush chairs closer so she could stand on it. It went against her grain to put her feet on the furniture, but these were definitely extraordinary circumstances.

She stood on the chair and took a closer look. The sculpture was beautiful, the detail absolutely amazing. She remembered being told that just down the mountain in Loveland, sculptors came from all over to display and sell their work during the annual invitational. She tried to lift the eagle, but it was very heavy. It would definitely take at least two hands. Good thing she worked out, she thought as she attempted to move the sculpture. It slid, but it would not come off. She heard a click, as if a latch unlocked.

She shined the flashlight from her perch, but saw nothing. Slowly she stepped down from the chair and searched for the source of the sound. Something caught her attention in the fireplace. Part of the back wall of the fireplace moved out. She froze. *Could this be a secret door?*

She reached in and tried to pull it open, but it wouldn't budge. Directly next to this area, she noticed a lever. As she lifted the lever, a small door opened. Victoria crouched down to its opening and shined in her flashlight. *Wow. This has to be one of those tunnels everyone's been talking about.*

Did curiosity kill the cat? Well, I won't let it kill this one, she thought as she moved in. It was a narrow passage that went back for about ten or so feet and then hooked to the right. Made sense. It probably went behind the registration area.

She crept cautiously through the tunnel listening for any of her furry friends. A creak sounded causing her to suck in her breath and stop. Quickly she turned off her light. Holding her breath, she quietly felt along the wall as the sound of a door opening and another shutting made her heart race. A light glow of light came from around the corner.

She stopped, careful not to make a sound. Being here alone was not such a good idea. After what happened to Sandy, a woman she knew could take care of herself, why should she think she could do better? *I need Christian here. This was not one of my brighter moments.* Slowly she felt her way back in the direction she came, counting her steps. But, when she came to the spot behind the fireplace, the door was closed. No longer an option.

Victoria made her way back to where it hooked right and decided to take her chances. Taking inventory of any self-defense weapons she had on her, she realized she left her purse in the room and only had a flashlight. Thankful she was well trained in the martial arts, she knew she had to rely on herself. Someone or something was around the corner.

She closed her eyes and meditated a few minutes before proceeding. Moving in stealth-like fashion, she rounded the bend.

****

For the first time, Elizabeth felt her spirits lift a little. "Thank you, Christian. You've saved my Brian once, and I have no doubt you, David, and Victoria will be like the Three Musketeers and do it again. You give me hope."

"We'll do our best. I've got additional resources ready should we need them." Christian stopped to open the door to the Macraven Room, located at the top of the grand staircase on the second floor.

"I never did know what you do for a living. Care to enlighten me?"

"Joe and I are partners in J.C. Classified. We're world-wide and specialize in search and rescue. We do a lot of government work."

"Then you are just what the doctor ordered. I can't thank you enough." Her new found hope could not be contained.

When they entered the room, Christian looked back. "Where's Victoria?"

"I thought she was right behind us."

"She's not. I don't like her going off on her own."

"Technically, she must have stayed where we were and we left her on her own. I was so caught up with our conversation and my belief we really have a chance to find Brian, I didn't realize she wasn't with us."

"Let's go right back."

"Christian, she's just down one flight of stairs and the reception desk is near her with employees coming and going. This is a small boardroom so it shouldn't take us too long to search it. It looks like it's one of those conference rooms reserved for businesses only."

He hesitated.

"She was taken with the painting of Lord Macraven. She's probably still studying it. Anyway, if something's amiss, we'll hear her."

Christian quickly searched the cabinets as she spoke. With the number of cabinets, it was taking longer than they thought.

"Christian, I've got something."

****

Victoria gasped. "Peter, what are you doing here?"

Peter's head snapped up. "I could ask the same thing of you."

Victoria sighed, thankful it wasn't someone dangerous, like the Raven. "We've been searching for Brian, and frankly, we started worrying about you when you weren't in your room and didn't check in with Elizabeth."

Peter shrugged. "I couldn't just sit and wait. I decided to start checking out the tunnels I know about."

"Did you toss your room?"

"No. I'm kind of a neatnik. I can't stand disorder of any kind." Peter frowned. "Why do you ask?"

"Your room was tossed. Every drawer was dumped. One of the lamps was on the floor, the shade broken. And the stench was something else. It smelled like something died in there." She wrinkled her nose as she spoke.

"It's nice to know you were worried." Peter swiftly closed the distance and took her by the shoulders. Stunned, she froze as he looked deep into her eyes and bent his head for a kiss.

Chapter 15

Victoria turned her head and Peter kissed her cheek. Taken totally by surprise, she was rattled and upset. *This is not something I need to deal with. Especially with a man who is not only a co-worker, but also a named partner.* In the distance, Victoria heard Christian and Elizabeth calling her name.

She stepped away from Peter and cupped her hands around her mouth. "Hey! We're in a tunnel!" she shouted.

Christian called back. "We hear you, but can't see you. Where are you?"

"Behind the fireplace near the Gregory Room. I have Peter with me."

Peter stepped around the bend and flipped the latch pushing open the fireplace door. "Hey, guys."

Elizabeth was relieved. "Peter, we were worried about you. Any luck finding Brian?"

"No. I had trouble just waiting, so I wanted to check out some of the lesser-known places I was familiar with. Anything happening on your end?"

Hands on hips, she was obviously upset. "Next time kindly let someone know what you're up to. We don't need two missing persons."

"Sorry I worried you. I'm not used to letting people know where I am," he said, striking a pose, "you know, being a bachelor and all that."

"Forgiven."

"I was just informed that my room's been tossed and literally it's a stinking mess." Peter rubbed his hand up and down his right thigh.

"That's right." Christian's eyes narrowed.

Peter bowed at Elizabeth. "With your permission, madame, I'd like to check it out."

She curtsied in return. "Permission granted."

As Peter left, Christian turned his attention to Victoria. "You look a little shaken." He raised his eyebrow in question.

"Nothing to share. You'd look a little shaken too if you were in my shoes."

"I bet." He couldn't knock the feeling that something was up.

Victoria brought them back on task. "Anything in the Macraven Boardroom?"

"Yes, there was," Elizabeth quickly piped in, "a lead off your list."

"What lead?" She was already on her way to the second floor.

"Just a minute, we need to catch up," Elizabeth said breathlessly.

Victoria was the first one in the room. Elizabeth led the way to one of the knobs on the far cabinet. "What do you see?"

"A knob."

"Look carefully at the knob."

"It has an engraving of a raven. What's so unusual about that? This is the Macraven Boardroom isn't it?"

"Yes it is," Christian interjected. "Look at the other knobs."

Victoria quickly looked at all of them. "All trees.

The Horse Whisperer mentioned a raven in a tree. Could he have meant this raven among all these trees?"

Christian shrugged. "Could be, but take another look at the raven."

She squat down to study the knob. "The raven appears to be sitting on a branch; therefore, this raven is in a tree. Well, this must mean something." She opened the cabinets one by one. "All empty except for the one by the phone system. That one has small hotel notebooks and about a dozen pens."

Christian took a Swiss Army pocket knife out of his pocket and squat until he was just about eye level with the knob. "I wanted to try one more thing." He opened it up and used the screwdriver to remove the knob.

Victoria stooped over his shoulder, resting her hands on his shoulders, her face glowing with anticipation as she peered inside the knob.

"Elizabeth, you were right. You definitely have something here." Victoria smiled as Christian removed a key from inside of the knob.

Elizabeth took the key and slowly turned it in her hand. "How odd. This looks like an original key for the hotel. It's very old. I wonder what it belongs to."

Victoria picked up the key and examined it. "I'm not sure, but it's too big for a small box. It most likely is a key to a door. But I'm no key expert. Why don't we ask Maggie?" She already had one foot out the door.

Christian took hold of her arm. "What directed you to the tunnel?"

"I was studying the portrait of Lord Macraven and his eyes were focused on a statue of the eagle on the mantel. The eagle was a sculpture of one flying, searching, and I remembered what the Horse Whisperer said about his vision quest. When I moved the eagle, the door unlatched and I went in."

Christian sighed and kept his voice low, so Elizabeth couldn't hear. "Not a good idea when you're alone you know, especially when we've got a missing person and possibly a connected murder. Next time, please don't go anywhere or do anything alone."

"I'm as worried as you are, but I'm not totally defenseless. If you only knew how much digging I did alone when I prosecuted cases. That's why I study the martial arts, where I compete at the black belt level. I like to know I can take care of myself. Plus, don't forget my 007 collection."

"And was your 007 collection on you?"

"Uh, no."

"What good is it then?"

"When we go back to the room, I promise I'll take it with me. By the way, sorry I snapped. I'm just frustrated, and I refuse to let fear get in my way."

"All right then, now enlighten me. How did you find Peter?

"We sort of ran into each other. He was checking out the tunnels he was familiar with, like he said, and I just happened to fall into the tunnel by accident, really." Victoria held Christian's eyes. "Why?"

"I don't know. I had an uneasy feeling, and my feelings are rarely wrong."

"Could it be because he seems to be interested in me? Perhaps you are experiencing a little jealousy."

"Nonsense. Let's find Maggie," Christian said as they approached the reception area.

The laughter began. They froze, trying to discern

the direction of the laughter. Victoria started for the Gregory Room. "He's back in the Gregory Room."

"I'm with you," he said right on Victoria's heels.

"Wait up, guys, don't leave me alone." Elizabeth ran to them trying to keep up.

Jimmy was center stage sitting on the throne. The laughter came to an abrupt end, and a new voice resonated from Jimmy. "You hold the answer in your hand."

A new voice arose. "Shut up, smart one."

The first voice returned. "I'll foil you yet, Macraven."

The second voice answered, "When hell freezes over."

Laughter resonated and then faded away as the flashlights blinked off. Christian shook his and flicked the switch. When he got it back on, Jimmy was gone.

Chapter 16

Victoria pulled the list Elizabeth gave her from her pocket. "Guys, let's go to the registration desk and see if any of the people on this list have checked in."

"Good idea. Ladies, after you." He swept his hand prompting them to move out ahead of himself.

Victoria smiled at the clerk and spotted Mike, the manager. "Hi. I see you've taken our suggestions to heart and got the door repaired."

"Yes, ma'am. We still can't get through to the police though."

"Please keep trying. In the meantime, we need to know if any of these people have checked in."

Mike took the list and checked out all the names. "Our computers are still down, but I know that Mr. Dennis Ryder and Ms. Sissy Tram have checked in. I know Mr. Teddy Whyler. He's a regular here at our restaurant and some of the activities, but he never stays. He has a family cottage walking distance from here, so he won't be checking in with us, but he's here."

"Where did you see him?"

"Right here in the reception area. He was talking to Ms. Tram."

"Any others on that list here?"

"Not that I know of." Mike turned to his clerk. "Do any of these other names look familiar to you?"

Her badge said Stacy. "No, sir. They don't."

Victoria took her list back. "Thank you. Can you tell us where Sissy Tram is staying?"

Mike looked at the key board. "Again, that information is in the computer system. We tried to keep the men together on the same floor, and the single women on a different floor. Couples are on the second, although exceptions were made. So, I could see what keys are missing and we could narrow it that way."

"Excuse me, Mike?" Stacy interrupted. "I was helping the wedding organizer, Renie, and I printed off the list of wedding guests and the rooms they're staying in for her. I bet she has it in her office."

Victoria's smiled widened. "Excellent. Where's her office?"

"Downstairs." Stacy smiled. "It's right next to the display outside the café. I'd be happy to take you."

Mike frowned. "I don't think that will be necessary. I'll just give you the key and let you check it out for yourself. I like the idea of pairs."

Christian said, "That's okay. We passed it earlier today."

Mike handed them the key. "No rush, just return the key when you're finished with it. I have another."

Christian took the key. "Thank you."

"Ladies, let's first go to the room and do a little brainstorming."

Elizabeth sighed. "I like that idea. I want to see if Brian came back."

As they started back, to the room, Victoria noticed Elizabeth kept her eyes on her. It's hard to be a good actress in front of someone who knew her the way Elizabeth did. Victoria smiled, but it did not appease her BFF.

"Hey girlfriend, I noticed when you first came to the room to get me that your eyes were red and puffy. I put it up to allergies in an old hotel, but they are looking better despite where we've just been. So, the only other alternative is crying. What's going on?"

"Allergies, stress, lack of sleep...."

She looked at Christian's grim expression. "There's something you're not sharing."

Victoria took her by the arm, fighting back more tears, and they proceeded upstairs. "Let's get back to the room first."

"Is it Brian?"

Victoria shook her head no.

As they entered the room, she said, "It's Sandy." Tears started sliding down her face. Christian came to Victoria's side while David led Elizabeth back to a seat and took her hands in his. "We did find Sandy...."

Elizabeth looked to Victoria and back to David. "She's dead, isn't she?"

He held her gaze and slightly nodded his head.

"God help us. How?" She hugged herself.

Victoria grabbed a tissue and blew her nose. "Sandy thought there might be an accomplice. She might have been right." More tears streamed down her cheek as Victoria explained how she found Sandy.

Elizabeth jumped up and grabbed hold of Victoria as they cried together.

Christian stood uncomfortably while David put a comforting hand on each shoulder.

As the crying started to subside, Christian cleared his throat. "Ladies, I know you are hurting, but we really need to get on with our search."

After another round of tissues, Victoria nodded.

"You're right. We need to focus on Brian."

Elizabeth rubbed her eyes. "Do you think whoever did this to Sandy is the one who has Brian?"

"We don't know at this point. Let's follow through with our initial plan and brainstorm. One of us may have a critical piece of information and not realize it, me included. What do you say?"

"Okay." Elizabeth's voice shook. "I feel like it's my fault. Maybe if I hadn't insisted she come for a break."

"It's not your fault. It may be mine though." Victoria looked down at the papers in her hands.

Christian cleared his throat. "Enough, ladies. Let's stop wasting time trying to place blame. It's nobody's fault."

Elizabeth plopped down on the bed, while Christian leaned against the dresser and David gazed out the window. Victoria sat at the desk, pen in hand and cleared her throat. "Let's start with who we know is up here."

"Good idea." David shook his head in thought.

"Teddy Whyler was the person in charge of marketing. Elizabeth, how did you meet him?"

"He came highly recommended by Peter."

"How did Peter know him?"

"I'm not sure, but he said that he's done work for some of his clients before and it was top notch. He has a great reputation in the industry."

"Okay." Victoria tapped the pen on the desk. "Have you been happy with what he's done so far?"

"Oh yes. He even found our building."

"But he's not a Realtor, is he?"

"No, but it's a great building."

"Who are the sellers?"

"LM Returns Corporation."

Victoria made notes. "Do you know anything about the company?"

"No. They didn't even show up at the closing. Their attorney provided signed documents."

Victoria read off Elizabeth's list. "Peter was the senior attorney, Sissy Tram was the associate, and Dennis Ryder, the paralegal. You also have the secretary, Louise Clarkston. Anyone else?"

"If there were, I didn't know about them."

"Good enough."

"Let's get back to Teddy Whyler. Did you ever visit him at his office?"

Elizabeth smiled. "I sure did, and I'll never forget it."

"A good experience?"

"Oh yes."

"Good." Victoria had an idea. "What I'd like you to do is lie down on the bed, close your eyes, and think back to the visit. I want you to tell me everything about it."

Elizabeth lay back on the bed and closed her eyes. "It was a rather nice visit, a step back in time. First I was met at the door by a woman in a traditional maid's uniform from the nineteenth century."

"Do you recall her name?"

"Margaret. She had me wait in the foyer. It felt like I walked into a time machine and ended up in the late eighteen hundreds. Rich, dark wood surrounded me along with a beautiful hand woven oriental area rug. Large porcelain vases graced the entry filled with fresh flowers."

"Your memory is amazing," David said.

"Not always, only when I am really impressed, which I was."

"Go on," Victoria prodded.

"Margaret came back, offered me English tea, and led me into the reception area, which in most homes would have been the living room. There was a beautiful stone fireplace with a comforting fire. More fresh flowers that matched the wallpaper in what looked like heirloom crystal vases. Heavy draperies adorned the windows. That was common in that era you know."

"Yes, I know."

"Then Teddy came in. He was so proper. He bowed over my hand as I extended it to shake his, and he kissed the top of it instead."

"Was this the first time you met Teddy Whyler?"

"Yes, it was."

"Could you describe him to us?"

"Sure. He was tall and lanky. His dark hair was peppered with gray while his side burns were almost all gray. His eyes were such an unusual shade of light blue, almost like ice, they sent a shiver up my spine."

"We walked down a long hallway to the back of the house. All along the walls were framed artworks displaying a sampling of his marketing pieces."

"Were you impressed?"

"Definitely. His staff is quite diversified."

"Did you meet any of his staff?"

Elizabeth thought, eyes still closed. "No. Only Margaret. But he did say he had a staff of fifteen, plus support staff. I kind of feel like I'm under cross examination."

Victoria smiled. "Sorry about that. It's an

occupational hazard."

"No problem. At this point I wasn't one hundred percent I was going to hire him so I wanted to know how long he'd been in business."

"And?"

"The firm was started by his grandfather right there. The house, which acted as his office, was the original home where his grandfather was raised. I thought that very interesting."

"Where did you go from the hallway?"

"Why, his personal office of course. It was impressive with deep mahogany bookcases filled with leather bound books. Artwork covered the walls. Another beautiful oriental rug created a sense of comfort. And the ambience was further topped off with another warm fireplace. What a work environment that is!"

"Obviously, you were impressed enough to hire him. What fees have you paid to date?"

"Ah, I'm not sure. Everything is billed through Brian's firm. I believe the real estate paralegal Dennis Ryder handled all that. I just paid whatever bill I got."

"Didn't you check them?"

"Sort of. I wasn't as careful as I usually am, it being Brian's firm and all that."

"Anything else you can remember about Teddy or his offices that was unusual?"

"Well, yes there was. I even mentioned it to him. Teddy seemed to have a thing for certain wildlife."

"Wildlife in the office of someone who is a real outdoorsman may not be so unusual. What was there about it that caught your attention?" Christian rearranged himself against the dresser.

"Well, there were all kinds, but there was a reoccurring theme of ravens and eagles."

"How were these themes displayed?"

"Pictures, mainly through paintings and photographs. There was also a sculpture of an eagle, and a sculpture of a raven."

"Good. Just relax and think back to every raven you saw. Where were they?"

"The fireplace set had ravens for handles. There was one sculpture on the fireplace and a painting over the fireplace. The painting was a mountain scene with a raven set as the focal point. And, Teddy wore an unusual ring. It had the profile of a raven with a diamond eye."

"Anything else?" Victoria hunched forward in her chair.

"Not that I can recall."

"How about Sissy Tram?"

"She's a cold one. Her office was very impersonal, no photos, personal books, nothing. It reminded me of a sterile hospital."

"How often did you meet with her?"

"Not very. She worked with Dennis on the real estate documents, but I tried to avoid her. I asked Brian why they would hire someone with so few interpersonal skills."

"What was Brian's reasoning?"

"He said he didn't. Sissy was Peter's hire. He usually lets Peter have his way with anything to do with the real estate end."

"How about Dennis?"

"A very hard worker. Frankly I think they can do without Sissy and just let Dennis handle most everything."

They heard a *swoosh, puh, puh, puh, swoosh.*
Victoria jumped up. "Sounds like a helicopter."

Chapter 17

Victoria was the first to the window. Under normal conditions, dawn would have lit the skies, but the heavy cloud cover made that impossible. David walked up behind her and Elizabeth joined them. The snow's reflection allowed them to see the chopper land. Christian left without another word, with the other three close behind.

Victoria watched from the front balcony as Christian made his way toward the pilot and grabbed him in a bear hug. Next to her, Elizabeth pulled her fleece jacket closer around her. "You'd have me fooled this was March."

"Yeah, me too."

"Obviously this chopper visit is Christian's doing. I really don't know much about him, I just heard all the stories about how he helped save Brian in Poland. Maybe the second time's a charm."

"I think the saying goes third time's the charm. Let's hope you're right though."

Elizabeth sighed. "Do you know anything about what this chopper is doing here?"

"No, but it must have something to do with finding Brian."

"Do you know anything about his company? I asked him, but his response was pretty vague, although he did assure me that search and rescue was one of their areas of expertise, which I found quite comforting."

"I don't know much more than you. As you know, Joe is his partner and was one of his former SEAL buddies." She studied the two men in the distance. "I wonder if that's Joe. He's a little shorter than Christian, but stockier, like a tree trunk. Hmm, he just gave Christian a hefty looking bag."

The guys started toward the hotel. Victoria couldn't help but see the extra spring to Christian's step and the grin that just about cut his face in half. The bag was obviously heavy.

"Ladies, I'd like you to meet my partner, Joe."

Elizabeth shook his hand first. "Thanks for coming. I am assuming you didn't brave this weather without a good reason."

"You're observant. Nice meeting you."

"My brother, David, you know." They shook hands.

"And this is Victoria."

"Wow! My partner sure knows how to surround himself with beautiful women. And by the way, the television doesn't do you justice." He smiled as he held her hand a little too long.

Christian bristled. "Okay, Joe's got to take off, but he'll be back with reinforcements."

Victoria blushed. "Thanks. And thanks for coming." She looked at the duffel. "Whatever you brought, I hope it helps find Brian."

"Yeah, well, anything to help. Like Christian said, there are a few more operational pieces needed for what he has in mind, and then I will be back."

She followed his gaze toward Christian. Something about those emerald green eyes and the confidence he exuded added strength to her resolve and hope in finding Brian before it was too late, not to mention the murderer. She cleared her throat. "I'm assuming you know about Brian's associate, Sandy?"

"Christian filled me in. We've got a killer loose here as well, and from the looks of it, he or she could have Brian."

"Yes, but let's hope not. You see, I either prosecuted the wrong man, or he had an accomplice, or we have a copycat for the Raven."

Christian stared into the distance and rubbed his jaw line. "That about sums it up. Now you know why I needed my special bag of tricks."

The little group stood in silence.

"Well, I've got to get going to take care of Phase II. I'll be back as soon as I can."

"You got it, partner."

Joe saluted the group and returned to his chopper.

They watched him take off, and then Christian broke their silence. "I'd like to go back to the crime scene and check out Renie's office to see if we can find the guest list and rooms. David, why don't you join me?"

Victoria interrupted. "That's a good idea. Elizabeth and I will return to the room and do more brainstorming."

Victoria grabbed David's upper arm. "Just be careful not to disturb the crime scene. Maybe I should go and you can go with Elizabeth."

Christian chuckled. "Although I'd love the company of a beautiful woman, it really won't be necessary. I don't think I need to remind you that handling crime scenes is part of what I do for a living."

"All right then. Let's separate and join back at our room."

"You got it."

Victoria watched the brothers descend the stairs. She realized she had been holding her breath, so she let it out slowly. "Let's go."

****

Back at the room, Victoria paced. "Have you gone through any of the gifts you've received so far?"

Elizabeth was sprawled on the bed facing the ceiling. "Well yes. We've gotten cards and gifts before today. I like to be prompt and not get behind on my thank you notes, so yes, I've gone through what we've received so far."

"Did anything strike you as unusual in any way, even in a small way?"

"As a matter of fact, I received an odd card."

"Odd in what way?"

"For starters, it's not signed by anyone. It was slipped under our door before you got here and I found that odd. And then the card was just weird."

"Do you have it?"

"Yeah. I was going to ask Brian about it. It's in my show Brian pile." She got up from the bed and walked to the pile on the desk.

Shuffling through a stack of cards, she pulled one out. "Here it is. See for yourself."

Victoria took the card. "The outside is a print. Not exactly wedding card material, but appropriate for Eustis Park. Huh. It seems to be a print depicting what was spoken to us by the Horse Whisperer."

"In what way?"

"There's a soaring eagle high above a tree. That's

in my notes. In the tree there's another bird guarding its nest." Victoria squinted. "What does this look like to you?"

She handed it back to Elizabeth.

"Kind of looks like a raven to me."

"Yeah. Me too." She opened the card and started reading aloud:

Where eagles soar above the clouds
Searching, searching.
Where eagles nest upon a tree,
There you will find the treasured key.
Deep within nature's hollow,
My dear friends you will follow.
Happily Ever After
You should seek,
A home to share,
As a pair,
A heartfelt treasure,
A life worth living together.
Forever your love will grow in unity,
Under the eagle's protection in continuity.
The rhythm of life,
As husband and wife,
Drumming in tune,
To a world of fortune,
The answer my friends,
Is within the map,
Tap, tap,
Click, click chimes the computer's keys.
Quoth the raven, "Nevermore."

Victoria took a deep sigh. "Whoever wrote this is no poet. This is a literary anomaly."

A knock sounded at the door, and Elizabeth

jumped.

"It's just us," David called through the door.

Elizabeth let them in while Victoria checked her watch. "You guys were pretty quick."

"Yeah, well, we didn't stay all that long at the crime scene, and we found the guest list right away." David took his perch on the dresser.

Christian leaned against the door.

"We have another piece of the puzzle to show you." She handed the card to Christian.

"This was slipped under our door. Elizabeth just showed it to me when I asked her if she got anything unusual for her wedding."

He frowned and handed it to David who looked up after reading. "This fits with the clues from the Horse Whisperer. I wonder if the key we found is the one referenced in this card."

Victoria slowly shook her head up and down in agreement. "It definitely seems to fit the clues, and that key might just be the one referenced. There is one more thing that may be important." Victoria took a deep breath and let it out slowly.

"Go on," Christian pried.

"When Elizabeth and I were brainstorming right before Joe's visit, remember that unusual gold ring she mentioned? It had a raven with a diamond eye. Well, the man I prosecuted wore a ring of the same description when he was captured."

"Now that's interesting and needs exploring. It's possible they belonged to a similar group, kind of like the Masons."

"I was thinking the same thing," Victoria said.

"Our first stop should be the Horse Whisperer.

Maybe he can now add to what you've already found, especially when it seems he's been right on the mark. Before we go though, I'd like to see that key again."

Victoria handed him the key and watched as he examined it.

"An old one all right, probably the age of this hotel." He handed it back. "Why don't we pay a visit to the Horse Whisperer now? Then, see if we can't locate some of our guests."

"Sounds good," David said as he pushed up from the dresser. "Even though we could probably get to the stables outside, let's use the tunnel."

Christian nodded and opened the door.

"Me too?" Elizabeth asked.

"Yeah, I really don't want you here alone." Victoria took Elizabeth by the hand and led her to the door. "Ah, just a minute, my purse." Victoria shot Christian a smile and clipped it to her waist.

The group took the stairs to the ground floor. David opened the hidden door to the tunnel and went first. Victoria and Elizabeth followed, and Christian brought up the rear.

Victoria heard the Ute chanting as David opened the door to the stables. Quietly, respectfully, they approached the Horse Whisperer and sat cross-legged in his presence. Again, Victoria was engulfed in a blanket of peace. She closed her eyes to drink it all in, steadying her breathing in her own meditation.

Victoria could hear David pray softly. "Lead us, oh Lord. Help us, oh Lord. Protect us, oh Lord. May your child Brian be safe."

The Horse Whisperer opened his eyes and greeted his visitors. "Welcome. I was expecting you."

Victoria asked, "How could you expect us?"

"Ah, Victorious One, you are in possession of leads resulting from my vision quest, but you know not what to do with them."

He looked at Christian, while continuing to speak to Victoria. "I see you brought with you the one who catches his prey and the bride."

Christian spoke up. "Thank you for seeing us. Have you had any more dreams or visions since you last spoke to us?"

"Time is running out. I see hunger, thirst, and cold. Direction can be found in the key." The Horse Whisperer closed his eyes and started to chant.

Victoria pulled out the key and held it up. "This key?"

But the Horse Whisperer was deep in a trance.

Chapter 18

Victoria studied both David and Christian as they left the Horse Whisperer. She saw the similarities, but there were genuine differences.

What is it with the Van der Kruis men? David first captured my heart, and then broke it. He made me leery of relationships, which may have saved me, but I don't know. I like my life, my freedom, no ties to anyone but whom I want to be tied to for the moment. But what I saw with Elizabeth and Brian, I don't know. It's special. She sighed.

"You okay?" David asked.

"Yeah. Just thinking."

"About?"

"Nothing that concerns you."

David shrugged.

Victoria looked at Christian. She was definitely drawn, and just like his brother, he seems to have the ability to see into her soul.

As they reentered the tunnel, Victoria stretched. "This is the second time the Horse Whisperer left me with two contrasting emotions, both peace and urgency. And I've only seen him twice."

"You're not the only one," David added.

Christian nodded. "He definitely has insight. In my experience, people like the Horse Whisperer have a gift that is reliable. Time is short. I believe Brian may still be alive, but not for long."

Victoria turned her attention back to Christian. "And what type of experiences have you had?"

He looked at her and smiled. "Oh, various sorts, but as I mentioned earlier, search and rescue have been a popular one for me."

"As the rescuee or searcher?" Victoria chided.

"Definitely the searcher. You mentioned clues from Jimmy. I came in at the end so I missed out. I think we should revisit him."

Father David answered. "I agree, and with you here, I'd like to try an exorcism. It may be helpful to both Jimmy and us in locating Brian. I know Jimmy's seen something. The demons within definitely know something."

"We're near the kitchen. Let's find Nate and see what we can do," Victoria said, heading for the kitchen.

Maggie was helping out and lifted her head as Victoria entered. David, Christian, and Elizabeth followed.

"Hi, Maggie. You still up?" Victoria smiled.

"A few of us were on all night duty, and I volunteered to stay on. The day shift hasn't been able to get here. Can I do something for you?"

David said, "As a matter of fact you can. Would you mind returning to the room with Elizabeth and keeping her company for a little while?"

She dried her hand on the towel and covered her mouth as she yawned. "Would love to."

Elizabeth sighed. "That's not necessary."

"Yes it is. I'd rather you not be here for what we have planned. We'll be right back if it's a no go."

"Okay."

Elizabeth left with Maggie.

Victoria found Nate at work in the back of the kitchen. "Would it be possible for David to perform that exorcism he spoke to you about?"

"Now would probably be best. Jimmy's asleep on the cot in my office. Let's go."

The office was on the other side of the fireplace in the kitchen. As they came upon the door, Nate placed his hand on the doorknob, and they were assaulted with ear piercing screams.

"My poor Jimmy has suffered from night terrors for quite a while now. Do you think the exorcism would relieve him of these?"

"It's very possible," David said, pulling out his rosary and prayer book containing the Ritual from his inside pocket. "When we go inside, it's important for all of us to pray. Christian, Nate, I may need you both to physically restrain Jimmy. And Nate, after we enter, please lock the door."

When the door locked behind them, David opened his prayer book and started with the first blessing and prayer of deliverance, the "Prayer against Malefice." "*Kyrie eleison.* God, our Lord, King of ages, All-powerful and All-mighty, you who made everything and who transforms everything simply by your will…"

Victoria prayed and watched, totally fascinated by what she was witnessing. David, totally engrossed in prayer and meditation called out to Jimmy after the first prayer. "Name yourself!"

Jimmy violently shook and sat straight up. A deep voice boomed, "You speak to Asmodeus."

David continued, "You are the chief demon, are you not?"

Laughter followed. "You got it, righteous one. But we are not ready to leave."

Holding the rosary, David continued to question him, "How many are you?"

"Legion, for we are many. Begone, man of God. Leave us alone! You have your own heart and soul to worry about. Yes, we know of your lasting love. It is your weakness as well as your own brother's. She stands next to you. Take her first and enjoy!" Laughing, Jimmy flew back seemingly pinned to his bed.

David started the second prayer of deliverance, Anima Christi. "Soul of Christ, sanctify me; Body of Christ, save me…"

Victoria was frightened. *I've never experienced anything quite like this. It seems that the demons know the hidden sins of everyone here. What have I learned? David still loves me, but he can't have both his ministry and me. The Church won't permit it. How does this make me feel? Comfort that my heart wasn't tossed aside because I wasn't loved. Sad for the forbidden love we both shared and for the anger and hate I harbored all these years. Frustrated at my own inability to easily forgive. And what about Christian? Has he had feelings for me all these years?*

Jimmy sprang from the bed and froze. A new voice emerged, "Welcome, beautiful lady. I especially love tangling with ice princesses. A good challenge excites me."

"Who are you?" Father David interrupted.

"We've met before. I call myself Lord Macraven." Jimmy bent over in laughter.

"Where is Brian Gregory?" David demanded.

"You've already asked me that question, righteous

one. Foolish one too I might add, with such a beauty within your grasp. Your ice princess holds the key."

"I command you in the name of Jesus, *begone*!"

Victoria watched as Jimmy went into convulsions. Christian grabbed him, steadying him while his body convulsed and went still.

Whimpering started deep within Jimmy. "Lord Macraven is gone. Quoth the raven, 'Nevermore.' "

"Who are you?" Father David commanded.

"The demon of fear. You have much to fear. Your friend suffers. He's cold. He's hungry. He thirsts."

"Where is Brian?"

"I do not know."

"*Begone*!" David commanded.

Jimmy heaved violently and then lay still.

Father David turned to the others in the room and said, "Repeat after me the words to the 'Prayer against Every Evil'…"

The prayer ended. Jimmy lay exhausted and asleep. "This is enough for now. Jimmy was possessed by many demons. Unfortunately the first one, Asmodeus, still remains. We will need to do another exorcism at a later date."

"Thank you, Father," Nate grabbed his hand. "And please, at the next soonest opportunity, please get rid of the last demon who has a hold on Jimmy."

"Rest assured, Nate, I wouldn't forget about Jimmy."

The group left Nate's office and a peacefully sleeping Jimmy. Victoria turned to David and Christian holding up the key, "We need to find the lock this key fits."

Nate stopped and stared. "That's an original key."

"That's right," Victoria answered.

"May I see it?"

Victoria handed over the key. Nate turned it over in his fingers, carefully examining the key. "There aren't too many places this key will fit."

"Where should we start?" Victoria asked.

"Probably some of the old cabinetry. This old hotel has a few original pieces. This looks like it most likely will go to one of those pieces rather than a regular door of that era."

"Thanks."

The threesome left Nate staring back at the bedroom door. Christian made a suggestion. "I think we return to room 217, and check out Elizabeth's computer and things. If Brian found anything that might have prompted his kidnapping, he may have left results of his investigation with the one person he trusted most, Elizabeth, instead of in a room shared by someone maybe he no longer trusted."

"Good point. Let's get back to my room then and see what we find, although I know we've been through everything and found nothing."

When they returned to their room, Victoria let them in. Maggie was gone.

"Elizabeth, you know none of us are to be left alone." Victoria reprimanded her friend.

"I know, but I locked the door and all. She was so tired. I told her to get to bed."

Christian shook his head. "If it's a staff member, don't you think they'd have a key?"

She looked at her feet and started rubbing her toes on the carpet. "You're right. Sorry."

Victoria hugged her, closing her eyes, she thought

of Sandy, her strength, kindness, dependability, and the horror she suffered. "I know you don't want to be a bother, but we need to take extra care."

Christian interrupted. "Although I know that the two of you searched your room for anything Brian may have put here, sometimes someone new comes with a different perspective and can find what's been overlooked. Do you mind if I go through your things once again?"

"As long as you wash your hands first before going through my underwear. Anything to help find my Brian." She kept wringing her hands.

Christian did as he was asked and started systematically going through Elizabeth's things. He found a bag labeled, "Wedding Night Surprise, KEEP OUT." He lifted it out of the drawer and turned toward Elizabeth. "I'm assuming this note was meant for Brian," he said with a smile.

She returned with a wicked smile. "What do you think?"

"I think you need to open it to see if Brian left something in there as well," Christian said as he handed the package to her.

"If he did, I'll kill him when we find him." She took the package and opened it up. Her expression changed. With a questioning look, she pulled an envelope from the package. The note on the outside read, "Sorry, babe, but I had to."

She handed it to Christian. He carefully opened it and said, "Well, well," as he pulled a flash drive from the envelope.

Chapter 19

"Let's check your computer." Christian strode through the room. The other three peered over his shoulder while he slipped in the flash drive. "It's password protected. Any ideas?"

"We can try one we share, *Elibri*."

Christian typed it in. "No go. Any other ideas?"

"Well, since all this stuff may be related to my new business, type that in and if that doesn't work, try the initials." Elizabeth started pacing.

"Try again."

Her pace quickened, and then she stopped abruptly. "How about his pet name for me, Cream Puff."

Victoria started to giggle. "You have got to be kidding me, Cream Puff?" She held her hand over her mouth to stifle an all out howl.

Christian shook his head. "I would hope he could come up with something better than Cream Puff."

"I love them. One evening I ate so many of them he told me I'd turn into one. The name sort of stuck."

"Yes! Cream Puff it is." Christian rubbed his hands together as the pictures uploaded. "Elizabeth, did you notice Brian taking pictures?"

"Yeah. He always has his camera. It's one of those high pixel little deals that's easy to carry. He's one of those frustrated photographers. I think he might have even done that for a living if given the opportunity."

"The first shots I can't seem to identify. The next set is of people who arrived for the rehearsal dinner. The last set of shots include silhouettes, furniture, and other items probably from around here. In all, there are quite a few photos. Brian must have considered at least some of them confidential, or he wouldn't have password protected it and hidden it in your lingerie."

Elizabeth bent over Christian's shoulder to take a closer look.

"Why don't you just have a seat here and let me know if anything comes to mind or if you can identify any of the places, objects, and people?" Christian stood up to give Elizabeth room to peruse the photos.

"The first grouping are places in my new building. Brian said he wanted to go over and sneak an unaccompanied peek if he could manage it. I guess he did."

"Do you know why Brian would have chosen to take these particular pictures?" Victoria asked.

"When we went on our walk-throughs, these were the areas we were whisked through. Either they only let us peek in the room, or they let us in, but only for very brief periods of time." She kept examining the photos.

"Didn't you find that strange?" Christian asked.

"Yes, and it made both Brian and me angry. I think he intended to go back if only to satisfy my negative feelings about a seller who would take huge deposits, and not let the buyer even have a satisfying look at what was going on. The contractor kept throwing the fact in my face that I signed that contract and had to abide by its terms."

"What terms?"

"Quite a few of them got my goat. First, I had no

control over how it was finished. They maintained that was for cost control since I didn't own it yet. Second, all inspections had to be accompanied by a seller's representative, and the seller could be selective on what could be seen by the buyer at various times." Elizabeth tugged her ear.

"Why didn't you just negotiate those provisions?" David asked.

"That's what I hired lawyers for. I was in a time crunch when the contract came up and since it was eighty some odd pages long, I relied on my fiancé's real estate department."

"That's understandable." David nodded.

"Yeah well, I shouldn't have. I didn't read it myself until it was too late. I had already signed on the dotted line. When I tried to inspect my property on my own and I wasn't permitted to, I read the contract I signed from cover to cover."

"Oh boy." Christian shook his head.

"That's an understatement. I was mad so I called Sissy. She assured me that provisions like that sometimes appeared in commercial contracts for safety reasons."

"Did she assuage your anger?" David asked.

"A little, but the closer it got to closing, the more agitated I became because I still didn't have unfettered access to the property. That's when my whining got Brian's attention and he asked Sandy…" She brushed at the new onslaught of tears with the back of her hand. Voice halting, she continued, "…to see what she could find." She brushed again, her tear-filled eyes never leaving the photos.

Victoria handed her a tissue. "Thank you."

"See right here?" She pressed the tissue against each eye. "This is the fireplace in a third floor room that's large enough to be a library, or even a lounge/café for waiting customers. These other four photos are of the same room. I wanted to spend time in there to decide how I wanted to use that space, but that was one of the rooms I wasn't permitted total access to." She blew her nose.

"That's odd. How about if we zoom in on the various portions of this fireplace and mantel. It seems very detailed. A lot of workmanship went into just this mantel alone. It must have cost a pretty penny." Christian moved in on the detail.

Victoria was looking over Elizabeth's right shoulder. "Let's take a look at that card again."

"I put it back in the show Brian pile. Hey, do you think any of this will help us find him?"

"That's what I'm hoping." Christian kept his eyes on the screen as he spoke. "We need to find him before it's too late."

Victoria retrieved the card from the show Brian pile and handed it over to Elizabeth to compare it to the photo on the computer. "Look, these engravings are depicted on the card." Elizabeth outlined the relevant portions to the others. "But this poem captures more than what's here."

Victoria pulled a chair closer and sat down. "Yeah, like the key we found behind the raven."

Christian said, "Probably does. Elizabeth, why don't you move to the next set of photos?"

"Okay."

"Anything odd about these people?"

Elizabeth shrugged. "They're all guests but this

one. This one is just staff cleaning up or something. But look, do you see these photos over here?" She pointed to a glass display case. "Let me zoom in."

"There are locks on the flip top portion of this case. And this looks like an original piece."

"It is. This is one of the three pieces Nate told you about." Elizabeth tapped on the screen. "Here, let me see if I can zoom further right here."

Victoria tried to get closer. "What does it say?"

"It's in the poem on the card," Elizabeth said.

"And when we were talking to Jimmy, the demons said, 'Happily ever after, not,' " David said.

Christian straightened up. "I saw this display cabinet on the ground floor. David and I passed it on our way to the spa. Am I right?"

"Yes."

"I'm going down to check it out."

"I'm coming with you," Victoria said as she got up from her chair.

"That's fine, but Elizabeth and David should continue examining these photos. Time is precious."

Victoria nodded in agreement.

"I've got my cell phone. Hopefully there'll be service. Call me if you find anything at all."

"Okay."

Victoria and Christian left them and made it two floors down in no time. They slowly approached the display cabinet while Christian shined his flashlight carefully so he wouldn't miss a thing.

"Hold the light right there, Christian. See the *Happily Ever After*?"

"I do, but it seems a little out of order from the photo, but it's there. And look directly above the card.

166

There's the lock. Pass me the key." After she handed it over, he put the key in the lock and it turned. "Can you hold this flashlight and shine it in as I open the top?"

"Absolutely." She took the flashlight and kept it shining in the cabinet.

There was a letter sized manila envelope. Christian took a pair of latex gloves out of his pocket and put them on while Victoria shined the light on the rest of the cabinet.

"Doesn't appear to be anything else up there except for some undisturbed dirt and cobwebs. Be careful when you reach in for the envelope."

Christian stopped midway and turned with raised eyebrows. "I know what I'm doing here. Just hold the light."

She grinned. "Just trying to help."

With the beam of the flashlight, he reached up and carefully extracted the envelope.

Victoria moved the flashlight over the disheveled wedding display. "You know, the hotel staff would keep this neat and tidy. This is disturbed."

"You're right. Keep your light shining on it while I check it out."

Christian lifted each piece of the wedding display, examined it, and put it back. Saving the artificial cake top for last, he lifted the plastic bride and groom piece. It came off.

"What did you find there?" Victoria asked.

"A memory card. Hold your light on it."

Christian carefully looked it over and with his latex gloves, he slipped it in a plastic bag.

"Check out the front of the envelope." Christian pointed. "A stamp of some kind and black ink must

167

have been used to imprint this raven."

"Let's take our booty up to the room and examine it more closely."

Chapter 20

Victoria attempted to put the access card in the door, but it just pushed open.

Christian shook his head as he came through the door. "Guys, this should have been locked."

David looked up from the computer. "But I was here."

"And do you believe that you're going to single-handedly stop a psycho killer? I don't think so."

"You're right."

"Let's try not to let up on our guard. We've got something here." Christian held up the envelope and memory card.

Christian headed directly for Elizabeth and her computer. Victoria reminded him, "Don't forget the latex gloves."

"Got them. Remember, I've done this sort of thing before."

Victoria grinned. "So you say."

"Ready when you are," Elizabeth said.

Slowly opening the envelope so as not to disturb any potential evidence, Christian lifted the flap and looked inside. "There's another envelope and a passport." Christian opened the passport, stunned.

"What is it?" Elizabeth asked.

"It's Brian's passport."

"What's his passport doing inside the cabinet?"

"That, I don't know. He's been out of the country before, but there are no stamps in this passport. It's brand new."

"That's odd. The only passport of Brian's I've seen is stamped by a number of countries." Elizabeth just shook her head, perplexed.

David tapped the desk. "Christian, open the envelope."

Carefully he opened the inside envelope and pulled out a one-way plane ticket. "This plane ticket is in Brian's name. The flight originates in Albuquerque, New Mexico, and terminates in Zurich, Switzerland. There's also a key, the type that typically opens a safety deposit box."

David shook his head. "What does all this mean? Why would Brian have a passport and a one way ticket to Switzerland when he's supposed to be getting married?"

Elizabeth's face was turning beat red. "That's not Brian's doing. I know him."

"Maybe not. People do funny things." Christian raised his right eyebrow.

David asked, "When is the departure date?"

"In three days."

"That's when we were supposed to finish with part one of our honeymoon, you know the hiking portion. Then it was to be sun and surf in Hawaii." Elizabeth's eyes swelled with tears.

Victoria gave her a hug. "If this is his passport and plane ticket, he won't be going anywhere. We have time to find him."

"I don't think he put it there. It's not like him. He loves me and wouldn't do this to me."

Christian rested a hand on her shoulder. "We'll find him, Elizabeth."

Victoria moved closer to the computer screen.

"By the way, how's your computer battery holding out?" Christian asked.

The portable printer chirped. "I'm always prepared with more than one fully charged back-up battery. Brian and I are workaholics. We're always ready." She grabbed hold of Victoria's hand and Christian's arm. "You have to find him."

"We will." Victoria squeezed Elizabeth's hand. Christian lifted his shirt and secured the file in a pouch next to his skin along with the key. "I don't think these should be left. Someone is going to want to get to these, and I'd rather they go through me."

David pointed to the computer. "There was another folder on the flash drive Brian left. You need to see this."

Elizabeth opened it. "You know that library in my new building? This new folder shows images starting at the fireplace. Look. It opens to an ornate elevator. Brian must have stepped into it and taken it down. It then opens to an area I didn't even know existed."

"It looks like a basement." Christian noted.

"Yes, but I was in the basement. This is another basement, possibly below the other, that none of us knew about." Elizabeth held her breath.

David pointed. "Now look at this."

"Holy," Victoria said, mouth still open.

"Holy isn't exactly the right word for this place. I'd say far from it. See that pentagram in the center of the floor?"

"There's also an altar there with some very large

knives. Their decorating has a lot to be desired with boar's heads and stuffed snakes on the walls." Christian studied the footage.

David pointed to the altar. "See here? Brian, or whoever he got to take this, zoomed in on the altar. It looks like marble."

Christian said, "Freeze it. Looks like blood stains in the carvings on the marble."

"It does. This appears to be a place of devil worship."

"And do you believe this is in the basement of the building I just bought?"

"Without checking it out, we don't know for sure yet."

Victoria suspected that Christian was trying to be comforting under the circumstances. It seemed pretty obvious to her that this was in Elizabeth's building.

"That's the last of it. There might have been more, but the files come up blank."

David said, "How about what's on that memory disc you found? Do you think it could have been left by a wedding guest?"

"If it was, the cabinet had to be unlocked at the time, or it was left by someone with access to the key. Hotel staff would never blatantly leave it in that messy condition, so it's got to be recent."

Christian looked intently at Elizabeth. "Sorry for my skepticism, it's part of my occupational hazard. We need to look at this, but I don't know what's on it. Are you up for this or do you want us to check it out first?"

Elizabeth blew her nose. "I'm staying."

Victoria put her hand on Elizabeth's shoulder. "Are you sure?"

Elizabeth held her breath for a moment. "Yes.

"Okay, here we go." Christian handed it to Elizabeth to put in the computer.

"It's a video feed. We seem to be back in the sub-basement of the building. This could almost be a continuation of what Brian left in your lingerie." Victoria brushed the hair off her face.

Elizabeth frowned. "Why wouldn't Brian have all of it if he took the pictures?"

"Maybe he didn't. Maybe someone passed that flash drive on to him and maybe the same person hid this in the wedding display. Let's look at the rest of it before we start jumping to conclusions."

David said, "It's starting at the altar, so we are in the same place."

"There's a small room." Elizabeth sat forward.

David got closer to the screen and glanced at Victoria. "Look here. This room is all about you. Elizabeth, zoom in if you can and look at what's on the walls up close."

Victoria took in a sudden breath. "I can't believe this. It seems as though every newspaper article ever written about me is there. It's my life starting with college graduation."

Elizabeth shook her head. "How creepy. And the lighting. There are candles strategically placed as part of a shrine to you."

Sound emanated from the disc. The video focused on a grandfather clock whose chimes sounded, "*Bong, bong, bong, bong, bong, bong, bong,*" and a raven came forth from the clock. "Quoth the raven, 'Nevermore.' "

Christian tightened his lips. "Any doubt now, Victoria?"

Elizabeth said, "There's more."

"We need to see what's here. I can't imagine it getting better." Victoria had Elizabeth scoot over on her chair so she could get closer.

Christian and David remained standing. As the disc unfolded what lay inside the final room, Elizabeth grabbed her mouth, running for the bathroom. Victoria stood transfixed. David grabbed the table. Christian stared, mouth set, face reddening in anger.

Christian, hands still arranging his belt, looked up at Victoria. "You better be especially careful. Whoever took Brian has something planned for you, and it isn't pretty. Don't go anywhere alone."

Elizabeth came out of the bathroom with a wet washcloth. "I'm sorry."

"We're all a little shocked here, and the quicker we get resolution, the better." Victoria picked up the file David and Christian took from the tour office. "We've also got the room numbers of the guests that worked on Elizabeth's new business. We should speak to them as well."

Christian nodded. "They need to be interviewed, no doubt. I think Victoria and I should do the interviewing."

"Why? They know me already." Elizabeth frowned.

"Yes, but they are now my associates, and we are more experienced in this sort of thing." Christian pulled the desk chair out. "Elizabeth, bring up those photos first, and set it up as a slide show in the order that Brian, or whoever, took them. This way we'll get a feel for everything on here, and whether there's anything specific relating one photo to the others. There might be some type of theme."

"Good idea." David rubbed the kink out of his neck and pulled up a chair closer to the screen. "I need to get a little more comfortable so I can focus."

Elizabeth slid her chair over to let him get closer while Christian remained standing and peered over their heads. "The first set is from my building. He took photos of the entire room and everything in it. Set as a slide show, it almost looks like a movie. He took a wide view as he entered the room. Boy, it's beautiful. I love that room. The cherry wood is so rich and welcoming. What I could do with it! Look at the detail on that cabinetry."

Victoria pointed to the screen. "Elizabeth, look at this room. Look at the initial wide view again. Doesn't anything strike you as unusual for a building still under construction, but sold?"

Elizabeth froze the frame and stared. "What is wrong with me? I was so struck by the beauty and warmth of the room, I never saw the obvious! This room is totally finished. Not just the construction, but it is completely decorated. There are pictures on the wall, books in the bookshelves; an expensive desk set enhanced the mahogany desk. The chair is top of the line leather with an ergonomic design. The windows have window treatments. Do you think that this is why Brian, I'm going to assume it's Brian, took so many photos of it, or was it just to let me get the full flavor of the room?"

"I don't know."

Christian reached between the two women and tapped the screen. "Do you have a way of measuring the height of the chair so we can get an idea of the height of whoever claimed it as his or her own?"

"I know the measurement of that room which we can use as the base for a program I have that can calculate close to its actual size. At least we'll be able to get an idea as to whether it was for someone big or small."

Elizabeth fiddled with the program. "Here we go. This chair is definitely for someone taller."

"When you say taller, is it possible to get a little more specific, like over or under six feet?" Victoria asked.

"Sure. I'd say someone taller than six feet. I'd go so far as to say this might be for someone over six feet three inches. It might be a custom chair."

"Great." Victoria smiled. "Now, did you take a look at the photos on the wall?"

"Not yet."

"Zoom in on them and let me know if you notice anything familiar. They appear to be photos of wildlife found in the Rocky Mountain National Park."

"One thing I recognize, the soaring eagle is also the same photo that I saw in Dennis Ryder's office."

"The real estate paralegal? How odd."

"There are also old photos from the early 1900s. These are from the same time period of the photos I saw in Teddy Whyler's office. Now, there may not be anything to it since Teddy is old time Colorado."

"These may just be common photos, but it would be interesting to see if the same people are captured in the photos in Whyler's office," David added.

Elizabeth cocked her head and tapped her chin. "I wouldn't bet my life or anything that drastic on it, but I would venture to guess they are of the same people in

Whyler's office. Okay, I'm going to continue with the slide show for that overall first impression and then zoom in where needed."

"Good idea." Victoria adjusted her chair.

As Elizabeth started again, she zoomed in on the photos of the library/office.

"Just a minute. I've seen that photo before. It's a smaller version of the one outside the Gregory Room."

"That's Lord Macraven! What's his photo doing in this room?"

"Good question. Also, look at the sculpture on the bookshelf next to the portrait of Lord Macraven. Does that look familiar to you?"

Elizabeth stared. "Isn't there a similar one on the mantel in the foyer downstairs?"

Christian nodded. "Not only is it similar, but I'd say it's the same one, a soaring eagle."

"Can you zoom in closer to the photos on the book shelves?" Victoria asked, getting excited.

"This is about as close as I can get. I can't really make out the people."

Victoria moved even closer. "No, you can't, but this is from the same time period as the photos which decorate the walls in this hotel."

"They sure are," David said.

Victoria's excitement was getting the best of her as she twirled her hair. "Hey, take a look at the furniture around the fireplace. It's beautiful, rich looking, definitely expensive, but can you see what I see?"

"There are a coffee table, a love seat, and two chairs on each side of the love seat with small end tables between each chair and the love seat," Elizabeth said.

"What is different about the chairs, David?"

"One is rather large and quite masculine. The other is smaller and delicate."

Victoria smiled and struck the desk palm side down. "That's right! This room at least has a woman visitor on a regular basis or why have the chair?"

Christian grinned. "You're good, maybe you want to join J.C. Classified?"

"I may be on a roll! Is it possible that she's more than a visitor? Take a look at the space on the other side of the room. It's finished differently, almost as if it was designed for a woman. There's another work space with a smaller desk."

Elizabeth nodded. "You're right. There's something here. Not that I've seen one quite like this one, but there's something familiar about it. I feel like I've been in the home or office of whoever decorated this room."

"Perhaps the same designer was used?" David asked.

"That's possible, but good designers tailor the room to the owner. So even if this was done by a designer I'm unfamiliar with, the room should still have the same flavor of the person the room was meant for." Elizabeth frowned. "This is going to nag at me until I can put my finger on this room's intended occupant."

"Maybe something else about the photos will prompt you. Let's keep looking."

"We're now up at the Preston Hotel in the photos," Elizabeth said deep in concentration.

Victoria nodded. "Brian saw the familiarity as well. Take a look. He's photographed Lord Macraven's portrait, the sculpture on the mantel, and the raven in

178

the Macraven Boardroom. Look guys! It's the same raven that's on the mantel in the office/library!"

"Sure is. That building in Denver is somehow tied to the Preston Hotel, or at least certain people who have ties to both. Do you see anything unusual about the photos containing people?"

"Something about the photos when we did the slide show bothered me, but I need to closely examine them to figure out why. There's something, I just don't know what yet." Elizabeth took a deep breath and held it, then looked at Victoria. "Any suggestions?"

"Do a slower slide show of just the photos with people, and let's see if we can figure out why these photos were taken."

Elizabeth sighed. "I wish I had a better handle on what was going on. Wait a minute. Do you see what I see?"

"Not sure, but there seems to be something similar about each picture. There." Christian tapped the screen. "And there. Each picture has a shadow of someone who is not part of the wedding party."

"That's right." Victoria twirled her hair faster. "In the first one, she looks to be a worker. She has on a uniform, but you can't see her face. On each of these pictures, there's someone who does not belong to the wedding party, but appears to be a staff member. The shots aren't clear. Elizabeth, try zooming in on each one to see if something better shows up."

Elizabeth worked the computer keys to adjust the photos. "Sorry, guys." She shrugged.

"The only thing we can tell is that it seems to be a woman," David added.

Victoria stood and picked up the file with the guest

list and room numbers. "Elizabeth, can you pass me the outline we put together? I'm going to speak to those guests on our outline first, and then see where I get from there."

"Not alone you're not," Christian said, moving toward the door. "Elizabeth, could you stay with David and study those photos to see if something jumps out at you?"

"Yes. Wait a minute. Let me give you something else." Elizabeth scribbled a note, signed and dated it and handed it to Victoria.

Victoria smiled. "I see Brian has rubbed off on you. Although technically I'm now a part of Brian's firm and also represent you, some of the people we interview might not feel comfortable talking to me anyway because of attorney/client privilege and the presence of Christian. This note waiving it and directing them to answer all our questions may prove helpful. Thanks."

"I'm going to work with Photoshop and see if I can figure out who that woman is. Get back with me."

"Will do." Victoria checked her bag and made for the door.

"Keep the door locked and when we leave, push that dresser in front of the door." Christian said as he pointed to the closest moveable dresser. "It'll make us feel better."

Chapter 21

Victoria opened up Elizabeth's staff outline.

"That's impressive," Christian said, reviewing it over her shoulders.

Business: Creation, Organization, Marketing
Brian Gregory—Partner in charge
Sandy Forrester—Associate, attending wedding
Ruth Peachtree—Administrative Assistant, invited, not attending wedding
Teddy Whyler—Managing Partner, Starlight, Limited, in charge of marketing, attending wedding

~*~

Real Estate Purchase
Peter Mack—Partner in charge, best man
Sissy Tram—Associate, attending wedding
Dennis Ryder—Paralegal for real estate and central billing, attending wedding
Louise Clarkson—Administrative Assistant, invited, not attending

Victoria pointed to Dennis Ryder's name. "What do you say we start here? He checked in, but no one has seen him." She pulled out the guest list file.

"David checked his room with Elizabeth, but he wasn't there. I was told his Dopp kit was open, laptop set up, and clothes put away."

"We need to see if he returned. Obviously he wasn't with Sandy."

Christian climbed the stairs closest to Elizabeth's room to the fourth floor two at a time with Victoria coming up quickly behind. They turned left and walked the floor briskly until they came to room 414. He knocked and they waited.

No answer.

He pounded harder.

But still no answer.

Christian took out the master key and opened the door. Dennis's room was as David found it, and his bed had not been slept in.

Victoria walked into the small bathroom. "The sink looks unused. Although the Dopp kit is open, the toothbrush is dry. This is not a good sign."

Christian opened the closet. "The clothes appear to be as David described."

Victoria twirled her hair. "We may have another missing person."

"Sure looks that way."

They left the room and closed the door. Victoria pulled out the list. "There's only one other person staying at the hotel who we haven't seen, but who was confirmed here. Sissy Tram, room 314."

"Let's go."

They took the stairs closest to room 407 down one flight of stairs, Christian taking them two at a time, Victoria close behind at a jog. At the third floor, they turned right and looked for 314. He stood outside the door, took a deep breath, and knocked.

"Who is it?"

"Victoria and Christian."

The door partially opened. "Is there something I can help you with?"

"Maybe," Victoria answered. "Did you know that Brian was missing?"

"Yes. Everyone knows by now."

"Really?"

"The guys from the bachelor party spread the word hoping maybe we might have seen him or something."

Victoria nodded. "That's right. We're still looking. I was wondering if I could ask you a few questions."

"Sure. Come on in. This room has a little table and two chairs. I'll just sit on the bed."

They came through the door and looked around. No bags were evident. Everything was neatly put away. Both glasses provided by housekeeping were upside down.

"You must be quite bored staying in your room by yourself," Christian said.

"Not really, I brought work." She smiled and tapped the back of a chair. "Please sit."

As they all sat, Victoria watched Sissy. She apparently was an early riser since it appeared as though she had been up a while. Sissy wore a black turtleneck sweater and black velour pants. She was fully made-up, her mid-length hair curled, and she wore what appeared to be a matching set of silver earrings, necklace, and ring. From this vantage point, she couldn't tell what the specific design of the set was.

"Have you seen Dennis Ryder?" Victoria asked.

"Briefly in the reception area when I was checking in, but I haven't seen him since."

"Do you know what his plans might have been?"

"Not a clue."

"Okay. Other than that brief meeting with Dennis, have you seen anyone from either your office or from anyone associated with Elizabeth's business?"

Sissy turned the earring in her right ear as she considered her answer. "Hmm, not that I can remember. Just Peter earlier to ask if I've seen Brian."

"What was Dennis's role in Elizabeth's venture?"

"I'm not too comfortable talking about any client of mine. You know, attorney/client privilege and all that."

Victoria smiled. "First, as I'm sure you know, I'm a partner with the firm, one of the bosses so to speak. I'm covered by the privilege. I also have a note from Elizabeth waiving the privilege, so you can feel comfortable speaking in front of Christian."

Sissy read the hastily drawn up document. "So she did," she said as she handed it back.

"Now, how about Dennis's role."

"He's our real estate paralegal."

"Did he do anything else for Elizabeth?"

"He centralized the billing so Elizabeth didn't get hit from all sides."

"Is that a common practice?" Christian asked.

"Only when there's a lot going on. It makes it easier for the client to deal with only one person. It cuts down on the confusion."

"Makes sense. How about Teddy Whyler?" Victoria asked.

Sissy sat up straighter in her chair.

"Did you have any involvement with him?"

"Sure. He found the property and brought the parties together."

"Oh, so you both met with the seller?"

"I didn't say that." Sissy turned her earring again.

"You said he brought the parties together. Since

you worked with him representing the buyer in this real estate transaction, I assumed then you met with the seller as well."

"No. Bringing the parties together was just in reference to the transaction. I never met them. I spoke to their attorney over the phone, but everything was couriered."

"Is Mr. Whyler a real estate broker as well?"

"No."

"So he didn't receive a commission?"

"No. He did it to help our mutual client."

"How much dealing have you had with Mr. Whyler?"

"Some."

"Have you had the opportunity to meet with him socially?"

"That's really none of your business." Sissy tossed her hair.

"What do you think of Mr. Whyler?"

They watched as she composed her answer. A light blush appeared on her fair skin. Ah, she hit a soft spot. "Very professional, hard worker, a real gentleman."

"I understand that Peter Mack introduced him to Elizabeth."

"That's right. Peter and Teddy have mutual clients."

"How far back do they go?"

Sissy looked down at her hand that was resting on the table. Christian watched her intensely gaze at that ring. "Not sure, but I think way back."

"I don't know if I've had the opportunity to meet him or not. Can you describe him to me?" She also watched Sissy staring at her hand.

"I guess he fits the coined phrase of tall, dark, and handsome, with ice blue eyes."

"Is he staying at the hotel?"

"No. He has a family cottage nearby."

"How close?"

"Walking distance."

"Have you seen him since you're here?"

"Briefly."

"So he's here. "

"Yes." She twisted the ring on her finger.

"When we asked if you saw anyone who worked on Elizabeth's business, why didn't you mention Teddy Whyler?"

"It was so brief, I forgot about it." She continued to twist her ring.

"Your jewelry is unique. I don't think I've ever seen anything like it. Is that silver?" Christian asked.

"White gold."

"Ah. Shame on me. May I take a closer look at your ring?"

"Sure." She held out her hand.

He took her hand in his and examined the ring, tipping her hand so that Victoria could also see—a raven with a diamond eye.

Chapter 22

Christian knocked on Elizabeth's door. "It's us."

"Just a minute. David has to push the dresser aside."

The door opened.

"I got something on those photos. I wasn't able to get a clear head-on shot, but I think I got enough to be identifiable. Two people show up regularly in more than one photo. A man and a woman."

"Great, let's see what you have." Victoria scooted onto Elizabeth's chair sharing it with her while David sat on another next to it, and Christian remained standing close behind.

"First, I've seen them both before. The woman is the one in uniform. She worked as a regular staff member at the dinner and at the beginning of the bachelorette party afterwards. The guy came with one of my bridesmaids, Jacqueline."

Victoria pointed to the screen. "Look here, the two are definitely conversing, and it doesn't look like he's just ordering a drink or asking for hors d'oeuvres. Do you think they have something going on?"

"I hope not. Jacqueline would be crushed. She isn't formally dating this guy. She just met him. I don't even know his name, but when she mentioned the wedding, he was interested in accompanying her. I know she's interested in him being more than an escort."

Christian cleared his throat. "That sounds strange to me. Most guys avoid weddings like the plague."

David added, "Unless you are officiating."

"Hey, as Jacqueline's escort, he should have been at the bachelor party. Did you see him?" Victoria asked.

"No, I didn't. But the woman looks like our tour guide, Renie. The shot's not too clear of her, and our tour guide was in costume, so I may be wrong."

"We need to speak to Jacqueline and find out more about this guy."

Elizabeth printed the best of the photos for both the staff member and Jacqueline's guest.

"Ready, Victoria?" Christian threw on his jacket and checked his pockets.

"Let's go. Elizabeth, do you mind staying with David and seeing if you come up with anything else?"

"No. You get going. I think we should be here anyway in case Brian or whoever tries to reach me."

"Lock it up and move the dresser again," he said, closing the door behind him.

Victoria pointed to the list. "Jacqueline is on the second floor here."

At the end of the hall, Christian stopped and knocked. "Who's there?" came the voice from the closed door.

"Christian and Victoria."

Jacqueline opened the door wide. "Come in please. Tell me what in the world is going on. Samantha and I have been frantic here, afraid to leave ever since Peter came by asking us if we've seen Brian. He told us to stay in our rooms until further notice. By the way, thank Elizabeth for us—the food baskets were glorious. Have you found Brian yet?"

"Uh, no. We need to ask you both a few questions."

"Sure, shoot."

"We're just trying to identify everyone who's here for Elizabeth's wedding, and get some information on those we don't know anything about."

Christian added, "And we wanted to know if either of you noticed anything that seemed unusual, or just something that caught your attention."

"Then you'd probably want to know about my date, since he's the new guy on the block." Jacqueline smiled. "He's a real cute one, don't you think?"

Victoria sat down in the chair to make Jacqueline more comfortable and smiled. "He's definitely cute. You mentioned at dinner that you met him just last month. Can you tell us a little more, like his name, where you met him, what he does? That sort of thing."

Jacqueline glanced at Christian and back to Victoria and looked at her folded hands. "I met him at my favorite Friday evening hang-out. You know, a few of the girls from work and I go out to dinner and listen to some music two days a month, usually the second and last Friday of the month. The second Friday gets us over the hump of the month, especially if it's been a grueling month, and the last to celebrate finishing the month and keeping our jobs."

"I didn't know things were getting rough at work?" Victoria frowned.

"Yeah well, the quarterly reports haven't shown any growth with the downturn in the economy and they're in the process of downsizing. We're all wondering when it'll be our turn. These Friday outings are a release for the stress." She pushed up her glasses.

"Well, Samantha usually is with us, but this time she had other plans."

"I had a date," Samantha said.

"We had just finished eating, and this cute guy came up to me, kissed my hand, and asked me to dance. Well, how can I turn something like that down? I can't, so we danced. After a few more dances, and let me tell you he's good, he thanked me, and kissed my hand. He left me in a daze, that's for sure."

"I'll say," Samantha giggled. "She called me as soon as she got home to tell me about her dream man."

"He didn't take my name or number, and didn't give me his, but on the last Friday of the month, there he was again. I just about thought I'd died and gone to heaven when I laid eyes on him. It started the same way. He kissed my hand, we danced, and after we danced, this time we talked. Keep in mind, it was only a week before the wedding and I still didn't have an escort, so I thought, what the hey!" She pushed up her glasses.

Samantha interrupted. "Takes guts, that's for sure, but I warned her. You don't know this guy from Adam."

"No, but I sure had that lovely butterfly feeling! When I asked him, he told me it would be an honor. An honor to escort me! Can you imagine?"

"How about his name," Victoria prodded. "When did he properly introduce himself?"

"He introduced himself when I asked him. He already knew my name, because his exact words were 'It would be an honor, Jacqueline.' "

"That didn't feel odd to you?" Christian asked.

"No, because when I seemed a little surprised, he

laughed deeply and told me that when he meets someone as special and as beautiful as me, he makes it a point of getting to know who that person is. He told me I captured his heart at first glance. Made me a little embarrassed that I didn't know his name."

Victoria sat forward. "Can you go over again, how you learned his name?"

"Sure. Right then when I asked him, he bowed, kissed my hand once again, and said, 'Let me introduce myself. I am Liam Newinn.' "

"Did you find out anything else about him? Like, what he does for a living?" Victoria was getting exasperated. She was in a rush, each second counted, but she didn't want them getting worried.

"Oh yes, I asked him to tell me more about himself. He's in public relations."

"Did you ask who any of his clients were?"

"I did, but he said that his client names were confidential."

"What else did you learn about him?" Christian asked.

"Oh, he's into the typical guy thing. He likes the outdoors: hunting, hiking, skiing, that sort of thing. And what impeccable manners! He must have had a great mother to have taught him so well."

"Do you know if Liam knew anyone else here, either in the wedding party or any staff members?"

"I have no idea. He never mentioned it."

Victoria added, "Did you see him spending time or speaking with anyone in particular?"

Jacqueline sat there in thought, then shook her head, "No, nothing that I can recall."

Samantha said, "Wait a minute, he spoke to that

server quite a bit you know."

"He was probably just asking for something."

"Then he asked for a lot of things from the same server. There were other servers, but he only spoke to one."

Victoria pulled out a picture of the female staff member and laid it on the table. "I'd like you to take a look at someone and let me know if you recognize her."

They looked at each other and up at Victoria. "That's her," Samantha said. "What does this mean?"

"At this point, nothing," Christian answered. "Have you seen Liam since Peter asked you to stay in your rooms?"

Jacqueline shook her head no. "I just thought everyone was asked to stay in their rooms with this storm and all."

"I'm sure you're right." Victoria took her by the hand. "Nothing to worry about at all, we're just turning over every rock. This was a vicious storm, and even though it's subsided, power is still down, and people may be injured."

"Just continue to stay here," Christian said as he headed for the door with Victoria. "We'll come back when all is clear."

"Next stop, Nate, the chef. He seems to know everyone here so he probably knows who this is." Victoria headed for the stairs.

Christian caught up with just a few well-placed strides. "Let's go."

They found Nate working tirelessly in the kitchen. He had his backup generators operating at full throttle. "Hi. Any luck finding Brian?"

"No. We were wondering if you can look at a

photo for us and tell us who it is."

"Sure, what have you got there?" He reached for the photo and smiled. "That's my Lenore."

"Nate, who's Lenore?" Victoria asked.

"My niece, my brother's daughter."

"Does she work here?" Christian asked.

"Yes. She's been here quite a long time. You may know her by Renie."

"Was she assigned to Elizabeth's wedding?"

"I'm sure she was. She's one of our best workers, and they always assign our best and brightest to our long time customers, which Miss Harrington and Mr. Gregory are."

"How long has she worked for this hotel?"

"She's been staying with me during the summers since she was a little girl. Once she turned fourteen, she started working. She's twenty-eight, so she's worked here for most of fourteen years now."

Victoria caught the caveat. "You said most of, what do you mean by that?"

"She did go to college, unlike the rest of her family. I think she's the first to go. While she was in school, she only worked summers. She worked hard to earn her degree in public relations."

Christian asked, "Why would she go to college to be a waitress?"

"Oh, she's not a waitress, she's a manager in charge of the wedding plans, putting her degree to good use. She even has a few employees who report to her."

Victoria pointed to her picture, "But isn't she wearing a server's outfit?"

Nate looked closely. "Yes, but she's been known to jump in and do whatever is necessary to make sure things run smoothly. It's possible that someone pulled a no-show. That's just like Renie."

Christian looked intently at Nate. "You're close with her, aren't you?"

"She's like a daughter to me. She was with me when Jimmy started up with the spirits. She stayed with him more hours than I can count. There are times he'd let no one near him but Renie. Jimmy loves her and trusts her dearly. Sometimes in the night when he starts, the voices will cry out for Renie." Nate shook his head.

"Does this still happen?" he prodded.

"Oh yes."

"And does Renie come?"

"When she knows he's calling, she does. And that's a special thing too. They are so close, that Jimmy will start up with the spirits in the dead of the night, and she'll just show up knowing he needs her."

"Does she hear him calling? Is that why she shows up?"

"I can't imagine her hearing him call. Her room isn't anywhere near where Jimmy and I live. It's just like she has a sixth sense or something."

Victoria pointed to the photo again. "Nate, do you recognize this man that Renie is talking to?"

Nate adjusted his reading glasses, carefully studying the photo. "There's something familiar about him, but I can't put my finger on it."

"Do you think you've seen them together?" Victoria asked.

He stared at the photo. "There is definitely something familiar. And it's possible he's familiar because I've seen him with Renie before, but I can't say for sure."

194

"Does she have a boyfriend?" Victoria asked.

"She's not serious with anyone that I know about, although you never know. As you can see, she's definitely a beauty with that almost jet black hair and piercing blue eyes. She's quite a package for such a tiny thing, barely five feet she is. That combination alone has had many a man stop to talk to her. It's possible that's all I've seen this man do. Just stop and talk to a beautiful woman."

"Is she back in her room?" David asked.

"I would assume she is. I haven't seen her since the storm broke. She's very conscientious, so if she's not in her room, I wouldn't be surprised if she was doing her best to help calm the guests and meet whatever needs they have. She turned out to be not only a beautiful, but a wonderful woman."

"Does Renie stay in the main hotel?"

"No. Her room is in the building next door, in the Manor House."

Victoria glanced at Christian. "What room number?"

"It's the only bedroom on the ground floor. I don't think it has a room number on it, but there's a small mailbox on the wall outside the door. Oh, it might be helpful to know, that although her room is on the ground floor, you need to climb up the exterior stairs to the main floor, then back down the interior stairs to get to her room."

"Thanks." Christian shook his hand.

Victoria turned to Christian outside the kitchen area. "I think we should try her next. Brian focused on her for a reason."

"Sounds good to me. Taking a position of someone

who knew nothing about Renie solicited more information than we may have otherwise obtained. Did you learn that in law school?"

"More like on the job training."

"My offer with J.C. Classified still stands." He grinned.

"I don't plan on jumping ship."

Once again, they passed the display and walked through the café. They walked along the covered area, up the stairs and into the main area of the Manor House.

Victoria pointed with her flashlight. "Look. Stairs ahead."

He nodded. "Let me go first. I don't know what we'll find here."

"The spa's on the ground floor."

"Yeah, I know."

Christian swept the stairs with his flashlight on their descent. When they got to the ground floor, he continued to sweep the area with the light. "Over there. A closed door with a mailbox outside. It's got to be her room."

They stood outside Renie's door and knocked, but no one answered. "Do you think your master key will open this door?"

"It's supposed to open every door in the hotel, that would include this too I would imagine." Christian took out the key Donald gave him and tried the lock. "It doesn't work. Let's find Maggie. She might know where Renie is if she's helping guests."

"Good idea. I noticed she was manning the front desk."

****

Maggie's face brightened when she saw them. "Oh,

it's good to see someone. My boss has me standing here, but truth to tell, no one's needed anything from me."

Christian smiled. "Hi, Maggie. Listen, do you know where Renie is helping out right now?"

"No. She's in charge of wedding plans, so it's possible she's in her office on the ground floor. You may want to check it out. Just head the way we went when we back tracked for the ghost tour."

"Thank you. I know just where it is."

They started back down the way they came.

Christian shined his flashlight. "She's not there unless she's working without a flashlight. It was dark when we passed just a minute ago."

"I know, but I wasn't with you and David when you got the list. I'd like to see her office anyway, even if she's not there."

"Good point."

Between Victoria and Christian's flashlights and the emergency lights, they found their way to Renie's office without a hitch. Renie wasn't in, as expected, but her office was open.

Victoria tripped just after she entered and landed in Christian's arms. Head in his chest, she said, "I seem to be making a habit of landing in your arms." When she looked up, what she saw in his eyes made her breath catch—unfettered desire. Bending, he cupped the back of her neck, drawing her close. He kissed her roughly, with no hint of the tentative kiss she first experienced. There was no holding back. She was consumed with internal fireworks, and she didn't want to put out the fire. *I have to have him.* She felt as if she were riding a powerful wave that took her to heights she never imagined possible in anticipation of the drop... and then the ride began. *This feels too good, unlike...no going back...*

****

He pulled back and searched her eyes. *Those big brown eyes make me crazy. I have wanted you for so long...thirsted for the taste of you...and you are so much more than even I imagined. Ah Victoria, I'll fight to the end for you...*"I hope you realize that I let you go once only because of my brother. No one will get in my way this time."

She lifted her hands and held his face, pulling his face down to hers for one more kiss, this time tender and teasing with a hint of what more could come. "It's been too long and I may regret this...it feels so right, but we need to explore this office."

"Hmmm. I guess this must wait." He stepped back. The hand that held her head now directed his flashlight.

Victoria spotted the bronze. "Look, another eagle lover. And doesn't this sketch look familiar?"

Christian moved closer. "Sure does. A raven in a tree. Hey, look at this photo."

Victoria turned her head to the direction he pointed. "These are the same folks in the photo in that beautiful office or library in Elizabeth's new building. Remember that chair? It was definitely not the standard size, it was quite small, possibly a special order. You wouldn't by any chance have a measuring tape with your Swiss army stuff, would you?"

"I sure do." He took out a small pocket measuring tape. "Can you write these measurements down?"

"Absolutely." Christian took the measurements from the top of the chair to the floor, from the seat to the floor, and the width of the chair and called them out to Victoria.

"Now, let me check it against Elizabeth's notes from her computer calculations." She flipped the pages of her notebook. "Here we go."

She smiled. "You know what they say about the shoe if it fits. I wonder if it works with a chair."

"Look's like it."

"Why don't you continue to check out Renie's office? I'm going down the hall to make a pit stop. Nature calls and she's not waiting."

"I don't think you should go alone."

"It's a stone's throw, and if anything happens I'll scream. It's not like you can come with me, you know."

"Scream loud."

She saluted. "Yes, sir."

Christian shook his head and grinned.

Victoria tossed her head and left. Flashlight in hand, she entered the ladies room and located the stall. While she finished up, she felt a draft and called out. "Christian, almost done, but not quite. I told you I'd scream if I needed you. Just give me a minute."

She shivered. Opening the door, she turned toward the draft. As she opened her mouth to scream, a chloroform-soaked cloth clamped over her mouth. She smelled a musty outdoor odor before she lost consciousness.

Chapter 23

Christian had an uneasy feeling. Victoria was taking too long. Women tended to take longer then men, but this long? He walked the short distance to the ladies room and called out, "Victoria, you okay?"

No answer.

He opened the ladies room and touched his pocket. "Victoria?" One by one, he opened the doors to each stall shining his flashlight over every inch as he went. Careful not to disturb anything, he quickly and methodically examined the room.

His phone vibrated. Hoping it was Victoria, he checked the text. It was David. *Where are you?*

Ladies room, ground floor. Can you come?

On my way.

Although he was experienced in handling difficult and hostile situations, it was different when it involved someone close, someone he loved. *I lost you once, I won't lose you again, especially like this.*

Wishing the electricity was back on, he moved toward the draft. In the corner, he saw something glitter and bent down to look. Using a handkerchief, he picked up the object, a silver and crystal bracelet with a poodle charm.

David appeared at his side and looked at the bracelet. "That's a gift Elizabeth gave to all the ladies at the rehearsal dinner."

"A bridesmaid's gift?"

"I guess. The crystal bracelet was a gift to all the bridesmaids, but I believe only Victoria had a poodle charm. Everyone else had a different dog. As the maid of honor, she also received a personalized white gold locket."

"Personalized with initials or something?"

"Don't know. Obviously I wasn't there when the gifts were opened, I just heard talk and saw the bracelet." David shrugged his shoulders and started to scope out the area.

"If we have her bracelet, Victoria was here, but she could have dropped it earlier."

"I don't think so. I remember seeing it on her as she sat cross-legged with the Horse Whisperer." He pulled his rosary out of his pocket and started fingering the beads.

"Not Victoria!" Mouth set in grim determination, fists clenched, he checked the window. "It's still locked. David, mark my words, I won't let them get away this! If she didn't leave this way, and she didn't pass by us outside the door.…" He stopped. "There's a draft around this garbage receptacle." Christian dropped to one knee while he searched the base of it.

"Anything?" David asked.

"I'm not sure yet." He felt around a crack behind the panel holding the garbage can. "It's definitely coming from this area." He found a thin lever-like piece and pulled. The entire panel opened to reveal a narrow passageway behind the wall. Christian shined his flashlight into the area and spotted a camouflaged handkerchief. Carefully he picked it up and smelled. "Chloroform. Someone must have been waiting for her."

He squeezed into the space.

"What do you see?"

"Nothing. It seems to lead nowhere and I can't find another opening. They could have just waited here for her and got her out quickly, or there's something we're missing. I just don't see a way out of here other than the way they came in."

"How would they know she'd need the bathroom?" David asked.

"You've been away from women far too long, brother. Whoever took her has kept tabs on her. Most women make a lot of pit stops. I would venture to guess Victoria was typical."

"If memory serves me correctly, every place we've ever been together, one of the key visitation points for us was the bathroom. I remember one professor commenting that I'll wait most my life outside the bathroom, waiting for one woman or another. You're right."

"Let's check out the area outside since I don't see a means of escape from inside."

Christian took a long hard look at his brother, the priest. "Did you make the right choice?"

They searched the hallway. "There's no doubt in my mind. My calling is hard and not without sacrifice, but what profession doesn't require sacrifices?"

"True, but some sacrifice more than others." Christian thought of Jimmie and what the spirits said. "Is it true that you still love her?" He walked into Renie's office.

David followed, shining his flashlight. "I will always love her, but the love I now feel is an agape love, not as a husband loves his wife. My calling doesn't allow me the luxury of both a love life and the priesthood. They don't go hand in hand. In the beginning, it was hard, because our relationship was heading toward marriage. When I recognized my calling, I didn't talk to her about it. My first step should have been prayer, followed by a heart to heart talk. I was immature and handled it poorly. I betrayed her love. My prayer is that she will forgive me so that she can love again. Without the ability to forgive, you can't be set free." He sighed.

"Forgiveness is always good, but if she does love again, won't that be painful for you?" Christian prodded the bookcase panels.

David's eyes rested on the eagle as he searched his heart. "In the beginning it might have been. But I think because of the type of love I feel for her I would be happy, and yes, free from the guilt I harbor. I want her to be able to love again if the right man comes into her life." His gaze moved to Christian. "My brother, are you that man?"

Christian stared at his brother. "I hope so. There's nothing here. Let's check the café and get back to Elizabeth. I don't like leaving her alone too long, especially now."

"What about Victoria?"

Christian looked at David with grim resolve. "She's not here. They planned this kidnapping carefully, and I plan to find her and whoever is responsible. I need to talk to Elizabeth first and get to the bottom of this. If it takes my last breath, I won't let anything happen to Victoria if I can help it."

****

Elizabeth paced while she waited. Interrupted by a knock at the door, she pulled it open, relieved it was David and Christian.

"Please be more careful when you open the door."

She moved out of their way and began to pace. "I'm a big girl, Christian."

"I understand that, but Victoria is now missing and we have a murder. I don't think you can be too careful."

"You're right, I'm sorry. What? Did you say Victoria is missing?" She stopped dead in her tracks, her mouth dropped open. "How? She was with you!"

"She had to use the restroom."

"Why didn't you go with her?"

"I tried. She wouldn't have it. Wish I didn't listen. We found this bracelet in the restroom," Christian said as he held up the bracelet.

She grabbed the bracelet, plopped into the chair, and put her head in her hands. "It's hers. I gave every lady a bracelet, but hers had a poodle. The other bracelets had a different dog. Did you find anything else of hers?"

"No."

"Good."

"Why?" David asked puzzled.

"Because then she still has the necklace I gave her."

"Is there something special about this necklace?" Christian asked.

"Yeah. It's personalized."

"David mentioned that, but how? Wait. Is this part of the 007 collection you started for her?"

"You bet. I never felt comfortable with Victoria's profession. It's way too dangerous, so I gave her a special gift that's pretty of course, but also could be used in case of emergency."

"Where did you buy it?"

"I had it specially designed and made for her. To my knowledge, it's a one of a kind gift." Her lips curled slightly into a tight smile.

"Go on."

"Well, for all intents and purposes, it looks like a locket. The outside is a poodle with sapphires for eyes and diamonds around the collar. When you open it, on the left side is a photo of the two of us at Notre Dame, but on the right, there's a watch. Behind the watch there's a mini tool kit and a tiny button which can activate a tracking device."

"How about the receiver?"

"Through satellite of course."

"We need to get that set up stat. Do you have the contact information for setting up the satellite?"

"My assistant does. Do you think we should go back to Brian's room? If he stumbled upon something, it's possible there's a clue among his things."

"We've been to the room a couple of times, but we could have easily missed something." Christian acknowledged. "After we get that satellite feed set up, we'll go back and carefully go through his things again."

Elizabeth called her assistant and followed her directions on the computer to set up the tracking. "Now we just have to wait until Victoria turns it on." Elizabeth checked her watch. "It's five hours before my wedding." She hugged herself. "Just missing the groom and maid of honor." Her eyes welled up with tears.

David rested his hand on her shoulder.

"We need you to let us know the minute Victoria turns on the tracker. Slide the dresser in front. David, let's go."

****

David knocked on Peter's door. No answer. He turned the knob, but it was locked. When he tried the master key, it did not work. "It worked earlier."

Christian tapped David's shoulder. "May I?"

"Certainly," he said as he stepped back.

Christian removed something from his pocket and within seconds had the door unlocked.

"What's that?"

"A tool I find comes in handy quite a bit." Christian opened the door. "What the…"

David stepped into the room. "It's Jimmy."

He was sitting in the middle of the bed crossed-legged and rocking in a trance-like state.

They slowly approached him. "Jimmy, can you hear me?" Father David asked.

Jimmy stopped rocking and looked at him. In an instant, he went from a trance-like state to hysteria. "David, David, you can't say I didn't warn you."

"Am I speaking to Asmodeus?" David asked.

More laughter. "Why of course. You never did get rid of me!"

"Are you the only one?"

"Yes, Mr. Righteous. You won't get rid of me that easily!"

"Where is Victoria?" David demanded.

"Ah. The heart, the heart, always so vulnerable."

"Do you know where she is?"

"I warned you, didn't I? Such a choice morsel. You two are not the only ones who long for her you know.

206

She is in the hands of yet another." Eerie laughter emanated from deep within Jimmy.

"Is she safe?" David asked.

More laughter. "Safe enough for now. I'd like her for myself you know. She took one of my best warriors."

"Who?"

"Why, Chuck Ramsey of course." Jimmy looked at David with dark frightening eyes and grinned slyly. "We warned her on more than one occasion. We've got her now, and we won't let her go. We'll play with her for a while, see what we can get, and then we'll steal her soul."

"Where is she?" Christian asked.

"Ah, the other one." Jimmy laughed even more deeply. "You think you always catch your prey!" The laughter continued. "Not this time!"

"Where is she?" David demanded.

"You have all the clues you will ever need. *Quoth the raven, 'Nevermore.'*" Jimmy doubled over in laughter.

David chose another prayer of deliverance. "My Lord, you are all powerful, you are God, you are Father…"

More laughter bubbled up from Jimmy. "So you think your little prayer of deliverance is going to do you any good?"

David removed the little book from his pocket, opened it, and with a bowed head began to pray the Ritual.

Jimmy screamed in torment as his clothes ignited. An immediate sulfur smell permeated the room, and the fire went out. Jimmy lay there somberly.

Christian checked him over—no burns.

David took a deep breath. "Asmodeus may have left him, but I'm not sure. We need to get him to his father where he can be watched, fed, and taken care of. Sleep wouldn't hurt him either. He has been in torment a long time."

"Let's do what we came here to do—search this room."

"Let's do it. At this point Jimmy is just sleeping anyway. If Peter returned, he didn't clean it. This place is still a mess."

"We don't want to disrupt a crime scene, if this is one. If Peter came back, he might have had the same thought. At this point, we're not sure who made the mess." Christian looked around, opening up his belt pack. Handing David latex gloves, he said, "Just be careful when you handle things."

"His tuxedo is still hanging in the closet." David noted as he slipped on the gloves.

"Check for Brian's hiking gear. Elizabeth said they were going hiking, so he should have under armor, boots, an outer shell, backpack, and other miscellaneous essentials."

David checked the closet while Christian went through the drawers. "Nothing. None of his gear is in the drawers. How about the closet?"

"Nothing."

"Why would he have brought work on his honeymoon?" David asked.

"Elizabeth mentioned that Brian never went anywhere without his laptop. Anything?"

"No."

"Speaking of computers, let's get back to Elizabeth

and see if something's come up on Victoria's beacon."

David walked toward Jimmy and touched his forehead. "You head back. I'll go via the kitchen and let Nate know where he can find Jimmy."

"Be careful, bro."

Chapter 24

Victoria slowly opened her eyes and tried to focus. She was enveloped by darkness. Her hands were tied behind her back; her legs were free. Listening for sounds, she only heard a deafening silence. Slowly she turned her head. A dim light from a crack in the corner of the ceiling was just enough to allow her eyes to adjust. *Where am I?*

No doubt, she was in a stone enclosure of some age. It smelled old and musty. The air was dank, the floor mere dirt. It was cold, yet not unbearably so. She felt like a sack of potatoes that had been dumped in storage for the winter. *Who brought me here?*

She was dry, so she had not been dragged through snow. Her clothing appeared intact, but the fanny pack she put on her waist before leaving her room had been taken off, dumped out, and tossed in a corner. Obviously, someone was looking for something, but what?

Victoria pulled herself to a sitting position and scooted to her purse. With her feet, she righted it and was able to peer inside. Her cell phone was gone. Her keys were gone. Her notebook was gone. Everything else was intact and already dumped on the floor, including the few girly gifts Elizabeth had given her.

She smiled. Elizabeth was one smart cookie, she thought as she reached with her mouth for her tube of lipstick, caught it between her teeth, and dropped it into the top of her UGG boot. She repeated this exercise for her perfume, compact, mascara, and storage case for tampons. Her high school ballet coupled with Pilates and yoga sure kept her nimble.

She stretched before she continued. *I love those UGG boots, like slippers, roomy, and my secret hiding place for all kinds of goodies. These could definitely come in handy.*

Too bad her hands were tied. She couldn't reach the locket, but at least she still had it around her neck. Carefully she looked around.

Am I on hotel property? How long have I been out? I don't remember seeing any stone buildings on the property, but there were quite a few stone outcroppings nearby. And, am I in a building or a shelter, or even a cave of some kind? She got her feet under her and stood up. The ceiling was tall enough, but lower than standard. No furniture. She looked for the exit, but one wasn't obvious. *Hmm. I got in here somehow*. Slowly she walked the perimeter of the room, carefully checking the walls as she went. The room had a small outcropping she followed around. *Ah, here we go*. A heavy wooden door, no more than four feet tall and three feet wide was located in the space. A modern deadbolt held the door.

Lovely, Victoria thought as she paced. What now? She heard an echoing sound, as if someone were walking through a tunnel. Quickly she looked around to make sure things were as she found them. She knocked her purse back over, spread the dirt around the floor so footprints were not obvious, and hoped no one noticed the missing items. She lay back down the way she was when she first arose.

Victoria waited and listened. She heard two voices speaking in hushed tones. She strained to hear specifics, but it was too garbled. Patience, patience, she reminded herself.

The sound of a deadbolt turning quickened her heart. She used relaxation techniques her grandfather taught her in high school to steady her breathing.

Slowly the door opened and the sound of two people entering the room greeted her. One had heavy footsteps, but the other had lighter. At least one of them was a man. Who were they?

"How long do the effects of chloroform last?" asked the one with a higher voice.

Sounds like a woman, Victoria thought. *But, she's speaking too softly for me to know if it's a voice I've heard before.*

"Not sure specifically, but from what I read, it should be wearing off," answered a man.

"Did you use too much?" asked the first.

"I don't think so, but she's a light weight, so maybe it lasts longer with lighter people."

"What are we going to do with her?" asked the higher voice.

"For one thing, find out where the key is. I thought for sure she had it on her," answered the man with the deep voice.

Victoria couldn't place the voice. *I don't think I've met this person before, local accent, nothing unique.*

"You mentioned one thing, therefore there must be a second thing. Is that second thing in addition to what I've been working on?"

"Maybe."

"Wipe that wicked grin off your face and answer my question."

"The Raven wants her for himself."

"Why?"

"I don't ask those questions. I only imagine the answer." The man laughed an eerily wicked laugh.

"Well, let's get out of here for now and come back later."

"Sounds like a plan. I'm starving," said the man.

"You're always starving," answered the higher voiced person.

The door opened, then closed, and Victoria heard the deadbolt click.

The Raven, Victoria thought as she sat back up. He keeps coming up even though I thought I prosecuted him. Sandy's concerns were real. Ramsey may not have been the Raven, but one of his soldiers. The demon possessing Jimmy mentioned him and the Horse Whisperer mentioned him. The key was found behind a raven. *Who is this Raven? And why does Jimmy always seem to add, Quoth the Raven, "Nevermore." Edgar Allen Poe wrote that poem. Let me go back to my literature course. I had to memorize that poem, let's see how good my memory is.* Victoria closed her eyes and moved back in time to high school and her recitation of that famous dark poem. Out loud she recited Poe's 1845 poem, "The Raven."

What a dark, sad poem, she thought. *I know that answers to what is going on lies within this poem. I just know it. I need to free my hands.* She looked around the room and saw the pen Elizabeth gave her for Christmas. She rose and walked to the corner where she saw its silver tip.

Pilates and yoga will always be a part of my daily routine if I get out of here. Be positive Victoria. When I get out of here. She sat with her back to the pen and leaned so she could grab it with her hands. Opening its top, she exposed the knife. Carefully she cut the rope holding her hands. Free at last. Well, almost, she thought as she stood and put the knife away.

She opened the exquisite locket Elizabeth gave her and pressed the tracking device.

The beauty of these gifts rested on the fact that they served multiple functions. They were what they purported to be, but they also would have rivaled anything James Bond, 007, used. It made her almost feel like a spy. She smiled as she opened the tampon box and removed a plastic high-powered flashlight.

Victoria slowly turned to get a better sense of the whole room. It looks like a cave with a door. Stone walls, natural in appearance, as if a hole had been blasted in the side of a mountain, and the floor was dirt. Victoria kicked at the dirt on the floor to see if anything was underneath. She found stone. Hmm. The dirt seemed to be added as carpet or something. And there was more than dirt here. There was hay in parts. *How odd*, she thought, as she moved toward the small door, heavy in structure. The deadbolt was definitely modern.

Victoria took out her mascara that coupled as a lock pick. Boy, was she glad she took that class Elizabeth insisted on. She worked the lock. Sighing, she rubbed her brow with the back of her hand and continued, slowly, deliberately, determined to keep her sense of touch fine-tuned. Bent close to the lock, she listened to the slightest click so she knew she was on the right track. This is a tough lock, tougher than any others she worked.

Click. *Yes! Keep going, steady as you go*. Intently, she continued to work the lock. Click.

Time was passing. She didn't know how long she worked; she just knew she had to get out before the Raven, whoever he was, came.

The mechanism clicked one last time, and the dead bolt released. "Yes!" Victoria did a little jump, fist raised, mascara in hand.

She closed the mascara and put it back into her UGG boot, grabbed her fanny pack, and put it on her waist. You never knew when it would come in handy. She pressed up against the door to listen, but it was so thick, it was hard to discern whether anyone was there. Slowly, she opened the heavy door, pushing with her left shoulder in a bent position.

She peeked out and saw a dark tunnel. Victoria flicked her flashlight back on and examined her surroundings. The tunnel was as high as the room, not very wide, probably could fit two to three people across. It only went straight about seven yards before disappearing to the left. She took a deep breath and proceeded forward. She moved quickly, but silently. When she approached the corner, she slowly peered around the bend and froze. Someone was coming.

Victoria frantically looked around, but there was nowhere else to go but back to the room, and she already decided, there was no other exit beside the one she took. She grabbed her perfume bottle from her boot and turned the top all the way to the right. Perfume was now bypassed for pepper spray.

She waited, her heart racing. Her body ready to pounce in a key kick-boxing move, which hopefully would do the trick. At least her training was never for naught.

The footsteps approached quietly. Whoever was approaching was trying not to be heard. She quieted the pounding of her heart, slowing it down as she concentrated on her breathing. As the footsteps approached, she determined it was someone with a long stride, probably tall, most likely a man, but not necessarily. Time seemed to stop as she waited.

The person stopped closer to the corner, being careful. They were almost at a standstill. Who would move first? Did this person hear her? Victoria wasn't sure if the hesitation was because she had made a noise, or because the person was just being cautious.

She raised the perfume bottle, knees bent, ready to spring and… waited.

In a whispered voice, she heard someone call her name. "Victoria?"

She was trying to identify the voice, but whispered voices weren't as easy to place.

"Victoria? I'm here to help you."

Peter stepped around the corner. "You trying to make me smell good?"

Victoria let out her breath heavily. "Something like that. How did you know that I was here?"

"I remembered some tunnels I played in as a child, and decided to check them out. I hid when I saw a couple of people coming, and heard them talk about you in the cave. I knew I had to get to you. Are you all right?"

Shivering, she said, "Yes, just frightened. They put a hanky over my face soaked in something that knocked me out, probably chloroform. I woke up before they came in, but pretended to be out. They mentioned that the Raven wanted something I had."

"Didn't you put the Raven away?" Peter had her by the shoulders searching her face with an expression of concern.

"They mentioned a key, and they took my phone. The man had an evil sounding laugh who thought it amusing to say that this Raven also wanted me for his personal use."

"What key do you think they're after?"

"I only found one key. That must be what they're after. When you went back to your room, we continued to the Macraven Boardroom. Behind one of the cabinet knobs, I found an old key. That must be the key they're looking for. I can't imagine they want the keys to my car or anything like that, although they took them."

"Where is this key now?"

"Christian or David has it. While we're here, shouldn't we see if Brian is someplace close by?"

"I've been looking, and so far, found no evidence that Brian has ever been here, but there's one more place we could check before we go."

"Let's do it."

Peter led the way.

"You seem to really know this place well. Did you know Brian growing up?"

"Not really."

"What does 'Not really' mean? Either you did or you didn't."

Halfway down the tunnel, another tunnel branched off, and Peter took the branch. "It means that I knew who he was, but I didn't know him personally."

"Where are we now?"

"This tunnel and the few rooms created from the mountain was a place a hermit stayed in a long time ago. Each room did have an escape route in case something happened. The room you were in was probably a living room or study of some sort. He created another area with even better circulation toward the mouth of the tunnel. He seemed to use it as his kitchen. We used to play like we were in a fort as kids."

"This is a short detour."

"That's right. It's straight ahead." Peter approached a similar door to the one Victoria just picked the lock on and listened. "Can you be the look-out while I see if I can get the door open?"

"Sure." Victoria backtracked, "Nothing." She turned back just as Peter slowly pushed open the door. Quietly, she moved closer to Peter to see what was behind the door.

He moved in first, and motioned for Victoria to follow.

****

As Christian and David entered the room, a signal sounded from Elizabeth's computer. "Can we figure out where Victoria is?"

Elizabeth studied the screen. "Her beacon has been turned on. The signal comes and goes and is weak, but it looks like it's because she's inside one of the ridges close by. See this?" She pointed to the screen, "This is the property line of the Preston Hotel. Over here is a ridge. It looks to be solid rock, but if Victoria's signal is fading in and out, she must be inside somewhere. Do you think she may be with Brian?" Elizabeth wiped her eyes with a tissue.

Christian leaned over the screen. "The signal hasn't

moved in a while. It seems as though Victoria is in one place, a place which must have some sort of reception, no matter how vague."

She grabbed hold of Christian's arm. "You have to find them."

"What I need to know is the best route to the last known location of Victoria's signal."

"I can point you to the general area, but I have to tell you, she's going to be difficult to find." Elizabeth walked to the set of windows behind the desk. "You see, it's just the ridge adjacent to the property, directly straight out from the side of this room. Legend has it that a hermit holed up there a hundred years ago or so, but I always thought it was just legend. We played hide-and-seek in the area as kids, but I never found an entrance into the ridge."

"It may not have been legend. If the signal's coming from the ridge, chances are she's inside somewhere. I've got to see what I find."

David walked in. "You leaving?" he asked Christian.

"Yeah." Christian opened the case Joe had given him earlier and removed a loaded backpack. He checked it carefully and added additional equipment.

"Where do you propose to start?"

"The Indian. He may know that ridge. I'll give you a heads up if I find a way in." Christian secured his backpack and left.

Chapter 25

Christian decided to enter the stables from the outside this time to take in a different perspective. Thankful he had the proper gear, he zipped his jacket to the top and slipped on his gloves. Although the cloud cover made it dark, the snow's reflection created light. The soft snow crunched under his boots as he made the short walk to the stables, lifted the latch, and quietly entered their warmth. The Horse Whisperer was brushing one of the horses, softly speaking in his ear.

The Ute lifted his gaze and met Christian's. "Welcome. You have come to seek direction, no?"

"Yes."

"It's the Victorious One you search for. She has been taken."

"How do you know?"

"I just know."

"Will she be all right?"

"That is up to you."

"I believe she is somewhere inside the ridge next to us. Is there a way in?"

"Yes. The ridge was the home of the religious one. My father taught him how to hunt, what berries were edible, how to survive. They spent time in meditation together. A good man."

"How do I enter the ridge?"

"Under the eagle's nest is the key."

"Where is this eagle's nest?"

"Come, join me in meditation. Let your worries escape you. Let your inner spirit join the Creator in worship. Then, you will find the eagle's nest."

They sat crossed legged in front of the fire. The Ute started his calming chant. Christian breathed deep as a sense of peace overtook his entire being. He let go. As David would say, "Let go and let God." He whispered a prayer of direction and safety for Victoria and Brian. Although he was not a deeply religious man, his brother did have a way of rubbing off on people. Even with his hardened past, there was something about the presence of God. *I know there is a God; it's the only thing that makes sense in this world.*

Christian released his entire being. He saw the sky in his mind. He saw a large stately tree, a mature evergreen. One not dense with young pine needles, but almost in a petrified form. An eagle soared above the tree, looking down, not for prey, but at her nest. He vividly saw the eagle's nest. The vision brought him from the stables to the nest. Deep within the hollow of the tree, he saw a key in his vision and opened his eyes. The Ute continued to chant, while Christian stood and made his way to the door. The vision clearly directed him to the hollow beneath the eagle's nest.

He was not far, and the nest was at the base of the ridge. Amazing. Christian looked up at the nest, his eyes searching beneath for the hollow. He put his hand in the hollow, but no key.

He closed his eyes and brought his mind back to his time of meditation with the Ute. Okay, a key could be just a figure of speech. He reached back in and pulled out a thick stick, about the size of the handle of a baseball bat. Smiling, he realized what he was holding, a map, or key so to speak. The start point was exactly where he stood. It was the floor plans of the hermit's dwelling inside the ridge. Christian smiled, closed his eyes and said, "Thank you."

He followed the map, but there was no obvious opening. He took out his flashlight and studied the map more carefully. There should be an outcropping of rocks and what looked like brush of some sort. Christian let the flashlight linger over the area. He found the outcropping, not too big, only about four and a half feet high by about four feet wide. Brush appeared to be behind and to the side. He moved carefully around the outcropping. Sure enough, he found the entrance.

Christian heard his heart pound, and tried to steady it. The last known location of Victoria's beacon was in this direction, but the signal still had not returned. He tried to slow his breathing. *I just want to get in and find them. I need to remain calm, stay on full alert, and be ready for anything.* As he entered, he heard a noise. Quickly catching the movement in the flashlight's high beams, he saw a furry animal frozen in fear, a fox. He smiled as the fox escaped deep within the cavern with Christian not far behind.

Based on the plans, there appeared to be a half dozen different rooms. He entered a rock tunnel. If this map was accurate, there should be a room coming up around the bend to the left. As he reached the bend, he stopped and listened.

Not a sound.

Christian continued slowly around the bend, and cautiously checked out his surroundings. He raised the collar of his jacket. It was colder inside the tunnel than out, like a refrigerator.

He entered the first room. Definitely for storage of some sort, perhaps for logs and other items intended for survival. It was small, but did not look like it had been used recently.

Voices sounded, coming his way. Christian tucked himself in the corner, a little cramped, but he fit. A man and a woman were talking in hushed tones, but getting louder the closer they came. He strained to hear what they were saying.

"The Raven's thrilled with Victoria as a bonus, but he's not happy we let the key slip by us." It was the man who spoke. Christian did not recognize his voice.

"She's secure, isn't she?" the woman asked.

Why does she sound familiar to me? He wondered if it was just the tone, or if he had actually heard that same voice before. He held his breath as they approached.

"Oh yeah, safely tucked inside the kitchen." Laughing he added, "She'll make a nice dish."

"What is the Raven planning on doing with her?" The woman seemed a little put out.

"Oh, he's got some very big plans for her."

"Why not for me?" She pouted.

"Trust me, you would not want to be a part of these plans."

"Why not? I want to be a part of his entire essence. I want him to have me in every way imaginable."

"Then try the unimaginable. He'll enjoy her to his fullest, but he's going to make sure no one else will."

Thoughts of the torture chamber filled his mind. *Does the Raven have anything to do with that sub-basement and the rooms of horror?*

Chapter 26

"It's definitely part of the hermit's living quarters. Take a look," Peter said as he stepped aside.

"This place is creepy. If I wasn't trying to find Brian, I'd say let's pass on the tour and get me out of here. But, I need to find him, so let's see." Victoria crossed over the threshold, slowly taking it all in. "Looks like a kitchen."

"It is."

"He spent a lot of time here and definitely used his surrounding resources. Look here…" She lightly brushed her hand on top of a rugged table made of stone slab. "Not very big; he certainly didn't have much company. And it's placed near the only opening which I imagine would allow light in. I wonder how comfortable his pine chair is. Only one way to find out," she said as she sat.

"It doesn't look very comfortable."

"Ah, but it is, which I find amazing since it's just wood. I think it's in the shape, almost as if this hermit naturally knew about ergonomics. And he must have hiked for exercise, or maybe he had a limp. There's a walking stick near the door."

She slowly stood as her eyes continued to take in her surroundings. Shelves were chiseled out of the stone walls, with storage containers carved from various trees. "He even managed to create a storage place. Not too big, but at least one person can fit inside."

"He must have hunted. He used antlers as light fixtures with the tips hallowed out to hold candles."

"I bet he made his own candles. A man like this hermit would have access to his own bee hive." She picked up one of the wooden canisters and lifted the lid. "Speaking of honey, this is his honey jar. I wonder if he died here or he just left?"

Peter shrugged. "Legend has it that he left, but who's to know for sure." He cocked his head, "Voices. Until I find out if it's friend or foe, hide in that storage area. I'll come for you when it's clear."

"What about you?"

"You were the one knocked out and taken captive. We know it's you they want, not me, so it's you I need to protect." In one fluid movement, Peter opened the cabinet and guided her in quickly.

From inside the cabinet, sounds were muffled. Victoria felt cold air, so she knew at least there was an oxygen source, although she didn't know from where. She shivered, pulling her jacket tighter around her shoulders. Her heart started to pound. *Did I see any spiders when I looked inside? I hate spiders.* She couldn't remember.

Victoria put her ears to the door area trying to hear something. She heard muffled voices and the sound of a door. Probably the door to the room she was in. She hoped Peter was all right. Victoria didn't like it. She didn't like feeling trapped. She didn't like the idea that someone was after her. Who would?

I wonder where Brian is…if he's still alive. Time seemed to move in slow motion. *How long have I been*

*in here? Do I dare turn on my light and check? How
sealed is this space from the kitchen? Will light seep
through?*

Silence.

No more muffled voices. No sound at all, just total
silence. She took out her pen light and examined the
space. Big enough for an adult, one larger than her,
with a narrower area, one from where the cold air
flowed. Hmm, the hermit might have used this space as
a refrigerator. Sure felt like it. She pressed her ear to the
door. Just silence. Slowly she cracked the door, and
dared to peek. No one there, not even Peter. *They took
Peter!*

Victoria slowly opened the door and crawled out.
Standing gently to work out the cramps in her legs, she
looked around. The door to the hallway was shut. She
made her way and tried to open it, but it wouldn't
budge. This door didn't have a lock on it from the
inside; something from the outside was keeping it shut,
but what?

Victoria walked to the only narrow window in the
room. It was dark outside now, so she wasn't sure what
was there, plus the window was so narrow, not even a
child could squeeze through. She went back to the
storage area that served as her hiding spot and took a
closer look. I need to know where the air is coming
from. Did it lead to another room? Did it lead outside?
It was cold, fresh air, so it might lead outside.

Crouching, she used her light slowly, carefully
covering every inch of the space. The front part was
solid stone, but the area bringing in air was the start of a
tunnel, but a very narrow tunnel. She checked for
spiders. Webs, but no spiders. *Yuck*, she shivered. *I*

don't even like spider webs. She backed out of the space. *I'm not touching it. I'll get that walking stick I saw.*

Victoria returned with the stick. Nice stick. It was not just a tree limb; care went into the carving of it. Victoria poked around the tunnel removing every trace of spider webs. This area was probably too cold for the spiders! She crawled in, craning her neck into the tunnel area. *The tunnel is smooth, but there is an outcropping that's not. Interesting.*

She carefully felt the entire area. It seemed to be shaped like a lever. How odd. She slowly shined her light over every inch. It wasn't a natural outcropping; it seemed to be a lever. Victoria tried to move it, but it was stuck. She pushed her head as far in as she could, maybe there was something she was missing. A sound. *A human sound, muffled, but I do believe human. Sounds like a muffled moan. This air flow was coming from an area where there was another human.*

I have to get this lever moved. But with what?

Victoria backed out to see if there was anything she could find. She opened the first canister, and was surprised by what she saw, saltines. Sealed packages to boot. Well, these didn't belong to the hermit. These are fresh. She went to the next canister, power bars.

Victoria frowned. *Who is staying here?*

The third canister was large, rectangular, and contained soups with pop-top lids, peanut butter and jelly, even cookies. There's enough food in here to keep someone going for a couple of weeks!

The next canister contained hot chocolate mixes, tea, even spiced apple cider mix. The last canister contained paper plates, plastic bowls, forks, spoons, knives, and napkins. Tucked on the corner of one of the shelves was a Sterno for cooking and cooking oil. The corner hid it from view when she first looked around. The cooking oil might work.

She took the oil back into the cabinet and poured it all around the lever. If she could work this oil into the lever, it just might move.

Victoria worked diligently trying to get the lever well oiled. She stopped and rubbed her hands. *So sore…it's got to budge sooner rather than later…I don't know how long my hands will hold out.*

Again, she worked the lever. The minutes ticked by and finally some movement. Click, she heard a mechanism slide, and the back wall opened to reveal a tunnel. The moaning was clear now. This tunnel definitely led to where the moaning originated. Victoria decided to follow the sound. She put the flashlight in her mouth and entered the tunnel.

The tunnel was small, perhaps a ventilation system of some sort.

The moaning ceased, but Victoria continued. She felt the tunnel close around her. *Thankfully, I'm not claustrophobic. Arachnophobic with my fear of spiders, but not claustrophobic.*

She stopped and buttoned her jacket as high as it would go. Even her adrenaline rush wasn't enough to keep her warm. And the deeper she went into the tunnel, the colder it got. *My knees hurt. This stone is not conducive to crawling, that's for sure.* She stopped and rubbed her knees, trying fruitlessly to make them feel better. *Maybe if I pull myself with my arms, at least it'll be a change.* She got into position, but hesitated, listening for the moans to resume.

Nothing.

She continued forward. *This is longer than I thought, but someone is in trouble and I need to reach whoever it is. Maybe it's Brian!*

The end of the tunnel was close. Victoria took the flashlight from her mouth to get a better look. It definitely ended just a few yards up. No light. Her hair was blowing away from her face. *There's an opening here somewhere.* She inched forward, careful not to venture into a hole. *Ah, there it is, but no light, hmm.*

Victoria stopped to listen. *I hear the moan. It's faint, but there. Someone is close.*

She shined her flashlight into the hole. *Wow, the ceiling is quite close to the ground, maybe only about four feet or so.* The space was bare just below her. *I'll have to hang through to get a better look. Good thing we added gymnastics to augment my dance competitions.* There was a petrified piece of wood longer than the opening. Victoria secured it across the hole and locked her knees around it, as if on the uneven bars. Slowly lowering her upper body, she swept the room. It was empty except for something large against the wall. Just then, she heard a soft moan from that wall. Definitely a person, definitely someone hurt. The room was otherwise empty. Carefully taking in the entire room, she noted two doors. *How odd. I wonder what this room was and where it went.*

Except for the person in the corner, the room was empty. Victoria pulled up, grabbed hold of the petrified wood with her hands, and unlocked her legs. She lowered herself down into a squatting position. The ceiling was too low to stand. *Boy, it's cold in here. Where's the wind coming from?* One of the doors had an opening with bars on it. Did it go outside?

Slowly she crept toward the body on the floor. The soft moans were more audible. Whoever this was needed medical attention. In a whisper, she asked, "Brian, is that you?"

"Help me."

It didn't sound like Brian, but it was too soft to be sure. She crept closer shining her flashlight. It was a man all right, bound hand and foot. Shivering, with cracked lips, disheveled brown hair matted with blood, but not Brian. "I'm here to help. Who are you?"

"I hurt."

"Where do you hurt?"

"All over. Need water. Need out."

Victoria looked all around. "There's no water here, but I know where to get some. Who are you?"

"Dennis." He looked toward Victoria. "Dennis Ryder."

"You work for Brian's firm, don't you?"

"Yes. Brian. Get him before it's too late."

"What do you mean get Brian before it's too late? Where is he?"

Dennis's head rocked to the side. "Need water."

"Can you get up and come with me?"

"Can't move. Too weak."

"I'll get water, but it'll take me a few minutes. It's in the kitchen."

Victoria went as fast as she could in a crouched position to get to the tunnel. As she pulled herself up on the petrified wood and into the tunnel, she heard voices and froze. One of the doors to the room which held Dennis opened followed by laughter. The same two voices she heard earlier. "Well, well, what have we here?" said the male voice. "Are you ready to talk yet?"

"Water. I need water."

"You'll get water when you tell us what we need to know. Where is the money?"

From where she froze, she could see Dennis's head loll to the side.

The woman's voice spoke. "You know he can't talk without water."

"Ha, ha, ha. I'll give you water."

Victoria heard water hitting something, or someone, and falling to the stone floor. She held her breath.

"That's only going to make him colder."

"Good. Maybe then he'll talk. Dennis, you tell us where the money is, and we'll give you water to drink and warm, dry clothes."

Dennis' response was silence.

The woman said, "He's passed out. How long can he take it?"

"He'll talk. Dennis, if you can hear me, know that I'll be back soon, and when I do, you'll talk. Ha, ha, ha. I'm going to have me a little fun. Can't wait."

Victoria heard feet shuffle and the door close. *I have to get back to the kitchen quickly. See what I can find.*

As Victoria approached the opening to the kitchen, she stopped and listened.

Silence.

Good. She pushed the hair out of her face and came through the opening she originally entered. She ran to the cupboard where she saw water and grabbed a bottle and an energy bar. She continued to search until she found a towel, bundled it all up, and returned to the

231

tunnel.

What have I gotten myself into now? Victoria took a deep breath and waited at the mouth of the tunnel to make sure the man and woman did not return.

Silence.

Into the tunnel she went on hands and knees, this time dragging her little bundle. As she approached the opening, she listened once again.

Silence.

She took her flashlight and shined it into the room. Dennis was where she left him, but he did not move.

"Dennis?" Victoria said in hushed tones.

No answer.

She lowered herself quickly and made it to his side.

"I have water. Please wake up and take some." She lifted his head and cradled it in her left arm.

His eyes opened slightly, followed by his mouth. Slowly she gave him water. He was wet and shaking from the cold. "I'm just going to dry you off a bit with this towel. I have a second one to cover you. We have to get you out of here."

Victoria took out the pen from her UGG boot and released the pocketknife. "I'm going to cut you free. Do you have enough energy to help me move you?"

"I—I don't know. My head hurts. What day is it?"

"This is Brian and Elizabeth's wedding day. They are supposed to get married in about five hours."

"Oh. Then I've had no food or drink in more than twenty-four hours. I've lost count." He coughed. "I'll try though."

"I've got a power bar here, but I think it's best if we get you out of here first, before they get back. Do you know them?"

"No."

Victoria helped him sit. "I'm going to help you get to the tunnel. It's warmer in the kitchen and there are more supplies, although I don't know how safe that will be. We know they're coming back for you. Do you know where Brian is?"

"No, but I know they have him." He coughed again.

She helped him crawl over to the opening in the ceiling. "Look up and follow my flashlight. Do you see that piece of wood?"

"Yes."

"If I help you stand, do you think you could take hold of it and help me get you up through that hole?"

"I'll try."

He struggled. Victoria pushed while he pulled.

"Whew. Move over while I get up."

She hoisted herself up, and then moved the wood. "This might come in handy. Let me squeeze past you so I can check out the kitchen. I'd hate to walk into a den of lions…Keep quiet now, so I can make sure all is clear."

Victoria shimmied through the tunnel cautiously, approaching the entry into the kitchen. "All clear. Come on."

When she safely got him into the kitchen, she realized there was a chest in the corner she didn't notice before. She opened it up, and with a big smile, she looked at Dennis. "We're in luck. I have some dry clothes for you." She gave him a set of men's sweats and boot socks. "Try these on for size. I'll turn around while you dress."

From over her shoulder, she asked, "What money

are they after?"

"You can turn around now. I can't tell you about the money." He slumped in the chair.

"Okay, what's going on here?" Hands on hips, she gave him the look.

"I'm not comfortable talking to you about this. You are Ms. Harrington's friend, aren't you?"

"Yes, that's right, but I'm sure you know I've just been hired by your firm. So technically, you can tell me anything you know, especially if it'll help find Brian and get us out of here. You better start talking. I don't know how much time we have here."

"I don't know everything that's going on, but I do know that Brian is in serious trouble."

"Do you know about Sandy's murder?" Victoria fought back more tears.

The stunned look on Dennis's face told her all she needed to know. "When did this happen?"

"Yesterday."

"Where?"

"The hotel spa."

He shook his head, and whispered. "How?"

"Have you been following the Raven murders?"

"Oh no. Not that." He put his head in his hands. "It's all my fault."

"What do you mean?"

Dennis shook his head slowly. "I came across some photos, and documents that were suspect. I did further research and your name kept coming up."

"I don't understand. What photos and what documents?"

"I received an untraceable call saying that you prosecuted the wrong person. Then, when I got here, there was an envelope that had been slipped under my door with pictures. Not long after, a note was slipped under the door telling me to go to the spa; it was a matter of life and death. I had the envelope with me, but had an uneasy feeling, so when I noticed the display cabinet was open on my way out, I hid it and flipped the latch so it locked."

"Why would you go without back up of some sort?"

"I didn't think about that. I went."

"Then what happened?"

"I'm not sure. I was drugged with something, but I don't know what. I remember calling Sandy, but that's all I remember. I've been in and out since then, but I know Brian is in danger, and that they took him."

Dennis rubbed his nose on his shirt sleeve. "Here." Victoria held out her hand. "A napkin is better than a sleeve."

"Thank you." Dennis sniffled. "I'm afraid it may be my fault Sandy is dead." He blew his nose.

"Do you know what money your captors are talking about?"

"I'm the real estate paralegal for Ms. Harrington's purchase. I was called into Peter Mack's office and told that as part of the negotiation of the property, he agreed to transfer the funds from the buyer in the manner specified by the seller's attorney. I would receive an encrypted file with specific directions for an electronic transfer. I would not have access to the code until the closing. Peter told me that I needed to follow the directions to the letter."

"Was it a large file?"

"No, quite small. I believe it was transfer

instructions to only one bank. I found the whole thing quite odd, so when Sandy came to see me asking questions, I told her about this encrypted file. She asked if she could look at my computer, and after working diligently on it for a while, she got excited. She followed it back to its source, and also managed to obtain another file linked to this one."

"How do you think this may have endangered her life?"

"When I received the code for the encrypted file, I gave it to her. I then followed Peter's instructions."

"Did you follow through with every aspect of the closing?"

"Not quite. I like to be the one who records the deed, especially when I represent the buyer, although it's not necessary. In this case, Peter let the seller's attorney handle it."

"Why?"

"I don't know."

"How did you end up here?"

"After the closing, I went back to my office. I like to go through my post-closing checklist while everything is fresh in my mind, and I thought I'd do that once I got up here. I checked in the day before the rehearsal dinner."

"Why did you come up a day early?"

"Peter asked me to so I can help out where needed."

"Okay, so you came up a day early. What then?"

"Well, as I mentioned, the envelope had already been slipped under the door before my arrival, so when I opened the door I found it and flipped it onto the desk. I unpacked, grabbed a quick bite, and when I returned, that's when I received the note."

"You didn't open the envelope before you left to eat?"

"No, I just thought it was something insignificant from housekeeping or something. I didn't give it much thought until I got the note."

"So you don't know what money they're talking about? Do you know anything about where you are?"

"Only that I'm still in Eustis Park somewhere."

"Yeah, you're in Eustis Park, but I'm not sure where we are either, just that a hermit used to live here."

"I heard them talking about Brian. If he's missing, then I think they have him."

"He's missing, and he went missing about the same time Sandy was murdered. She may have been murdered a few hours before."

The door leading to the tunnel where Victoria found Dennis was open. Another door creaked, and they froze. A man's voice spoke first. "What the? Where is he? When we left him, he was in no shape to be able to move anywhere. Do you know if the Raven has him? Perhaps he has his own plans for Dennis."

The woman answered. "I don't know. He never told me. As you said though, Dennis was in no condition to leave of his own accord. The Raven must have him."

"Let's check on Victoria. We don't want to leave her unattended for too long."

Dennis held his breath. "It's not safe here. They're coming to check on you."

"Those two left me in another room, so I'm sure they'll return there. I think we're safe here for a while."

"If they left you in another room, how did you end up here?"

They heard the sound of shoes coming down the hall. Two sets, one heavier than the other, and then voices, a man and a woman.

Dennis frowned. "They're coming here, not where they left you. How do they know where you are?"

"There's only one person who knew I was here, but maybe that person was taken, and he talked. Regardless, we've got to get out of here. Into the tunnel, Dennis, I'll follow."

He scurried back, adrenaline giving him the added speed. Victoria was fast on his heels, but she heard the door open to the kitchen. "Move faster."

A large hand grabbed her ankles as she tried to crawl to safety. It felt like a vise. "Well, well, what have we here? Little Miss Victoria being creative." Laughter. "You're just going to make things a little more fun for me, that's all, such nice legs. Easy to hold." More laughter.

Victoria tried to wriggle free. She looked up and saw Dennis's frightened face and motioned him forward as she was dragged backward.

Chapter 27

Elizabeth pored over files and kept track of the signal as it came and went. A knock sounded at the door. David stood and put his ear to the door. "Who is it?"

"It's Nate."

Father David opened the door to Nate, ringing his hands. "Jimmy wasn't in Brian's room. He's gone. I thought he was too exhausted to move."

"I'm sure he was exhausted. Look, you go back to his room. We'll go to the Gregory Room. He'll show up in one of those places."

"Thank you, Father."

Nate's footsteps diminished quickly. "Do you want to stay here, Elizabeth?"

"No. I'll come with you. If we find Jimmy, let's prod him for more information. Maybe my presence will help."

He rubbed his brow. "I exorcized a number of spirits, but one has a strong hold on him. You know, I've been thinking about what Nate said earlier. The only way I feel Renie could know when to go to Jimmy is if she has some connection to that demon."

"That's creepy."

"It is, but demon possession is dangerous and creepy business. Let's go to the Gregory Room and see if Jimmy's in his favorite spot."

Elizabeth stayed behind Father David as they approached the Gregory Room. He grabbed hold of the door handle and slowly opened the door, cringing as it creaked. Stepping into the room, he carefully looked around, trying not to frighten Jimmy. Candles lit the stage and Jimmy sat in the center.

"You dare return?" Jimmy's head jerked in David's direction, his eyes on fire.

Elizabeth quickly took in her breath and placed her hand over her mouth trying to remain quiet.

"Ah, I see you have a new one, Father. Did the other one get old already? Ha, ha, ha," Jimmy held his stomach as he continued to laugh uncontrollably.

Crazed laughter resonated throughout the Gregory Room. Father David held his prayer book tight with one hand, and rubbed his rosary beads in his other.

"That didn't work last time, do you think it will work this time?" More laughter.

"Who is Renie?"

"Ah, so it's question time again is it? I bet you want some answers to go with your questions, don't you?"

"Who is Renie?"

"Hmm, should I answer? Or not? Hmm. Why do you want to know?"

"Renie is a child of God, and I'm going to pray for her."

"Father, you can pray all you want, but she's mine and you'll never have her."

"How is she yours?"

"In ways you will never imagine, she's mine." Jimmy licked his lips slowly and deliberately, his eyes never leaving David's.

240

"Where is Renie?"

"Wouldn't you like to know? She is one of my most reliable foot soldiers, selected for her skills."

"What do you have in store?"

"That's for me to know, foolish one, and you to find out." Deep laughter mocked him.

"Is she with Victoria?"

"Ah, still sweet on her, are you, Father? I bet you'd give anything to get her back. How about your soul? Will you trade your soul for her? I can give her to you, safe, sound, and totally in love with you. You can have a life with her like no other you can even imagine. A life of love, joy, sex, companionship. Everything a man should have. You'd like that. I know you."

"Where is Victoria?" Father David demanded.

"She is where I want her. She is a gift we will make perfect for Lucifer." Jimmy rubbed his hands together. "She will be enjoyed as she was meant to be enjoyed."

Father David prayed fervently from his book of prayers.

"Begone, evil one!" he commanded.

Jimmy shuddered and slumped.

Elizabeth timidly approached David. "Is the demon gone?"

"I don't know, but I didn't like what I uncovered. We learned a couple of things; one is that Victoria is alive because they have plans for her."

"Frightening plans."

"Yes, they are. Two, Renie is somehow a part of what is going on. That is probably why Brian photographed her so much. I think he was doing some investigating on his own. I think he was probably working with Sandy on some things that weren't right. Sandy paid with her life, but they may still want something from Brian."

"You don't think he's in on it then?" Elizabeth asked.

"You know Brian better than I do. What do you think he's capable of?"

"Stepping in it by doing his own investigating."

"That's what I think."

"But what about that passport?"

"I don't know about that. That's something Christian could probably find out about if needed."

"Let's get back to my room. I want to check on Victoria's signal and see if we can reach Christian."

****

Back at the room, Elizabeth made her way to the computer. "The signal's gone."

"Can I use your phone to call Christian?"

"Yes. I asked my assistant to do a background check on Renie while you and Christian were gone, so I'm going to see what she found. Our company does background checks all the time, and we have great access. We use a program not available to just anybody. It's a similar type program used by the FBI and Homeland Security."

David tried his brother. "No answer."

"Try to text." Elizabeth continued to type away.

"Nothing."

"Okay. But I think I should give my assistant a raise. We just hit the jackpot." She rubbed her hands together.

"What do you mean?"

"I got some great intel on Renie, legally named

Lenore Wyndham Colter."

"That's definitely an unusual name. Go on."

"Yes, it is. Most family names are a little unusual. Just like Nate told you, she spent summers with him from the time she was about four years old. Her father is in a construction industry that moves him around the country quite a bit. Mom deserted her husband and child when Renie was only three, so she probably has limited memories of her mother. She's been nick named 'Renie' from birth.

"Renie's family ties go way back in Eustis Park. My assistant did a family tree to see how strong her ties went and who in this case she may be tied to."

"We already know she's related to the hotel's chef and troubled son."

"You're right about that, but that's nothing compared to the other relatives I dug up. By the way, as the web grew, my team added other individuals to the family tree. We have a relative forest here developing. Pretty interesting really."

"Let's hear what you've got."

"How much of Eustis Park's history do you know?"

"None."

"Well, the history is important. We saw photos in a number of people's offices that are from the same time period, around the turn of the twentieth century. In other words, these photos date back to the land purchase by Lord Macraven, as well as the building of the Preston Hotel."

David sat back in his chair. "You do know we're working on a tight schedule?"

"Yes I do, but what we learn here may expedite

matters."

"Okay. Let's hear it. This sounds like it's going to be good."

"Oh, it is. Let's just say, they could make a great movie out of all of this. You are aware that Lord Macraven was a ladies' man, aren't you?"

"Yes, I am."

"Lord Macraven is an important link. When he first came to Eustis Valley, it was 1872. This was a place where he could do some major hunting and fishing, and he envisioned a lodge where he could entertain his friends."

"Is Macraven his given name?"

"No. His real name is the Honorable Wyndham James, the Fourth Earl of Macraven. He was an Irish nobleman. Renie has connections to Lord Macraven. You could only buy land under the Homestead Act if you were an American citizen, so he enlisted the help of an Irish Canadian named Theodore Whyler. Name sound familiar?"

"Isn't that the marketing guy I still haven't met?"

"Yes. The original Theodore Whyler had questionable ethics to say the least."

"What did he do?"

"He paid people to come to Eustis Park to file fraudulent claims on 160 acre blocks of land. The only thing each landowner had to do was improve it by creating a foundation seemingly to build a cabin by placing four logs in a square. These people then sold their land for five dollars, and sometimes as little as three dollars to a company formed and owned by Lord Macraven, initially called the 'Irish Company' and later changed to the 'Eustis Park Company.' "

"And this worked?"

"Apparently. It was quite successful and allowed Lord Macraven to accumulate somewhere around 10,000 acres. Now, not everyone did what they agreed to do and held onto their land. Neither Whyler nor Lord Macraven could do anything about that since the whole transaction was fraudulent."

"So, Renie is related somehow to Lord Macraven, and Teddy Whyler's ancestor was involved in the original scheme." David leaned forward.

"It gets better." She was like a child in the middle of an exciting storybook. "All right. We now have historical ties between Lord Macraven and Theodore Whyler. At around the same time, a United Brethren minister came riding into town and fell in love with the area. In 1875, he built a home at the base of Longs Peak and gave up his missionary work to give guided tours, farm, and run a lodge. This minister's name was Reverend Elkanah Colter."

"Don't tell me Renie is also related to the minister."

"Oh, this is good. Elkanah Colter was one of those settlers who refused to sell to Lord Macraven. He felt that anyone who worked with the Earl of Macraven was 'prepared to sell their souls for a mess of pottage at the dictation of a foreign lord.' Elkanah Colter and his son Lyle stayed in the area."

"And how does this relate?" David pyramided his fingers together.

"Sorry, I got a little side tracked. It's so interesting."

"Only hit the important points please. Later you can share the other stuff."

"The important stuff is that Renie's mother is a descendant of Lord Macraven. Her predecessor is actually born of one of the earl's sordid affairs. Renie's father is a descendant of Elkanah Colter. Teddy Whyler is a descendant of Theodore Whyler, that rogue Irish Canadian."

"And this brings us to present day," David said.

"Renie went to college at the university right here in Colorado and got her degree in public relations and advertising. She interned for Teddy Whyler as part of her studies during one semester and then worked for him throughout the year, except for the summers, when she worked for the Preston Hotel."

David tipped his head as he thought about what he just heard. "That's strange. Why would you work for someone in the area of your major for a limited time throughout the year, but then work for a hotel in the summer? Could she have been helping out with public relations or marketing or something?"

"Remember what Nate told you. He only referred to what she did as help out where needed, whether it was as a maid, server in the restaurant, wherever. It did not seem to be related to her studies. You're right, this is odd."

Elizabeth shrugged. "There's more. There are reports of interviews that came up, probably for a job or something. But these are interviews with a few former classmates. They said she was nice, but very stand-offish. She didn't seem to have a best friend, at least none that ever was around. She wears what she referred to as a promise ring on her ring finger, but no one has ever met a boyfriend."

"Wait a minute." David interrupted. "Why would

246

anyone remember someone wearing a promise ring, especially when they weren't good friends?"

"Ah, you've got the same thought I had. This ring was not a typical promise ring. It was a raven with a diamond eye. These former classmates noticed it because they had never seen anything like it. When they questioned her about why a raven for a promise ring, she gave them an odd smile. They said it was pretty creepy. She loved ravens, and her favorite poem was by Edgar Allen Poe."

"Whoa, full circle here." David leaned back. "Her real name is Lenore. Poe's poem, 'The Raven,' was about a Lenore."

"There's more. One of these classmates, Pat, invited her to church a few times, but Renie never went. She said she worshiped the lord over the earth. When asked what church she attended, Renie just laughed. Some pets started to disappear. They never associated it with Renie, until the disappearances stopped when Renie left."

She hesitated. "Do you think Renie had anything to do with what we saw in the basement?"

"That's possible. How about this guy she was photographed with, Liam Newinn?"

"Well, as you know he's Jacqueline's date, but we have another connection. He was one of Renie's public relations professors. He still teaches at the university, but he makes most of his money as a consultant."

"Who does he consult for?"

"He's worked a lot with Teddy Whyler's firm."

Chapter 28

Laughing, the man pulled a struggling Victoria all the way out and onto the floor of the kitchen. While in the tunnel, she had been too cramped to get herself into a gainful position, but as soon as she hit the floor, she rolled, swept his right leg causing him to fall, and grabbed his left foot in a toehold. Seconds from breaking his knee, she found herself staring into the barrel of a pistol, a woman at its grip.

"Well now, Victoria, didn't see that coming. You all right, Liam?"

He growled as he carefully pulled himself into a standing position. "I'll live."

Pain etched his face as he stood over her and grabbed her hair, pulling her head back. He started laughing, but the laughter didn't reach his pale blue eyes. Victoria shivered, so cold. She tried to scoot back.

"You aren't going anywhere, my pretty," he said as his other hand grabbed her forearm. "Your little stunt just made your life a little harder. Don't even think of trying something like that again." He pulled harder. "Get me?"

She looked at his hand on her arm and saw a ring she had seen before. Startled she looked up at the man. "Who are you?"

"Ah, that's not important. What is important is that I know who you are."

Victoria looked around. The woman was gone, but she heard her voice and then a step-drag, step-drag. The kitchen door was kicked open and the same petite beauty came through dragging Dennis behind her. Where did she get that kind of strength for such a little woman? Victoria stared at her face. "I know you."

"I wouldn't say you know me. Let's say you've seen me, but I know you."

She kicked Dennis into the corner.

Victoria heard him moan. "Dennis, you all right?"

No answer.

"What have you done to him?" Victoria demanded.

As the woman brushed her bangs, Victoria noticed the ring. "Don't worry your little head over Dennis. I'll see to him."

"Where's Brian?"

The man laughed. "You'll be with him soon enough." He reached forward and lightly stroked the contours of Victoria's face.

She pulled back. "Don't touch me."

"Oooh, still tough, are we?" He laughed. "I'm not only going to touch you when I wish, I will touch you where I wish, and you'll enjoy it. As a matter of fact, you're going to be enjoyed by a lot of people, but saved for the very best, your groom."

Victoria shuddered.

"Let me introduce myself," he said as he bowed. "I am Liam Newinn. This is my partner, Renie. She will be getting you ready for your wedding, and I will provide the offering." He looked at Dennis. "Of course, I will have to be the one to make sure you are properly ready in every way." His grin brought another shudder.

Renie lit the candles placed on top of the lower

shelves. She opened one of the cupboards, brought down a mirror, and placed it on the counter before a chair. Next to it, she opened her large bag and brought out a perfume she sprayed in Victoria's direction. "Like it?"

She couldn't help but smell it. It had a musky smell, one she might associate with a sex goddess.

Renie shrugged and took out makeup and various makeup brushes from her bag, as well as a hairbrush.

Liam smiled and said, "I love to watch Renie work. She is such an artist and can do amazing things to enhance anyone's beauty." He rubbed his hands together, "Although I have dallied in art, which I'm sure you have already seen in the Billiard Room…."

Renie cut him off with a laugh. "I would not call your writing, *Quoth the Raven, 'Nevermore,*' art, Liam."

"Regardless, I can't wait to see what Renie does with someone who already is a beauty." He tapped the seat in front of the mirror. "Sit."

When she didn't move, he smiled. "You're not going to want to make this more enjoyable for me than it already is, are you? I'd love to force you into that chair, and trust me, it will be quite arousing."

She sat.

"Good girl. That's a very good girl. Enjoy this. All females like to be pampered. Consider this your time to be pampered. Pretend you're at a spa. You'll be at a real one sooner than you think." He laughed, such an eerie laugh it made her cringe.

She thought of Sandy and shook her head. "Did you leave the note at the front desk that said Sandy was fending off a migraine and was not to be disturbed?"

He laughed. "Smart cookie."

The fact that he kept messaging his knee gave Victoria some form of solace.

Renie kept Victoria's hair back with two large clips. She rubbed a very pale foundation onto Victoria's already pale skin. It made her almost ghostlike in appearance. Then she worked on Victoria's big brown eyes and made them appear even larger. The make-up was put on the way an artist would create a work of art. She thought briefly about the cover girl models. It couldn't be fun work, despite the illusion.

Renie smiled. "We're not there yet. You may be my most beautiful creation yet." She let out a long sigh of contentment. "The best is yet to come." Her eyes roamed Victoria's entire body, like a master sculptor examining her clay, picturing what would soon be born.

"One hundred strokes makes the hair glow naturally." She brushed Victoria's hair slowly, enjoying every stroke of what she thought of as her creation.

"Do you two belong to the same organization?"

This brought more laughter from Liam. "You might say that," he answered for Renie.

"How long have you known each other?"

Renie stopped and pulled Victoria's face toward her by her chin. Staring into Victoria's eyes, she said, "About as long as we have known you, which is quite a few years."

Stunned, she stared back. "I don't understand."

"Maybe not, but we have been following you very closely." She continued to stroke Victoria's hair with the wide brush. Under any other circumstances, it would have felt good.

"Beautiful, Renie. Why don't you dress the bride?"

Victoria clutched onto the seat of the chair. "I can dress myself."

Liam's laughter seemed to shake the room. "No, you can't. Plus, it wouldn't be as interesting if you dressed yourself. Renie is the artist. She will dress you. After all, you are her creation. I will not allow you to deprive her or me of the pleasure.

"Continue, Renie. Victoria, if you don't let her make you into what you must become, I will be forced to help. I must say, I would enjoy that more. I leave it up to you though. What will it be?"

She looked down at her hands. "I prefer Renie to you."

"I thought so. Continue then."

Renie laid out a large white shag rug. "Remove your boots please and stand on the rug."

Victoria did as she was told, carefully removing her boots so as not to lose her tools within. Unfortunately, a gun was not a part of her tool kit. Her mind floated back to Chuck Ramsey's last words as he was dragged from the courtroom, "The Raven will stop at nothing until he owns you Victoria—heart, soul, and body. Remember me when you belong to him. I'll see you in hell." When Ramsey was captured, he was wearing the same ring she saw on Liam and Renie, the same on Sissy—a raven with a diamond eye.

"Is Renie a nickname or your given name?" Victoria asked, standing in her socks on the white rug.

"My given name is Lenore."

"Like in Edgar Allen Poe's poem, *The Raven*."

"That's right. Can you remove your boot socks, please? They don't exactly match your wedding dress."

Victoria slipped off the socks.

"Now remove your warm-up outfit, please."

"Ah, now that's nice. See Renie, all her sit-ups, karate, and running really pays off. Beautiful. And no granny panties on this one. Remove the rest of it please."

Victoria didn't move.

"Do as he says, it won't work with the wedding dress." Renie pulled a gown out of a very narrow closet that seemed to be a part of the cupboard and beamed. "I designed this gown and hand stitched it myself."

Liam clapped. "It's a beautiful work of art, and it will look even better on the bride. Please continue."

She looked at the sheer dress, adorned with tiny Swarovski crystals laced as a trim, and centered on what would be her private area. *This looks like a dress Lady Gaga would wear*.

"Raise your arms and let me put this over your head."

She did as she was told. Renie pulled the dress down, smoothing the dress so that it fit like a second skin. It was a perfect fit. Renie picked up the locket around Victoria's neck. "Beautiful, if you like dogs. I prefer cats, black cats, and of course ravens. The dog will have to go." Renie jerked the necklace off her neck breaking the chain.

Totally stripped, Victoria thought. *I'm left with nothing but my training*.

Renie next pulled out a pair of sandals decorated with Swarovski crystals and handed them to Victoria. "Put these on."

She did as she was told. Under any other circumstance, she would have loved to try something like that on. They were incredible and must have cost a fortune, along with the materials in this gown. She stood.

She could see the pride in Renie as she beamed while placing a crown of Swarovski crystals on Victoria's head.

Liam clapped even louder than before. "Magnificent! The groom will be beside himself. Only one more thing is needed."

He reached in his pocket and pulled out a little box. "Your hand my dear." Victoria handed him her right hand. "No, I need your left ring finger. You will be presented to the groom complete, ring and all." When she didn't move, he reached over and grabbed her left hand holding it as if in a vice while he lifted the box top and removed a gold ring—a raven with a diamond eye.

Victoria had never been so frightened in her life. *Will anyone find me? With the beacon, I had hope.* She closed her eyes and prayed. As she prayed, she thought back over the previous couple of days. *Ah David, Father David, I know you are doing what you are supposed to do. Pray for me. Let God lead Christian to me, Brian, and Dennis too.*

She opened her eyes and caught Liam slowly taking her in. "Renie, you outdid yourself with this one. She will make an exquisite bride. Come, Victoria, the groom awaits."

He turned the raven knob, and the cabinet opened into an ornate elevator. Renie grabbed Dennis by the back of the collar, and dragged him into the elevator. "He can be useful," she said with a grin.

While her captors were distracted, she pulled off a few crystals, placed them in strategic locations, and slid the necklace toward the elevator with her sandal.

They entered the elevator and the doors closed behind them. Victoria tried to count floors. Three floors down, the elevator stopped, and the doors opened.

Chapter 29

When the footsteps and voices diminished, Christian stepped out of his cramped hiding place. He needed to find the area where Victoria's beacon first became live. He studied the key map with his flashlight. *Interesting map. It not only lays out the rooms, but tunnels, vents, and windows. I guess the hermit liked being alone, but didn't want to stay in rock for all eternity. He left this for his Indian friend. Smart man. Looks like it's his study.*

He checked his watch. He'd been gone almost an hour. There was quite a distance between the storage area he found himself in and the study. All told, there are about seven rooms and an equivalent number of tunnels or crawl spaces, with only a few exits to the outside. It seemed the hermit did allow himself a few escape routes equally separated in his mountain home.

Stealth-like, he made his way down the hallway. *I wonder where the man and woman are? I wonder who they are. Not remembering where I heard her voice is really bothering me, but first things first. I need to get to Victoria and find Brian.* He stopped at the curve in the bend and listened.

Silence.

If the man and woman went to the study for Victoria, I should hear something, even if it's muffled. Maybe they were heading elsewhere first. That would be best for me. I could get her out.

He slid down the wall in a crouched position and put on his night vision glasses. Slowly, he peered around the corner.

Nothing.

In front of the "study," he noticed the room had a deadbolt that wasn't locked. He stopped and listened.

Nothing. He slowly opened the door. It was empty. He entered, his eyes taking everything in. This room had been occupied recently.

He removed his night vision glasses and placed them on top of his head. After he let his eyes refocus, he took out his high-powered flashlight and carefully examined the corner that caught his interest. Cut ropes lay heaped in a pile. He squatted down and picked them up. They were frayed in such a manner that they were probably cut by a pocketknife of some sort. There was pink fuzz caught in the cord. This confirmed that Victoria was in fact here. This was the same color as her warm-up jacket.

Rolled in the corner was the cap to most likely a perfume bottle or something similar. Christian smiled to himself. She was using the tools Elizabeth gave her.

Christian stood and made his way back to the door, carefully examining the lock. It was picked. *Good going, Victoria.* She must have gotten herself out of this room. *But were you alone? Were you caught? Did you find someone else?*

There was a little window, so this was where she most likely was when the beacon picked her up. His phone vibrated. A text came through from David. *Victoria's last signal.* Christian checked his map. It was from the kitchen. He shook his head leaving the room behind and settled the night vision goggles back on.

The hermit's bedroom was just on the right. That door contained a modern lock as well. *Someone definitely uses this place, and it doesn't seem to be for wholesome purposes.* It was unlocked. He stopped, listened, and entered.

There was nothing more than a cot in the corner, a shelf just above it, and a cupboard right across. The cot had impressions on it. *Are these recent or from years past?* The modern lock and supplies indicated that this area was being used. This room must have been used as well. He checked his map. The kitchen should be coming up.

Based on the map, he had arrived. There was an exterior pull lock that could secure someone inside, but it wasn't drawn over. He turned the handle and slowly opened it.

Nothing.

Victoria was supposed to be here. This was the last known beacon signal.

He opened each of the cabinets looking for a clue to something. In a chest, he found wet and bloodied clothing. There were also empty Band-Aid wrappers and a water bottle. The clothes belonged to a man. He lifted the clothes with his gloved hand careful not to smear any evidence that might be present. Too small to be Brian's. They either put Victoria in these clothes or they had someone else hostage as well. The blood was fresh.

The door to the pantry containing the tunnel was open, and he looked inside, listening for any sounds from the room below. He looked around and made sure he put everything back in the exact same spot it was in when he found it. It was best to be able to take these people by surprise.

He slipped into the tunnel and quietly made his way to the opening of the room below. He stopped and listened. The scampering of a mouse was the only thing he heard. He dropped his head down, slowly turning to inspect every inch before letting himself down.

Nothing.

No one is here. Where have they taken her? Victoria was not here, but there was blood on the wall opposite the tunnel. The blood was fresh. It might belong to whoever was wearing the bloodied clothes in the kitchen. He lifted himself back into the tunnel and followed it back to the kitchen.

Standing just before the opening he looked around once again. For the second time he opened each cupboard, but there was nothing. He removed his glasses and brought out the flashlight.

Pink fiber was caught in the tunnel in two trails as if it came from her knees. There was a petrified piece of wood that had red on the end. It looked like paint. Maybe a nail polish scuff. She was wearing red nail polish. It looked as if she had been pulled out of the tunnel. Perhaps she'd been making her way into it and got caught and dragged out.

He squatted down to examine the floor more thoroughly. Faint scuff marks, probably from the boots she was wearing. *Based on the fiber, she's still in her pink outfit, so there must be someone else who is injured.*

These are drag marks coupled with marks that appear as though someone dug in. Perhaps there was a struggle. It stops in the middle of the room. He felt the candle wicks in the candles along the shelves. Warm. There was a makeup top and something glittering. He picked it up. A crystal. He looked carefully along the floor. Another crystal leading to the wooden cupboard. The narrow door to the right of it was shut, but not properly latched, as if someone had been in a hurry. He opened it.

On the floor in a ball was Victoria's pink warm-up. Her boots were under it. Christian peered inside the boots. There was a zipper compartment along the side. He unzipped it and found Victoria's tools. In front of the cupboard, he noticed something shiny. He squatted down and lifted the chain off the ground. On the end was a pendant of a dog that was described to him as the beacon. It was on, and this was one reason the beacon led here. This was an odd place for it.

Victoria, was this thrown here by your kidnappers, or did you intentionally put this here for direction? If so, where is it leading? It stops right in front of the cupboard, but the door doesn't open. There's no lock, so no key. He rubbed his hands along the top and bottom of the shelves. *Wait a minute. This is a wooden cupboard. Nothing from the time of the hermit was wood except for his chairs, and that looked old. This is new cabinetry. The knob to the cupboard has a raven on it. We've seen this before.* He pulled the knob even harder trying to open the cupboard, but it wouldn't open. *Let me try turning the knob.* The door opened to an elevator shaft.

Christian sent his partner a message. "Be on standby. Put one in air with Team 1. Scope out ridge where beacon last signaled. She's not with beacon, but I believe she is below where I am standing. See if a heat sensor can detect human activity. At my signal make entry."

He next sent a text to David. "Going in."

"Wait for me. Evil present. Must be there."

"Get here *stat*. In hermit kitchen. Directions follow…"

****

David's silhouette appeared at the door. "Hey."

"Good to see you, bro. Under normal circumstances I would have handled it myself, but after what I witnessed earlier and seeing what was in that sub-basement, I know we're up against something in two worlds, ours and another."

"No doubt."

He grabbed David's arm, noticing the prayer book and rosary and spoke in hushed tones. "Are you in for a little cave climbing, or I should say, a descent?"

"Whatever it takes."

"Good. I put my team on alert and they're close by, but I don't want anyone hurt. I found Victoria's clothing and boots. There's a makeup mirror." He pointed to the mirror as he spoke. "And evidence of a makeover. I believe they may be preparing her for something frightful. I found her necklace with the beacon, so she is no longer wearing it, but everything points down that shaft."

David tucked his prayer book and rosary inside his pocket. He took out the holy water with salt and oil and anointed the opening of the shaft with prayer. "Let's go," he said as he grabbed for the steel cable.

"Me first, little brother."

Christian descended silently, stopping on the roof of the elevator car. David followed. Christian removed the emergency exit door at his feet and lowered himself inside. The car itself did not have a door, but where it stopped did. The door wasn't closed all the way, and they could hear a choir of some sort creating eerie chant-like sounds. A man was speaking in Latin.

David listened and grabbed Christian's arm. "It's a satanic marriage ritual," he whispered with an edge to his voice. "We have to do something."

"That's why we're here. I need to scope out the area to see what our best form of attack is. Keep listening to what is said. I'm glad you learned Latin."

Christian crouched and slowly rounded the corner. He wasn't gone long, it only seemed that way to David. He listened and prayed for wisdom and a safe rescue. There was no doubt in his mind the bride was his beloved Victoria.

"You're right, little brother. I counted a hooded choir of nine. There is a wedding going on, and Victoria is the bride. There is a man strapped onto a table naked."

David cocked his head listening. "We need to act fast. The person performing the ceremony plans on sealing it with a beating heart."

"This is what I propose. You use that gift the good Lord gave you, and I'll use mine. Hopefully my team will find their way in before it's all over."

"Remember, Christian, pray." He took his prayer book, holy water, salt, and oil. He rubbed the oil and sprinkled the holy water and salt over the doorway to the place where it was all happening, praying in earnest.

He then entered the room praying and sprinkling the holy salted water. As he walked in, he saw Victoria first. David's breath caught for a moment. They had her in white, but it certainly wasn't something a bride would be seen wearing in public. She was frightened.

The naked man lay behind the satanic priest performing the ceremony. A rather large knife rested on a satin pillow along the side of the man. Victoria's right hand and right leg were tied to the hooded groom.

As David entered praying, the ceremony paused and the priest turned to him. "Begone, you coward. You lost your chance with Victoria. She is now ours." He laughed. "Maybe you'd like to be a witness to the wedding?"

He continued to pray, sprinkling sacramentals as he went. "*Kyrie eleison,* God, our Lord, King of ages, All-powerful and All-mighty…"

The satanic priest pointed at the smallest of the hooded choir and said, "Constrain him. Let him be tormented as he watches the love of his life marry someone so much better than he. Raven, my lord, show him what will be in store for her."

The little one grabbed David with incomprehensible strength. He knew that type of strength could only come from one source, Satan himself. Father David prayed and watched. The groom turned toward him and removed his hood. David gasped, "I knew something was wrong the moment I met you. It didn't feel right. There was no peace, only discontent. I sensed your essence, pure evil."

The groom looked at Victoria and said, "I've been waiting for this a long time. You are mine."

She looked at the groom in disgust. "You have got to be kidding me. You are the Raven! Brian trusted you! Elizabeth trusted you! Sandy trusted you! Do you really think that just because you want me, you can have me? Not! I will never belong to you, you spineless worm!" And she spit in his face.

The Raven struck her with his right hand and grabbed the back of her head and pulled it close. "Don't fight me. If you do, we'll share in two hearts."

She looked at David, constrained by the little Renie. She pulled away from David's face and glared at the Raven, fear turning to challenge. "I won't fight you, but I'll never belong to you."

The Raven laughed. "This is just a taste of what's in store for you, made better by the presence of your former love." The Raven kissed her with the pent up passion he possessed for too many years. "You will enjoy me as I enjoy you."

The groom looked back at David and grinned an evil grin. "It excites me no end to have you witness the greatest moment of my life."

****

Christian made his way down the narrow hall he spotted earlier. *Hopefully, this will bring me around behind that priest or whatever he is.* There was a door on his right, but the hall continued down and turned abruptly to the left. The floor was pitched, steadily gaining altitude. He needed his flashlight at this point. The lighting at the lower level was just not making it.

The tunnel came to an abrupt end. There was a ladder. Christian followed the rungs of the ladder with his flashlight until it came to a circular hatch. It was the type of hatch seen on submarines. He quickly moved up the rungs and turned the wheel on the hatch. Using all the strength he could muster, he pushed it up and over. A grin spread across his face as he sent his partner, Joe, a message.

The hole was camouflaged well and would be hard to find, even with the lid open. Christian reached in his pocket and pulled out Victoria's locket containing the beacon. "Thank you Lord! David said you answered prayers."

He left the latch open and hurried down to the door he had seen earlier. It was locked, so he took out his lock picking tool kit, and released the lock. He pushed the door open. There was a glow of light coming from a group of candles. Christian carefully slipped inside. As he looked around, he saw another door which must open to the area where David was. A gurney sat next to it. Someone was on the gurney. There was an I.V. hooked up to whoever was in the bed.

He approached carefully and sent up another prayer of thanks. "Brian, it's Christian. Are you all right?"

Brian moaned and slightly turned his head toward him.

"Do you understand me?" Christian looked into glazed eyes.

Brian's lips had trouble forming words, they made a motor sound like you make when you are playing with an infant. He was alive, but they had drugged him with something. Christian carefully removed the I.V. "Ah, poor buddy, you've lost weight."

Brian tried to talk.

"Don't worry; I'll get you out of here." He wrapped him in the blanket, and put him over his shoulders using the fireman's carry. He moved quickly, getting Brian up and out that escape he found and gently laid him on the ground. He messaged Joe and received one in return. "Just minutes from you. Will get Brian."

265

"I need to get back in there. Help is on the way."

He moaned again, trying to talk. He was getting agitated as he tried to hold Christian's sleeve.

He looked down and touched Brian's hand. "What is it?"

Brian tried to talk. Christian bent his head down to listen.

Christian raised his head and looked at Brian intently. "Are you trying to tell me he's the killer known as the Raven?"

Brian nodded slightly.

"I've got to get back in there. Joe will be right here. Don't worry."

Christian came back down the tunnel and into the room where he had found Brian. He approached the other door and quietly cracked it open. The chanting was getting louder. The door opened to an area that looked like the back stage of a theater.

Just perfect. Heavy drapes, the ones he saw behind the table with the naked man, were right before him. The drapes left an opening. Christian peered through and saw David praying. His prayers got louder, but amazingly, a little cloaked person held him.

Christian crept below the table holding the naked man. He was frightened and his eyes widened even further when he realized Christian was there. He held his finger to his lips and motioned for him to continue to look up, as he had been doing. Christian released him from his bindings and whispered. "Don't move until you see my signal, then get off the table as fast as you can and run through those drapes."

David shouted, "Begone! I command you in the name of God, our Almighty Father, Creator of the heavens and the earth!"

The person restraining David dropped to the floor. The Raven turned and grabbed Victoria to himself with the hand bound to Victoria's and reached for the knife.

Christian shouted, "Now!"

The naked man rolled off the table and onto the floor. Christian dove for the knife while David tackled the Raven at his knees. He released his tight grip on Victoria, although she followed suit, since their hands and feet were still bound.

Just then, the team Joe had in place came through the doors, rifles poised. The hooded choir attacked with knives and guns concealed within their robes. David cut Victoria loose while Christian took pleasure in cuffing Peter Mack, otherwise known as the Raven.

Shots rang out as the team took a defensive stand against the hooded ruffians. Out of the original nine, five were dead. Victoria stared at the little one and looked back toward David and Christian.

"That's Renie. She was the wedding planner for Elizabeth's and Brian's wedding and also helped out serving. And that"—she spat as she wiped her mouth with the back of her hand—"is the psycho who likes to call himself the Raven."

She gave him the most pitying stare she could muster as she stood. "You disgust me, you worthless excuse of a man." David took off his jacket and covered her, averting his eyes. Christian noticed the naked man crouched in the corner and handed him the sheet from the table. "You better cover yourself; you might catch cold. Who are you, by the way?"

"Dennis Ryder. Very pleased to meet you, sir. Thank you," he stammered.

Movement caught Victoria's eye as she saw Liam heading for the elevator. His limp gave her satisfaction as she shouted, "Grab him!"

Joe had just entered when he saw what was happening. He ran after the guy, threw himself on top of him and knocked him to the ground, grabbing him in a headlock. Joe smiled and nodded to Christian. "Who have we here?"

Victoria held David's jacket close as she swiftly joined Joe who was just getting up with his catch. "That is Liam Newinn, Jacqueline's date." She moved closer to him. "You sure enjoyed the benefits of my training earlier, but you didn't get the full effect." She smiled a lopsided smile, dropped the jacket, and hiked her gown high enough to free her legs. She spun and kicked him where it counted. He doubled over grabbing himself as she picked up David's jacket and pulled it together. Taking off the ring, she threw it at him.

"Now you can experience the full effect of what I consider art, and I can admire my own hard work."

One of Christian's team members ran after them. "Christian, we have a problem."

"What is it?"

"Two of the hooded participants got away from us; one was the person performing the ceremony."

Victoria stopped. "I would bet you it's Teddy Whyler and Sissy Tram." Victoria looked at Liam. "Am I right?"

"As if I'm going to tell you." He pushed out a half-hearted laugh.

"Give me a hand, will you?" Christian asked David as he yanked Peter up. "Your cohorts left you, Peter. Who are they and where did they go?"

"Get real. Do you think I'd tell you? You haven't heard the last of me."

Christian got rough with him as he threw him into the hands of one of his backup team members.

"We better get back to Elizabeth. Two escaped and they are desperate enough to take another to sacrifice in the hopes of incurring Satan's favor." Victoria turned on her heels to leave, but Christian caught her arm.

"Let's take the quickest route and exit the way my team came in."

Joe handed over Liam to another and caught up with the three of them. "You may need my help. And I have two ATVs in my chopper."

"Why would you bring those?" David asked.

"Christian suggested it. He thought they might prove helpful." He gave them a crooked grin.

They ran to the chopper and Joe let out the ramp. He and Christian climbed on board; each jumped on an ATV, cranked it up, and drove it off. "David, hop on," Joe called.

"Victoria, I'm not leaving you behind," Christian called.

Victoria hiked up her gown, jumped on back, and put her arms around Christian's waist and held tight. "Ready." His muscles were so defined she felt them through his clothing. *You have to work out actively to maintain this type of body. No doubt, I can get lost in him—physically and emotionally. What would life be like with him? Hmmm. Do I want to find out?*

They sped down the trail toward the hotel. Stopping in front, they jumped off the ATVs and ran up the front stairs, into the hotel, and up to the second floor. A loud crash sounded from room 222. Sneakers and other hard articles were strewn on the floor outside the room. Christian, Joe, and David ran in first.

A man had his arm around Elizabeth's neck with a knife touching her throat. His back was to the opened front window. "You will step back and let us go, or she dies."

Christian smiled. "You must be Teddy Whyler."

The man smiled. "Why would you think that?"

"Just by the powers of deduction."

"Who I am is irrelevant. What is relevant is that you must step back and let us leave."

Victoria had sized up the situation and spotted Elizabeth and the man. She knew she needed to get to the window from the outside and she knew just how she could do it, the fire escape. She grabbed her sneakers, which were among the stuff strewn on the floor, slipped off the sandals, slid into the sneakers, and ran to the adjacent room.

I have never been so thankful for my gymnastics and karate as I am right now. She tried the door and found it wasn't latched all the way. She gently pushed it open and ran to the window, opened it, and carefully climbed out. Holding onto the fire escape, she cautiously shimmied toward her best friend and the man.

Christian was still talking to him, but the man was getting more agitated. When she peered through the window Christian saw her. Using a directional signal, she let him know where she intended to strike. She needed both hands, so she steadied herself on the fire escape, hooked her leg through the rail, and in a quick motion, boxed the man's ears. As she made her move, Christian went for the knife and Joe dove for his knees.

Teddy screamed in pain and went down as Christian grabbed his wrist with the knife, brought his arms behind him, and cuffed him. Simultaneously, David grabbed Elizabeth and rolled her off to the side and out of harm's way. Joe tied up Teddy's ankles.

Victoria climbed through the window, trying to rub the circulation back into her hands and legs.

Elizabeth pushed herself up. "Sissy, get to Sissy's room, fast."

"Just a minute." Christian bound Teddy to the bed.

"Joe, do you mind watching him? Police should be here shortly."

"My pleasure," he said, grabbing the pistol from his belt. He released the safety and trained it on Teddy.

Victoria tossed her hair as she turned to look at him. "Let's go guys, Elizabeth."

The three of them quickly caught up to Victoria who grabbed Elizabeth by the hand. "Brian's going to be just fine. They're taking him to National Lux Medical Center."

"Thank God."

Up one more flight of stairs, and they were at Sissy's room. Christian stood to the side of the door, and waved David to the other side. The ladies stayed farther over.

Christian held up his hand, counting one, two, three, and kicked in the door.

Sissy turned around quickly with a gun in her hand. "Stop where you are. I'm not afraid to use this."

Her hand shook. Victoria approached the door and stepped inside. "Sissy, you don't want to do this."

She laughed. "Of course I do. What other option do I have?"

"Drop the gun, and turn yourself in. You can cut a deal for yourself. You weren't the instigator, you were used."

"No, I wasn't. I didn't do anything wrong but fall in love."

"He's a murderer, Sissy. Although Peter is the Raven, Teddy was his accomplice and right hand person, responsible for killing many women. By association, you are guilty."

"That's ridiculous. Teddy's no murderer."

"Your denial won't change the facts."

"Not possible." Her hand shook. "I didn't even know about that. Teddy and I were to be married in Switzerland."

Elizabeth piped in. "Sissy, have you ever been in the sub-basement of my new building?"

"No. Why, should I have been?"

Victoria added, "If you had been, you would know that Teddy is not capable of love."

Sissy shook her head side to side. "We were getting married. He wouldn't marry me if he didn't love me."

"Have you ever thought that he just might be marrying you to use the marital privilege? You're a lawyer. You know that means you could not be made to testify against him."

Sissy sniffed and broke into sobs letting her gun hand drop. Christian stepped up and took the gun from her hand.

Joe appeared at the door. "Police finally arrived. Another one coming down the hall."

Victoria smiled at the officer entering the room. "You'll want to book her."

The officer read Sissy her rights, cuffed her, and led her out the door.

Joe rubbed his hands together. "Elizabeth, I'm sure you're interested in a lift to your groom. Shall we?" He bowed and swept his arm toward the door.

Elizabeth turned to Victoria. "Do you mind?"

"Of course not. You go. I'll get out of this dress, pack your stuff, and be there shortly." She gave her a hug. "Get going."

Joe held out his arm and Elizabeth took it. "Madame, your air limo is just outside."

After Joe and Elizabeth left, Victoria started to twirl her hair. "Guys, I have an idea."

Chapter 30

Brian was sitting up, waiting to be officially released from the hospital when Victoria knocked on his hospital room door. Elizabeth was at his side, holding his hand.

"How are the love birds?" she asked, giving them each a hug.

"Couldn't be better." Brian provided his famous lopsided grin. "Just glad to be finally leaving. A hospital stay was not in my itinerary." He looked at Elizabeth and gave her a kiss. "We are ready to get back to our lives.

A rap sounded at the door and the doctor entered. "I bet you're ready to get out."

"You got that right, doctor."

"I understand that Ms. Bailey here will be taking you home." The doctor smiled at Victoria and winked. "I have the wheelchair outside the door, and I've already signed off on your release. I'll be doing the honors of wheeling you out today."

Elizabeth cocked her head. "Doctor, isn't that highly unusual?"

"I wouldn't say highly unusual, but unusual, yes. We've got something going on that's taking up staff time, and I thought that with all you've been through, you'd rather me push you rather than wait any longer."

"Absolutely," Brian said as he got up from the bed

274

and walked over to the chair.

Brian followed the doctor's direction with a smile and sat. The doctor set the foot rests so he could get his feet off the ground and they were ready.

The doctor steered the wheelchair to the elevator. "What's the first thing you want to do when you get out of here?"

"That's easy." Brian took Elizabeth's hand and smiled. "Take up where we left off before this horrific ordeal."

"Sounds good to me." He pressed the button.

The door opened and Victoria, then Elizabeth got in. The doctor pushed Brian in and rotated him so that he could continue to talk to Elizabeth. He turned his back on Brian, inserted a key, and pressed the top button, authorized only by certain personnel. The lovebirds were so engrossed in new plans, that they didn't notice. Victoria watched and nodded to the doctor. He turned and gave her his infectious smile.

The elevator started moving up. It stopped at the top. When the doors opened, they were hit by the wind from the helicopter props.

Brian shouted something, but they could not hear him above the noise.

Victoria led the way to the helicopter while the doctor followed with Brian and Elizabeth. She waved at the pilot. "Hey, Joe. Thanks for coming."

"Definitely my pleasure," he said grinning.

Brian asked, "What's going on here?"

The doctor released the footrests and looked at his patient. "You said you wanted to take off where you left off. That is precisely what Ms. Bailey arranged for you to do."

Brian and Elizabeth looked at Victoria with a perplexed expression.

She chuckled. "Your ride awaits."

Brian approached the helicopter door and looked at the pilot. "Joe, I haven't seen you in a while. What are you doing here?"

"You might not have seen me, but I have definitely seen you. I was among the crew who rescued you and brought you here. You were out of it, so I don't expect you to remember much. This will be a much nicer ride, I promise. Please get in."

Brian and Elizabeth climbed aboard and settled into the back row. Victoria climbed into the front with Joe, snapped her belt on, and turned to the doctor. "Thanks for helping."

"No problem. I love stuff like this. I'm a romantic at heart."

They all waved as the chopper lifted off.

"Where are we heading?"

Victoria turned and smiled. "You'll see. It won't be a long ride."

They headed toward the mountains. "No wonder you love flying. When you see the view from here, you have to know that something this magnificent could not have happened by spontaneous combustion. There has to be a God, the Creator of all this." Victoria held her hand out front, palm up.

"Yes, ma'am. I have to agree."

Elizabeth pointed. "There's the Preston Hotel!"

"Yes, it is," Joe said as he turned the helicopter to the left.

"I thought that was our destination." She looked deflated.

"Sorry to disappoint," Joe said and gave Victoria a side glance and wink.

She grinned.

Joe started to bring the helicopter down.

"Isn't that St. Malo's?"

Victoria twisted in her seat to face Elizabeth. "Sure is."

Joe landed the chopper in a predetermined location near the chapel, Saint Catherine Siena's Chapel at St. Malo's, also known as the Chapel on the Rock.

Victoria saw the horse drawn carriage parked in front and enjoyed the shocked expression on her best friend's face.

Elizabeth shook her head. "You didn't."

"I didn't, we did." She pointed to the front of the chapel as the rest of the bridesmaids came running down.

When the passengers disembarked, Samantha ran up and looped her arm into Elizabeth's. "Come with me. We don't have much time."

Father David and Christian came out next. Brian met them halfway. "I don't know how to thank you for all you've done."

David smiled. "What are friends for," he said as he grabbed Brian in a hug.

"You're back, Christian?"

"Yes. Obviously I had unfinished business. And, since your best man is rather tied up, I'm available." He grabbed Brian in a hug.

"I wouldn't want anyone other than you. Thanks." Tears filled Brian's eyes.

****

Victoria stood back and watched Christian, a

feeling of pleasure and anticipation overwhelmed her. She was free to love, and love she did. The possibilities were endless…God certainly was good.

Christian cocked his head toward Victoria, gave her his crooked smile, and walked toward her. She smiled and closed the space between them, drawn like a magnet. He took her by the shoulders and stared deep into her eyes. "I have loved you forever." Lowering his head, he held her tight and kissed her with such passion her soul shook. Her response matched his, giving as much as she took.

He pulled away out of breath and cupped her face in his hands. "I need to ask you something."

"Ask me what? You can't ignite the fuse and pull away. Do you know what you do to me?"

Grinning, he said, "No more than you do to me." Kneeling, he took her hands in his. "Will you marry me?"

Shocked, she could barely speak. "Yes," came out in a whisper.

"I was hoping you'd say that." He reached in his pocket, pulled out a black velvet box, and opened it.

Her mouth dropped open. "It's gorgeous." She picked it up and just stared at the heart shaped diamond accented with emerald cut diamonds in a wide band.

"May I?" He took the ring and placed it on her left hand.

"It's perfect." She looked up at him.

"Yeah, I thought so. If you noticed, it's a little wider than a typical engagement ring, which leads me to my second question."

With a raised eyebrow, she asked, "Wow, I thought this was the big question."

"Not quite. Will you marry me now?"

"You mean right now?"

"You aren't the only one who's been planning. I will not risk losing you ever again. Your family is here, and your mother brought her wedding gown, the one worn by your grandmother."

"What about Elizabeth and Brian? This is their special day."

"I just ran it by them. They are as excited as I am about the possibilities. What do you say?"

"Yes!"

He took her hand and placed it in the crook of his arm. "I was hoping you'd say that too. I love you more than life itself."

Chapter 31

Three months later, the wind caught Victoria's hair as she walked out of the courthouse. She couldn't even get a full lung of air. The reporters penetrated her personal space with microphones and questions.

"Ms. Bailey, how did it feel to be in the witness stand looking out, rather than the attorney looking in for a change?"

"I prefer my usual station as the attorney, but I feel good that justice has been served."

"When did you realize that the Raven had accomplices?"

"When my associate, Sandy, was murdered." Her eyes swelled, and she quickly brushed a tear from her face. "Sorry."

"We should be the ones sorry. Your tears just make you human."

Victoria nodded.

"Did you ever doubt your initial prosecution of Chuck Ramsey?"

"No. I knew I prosecuted the right man. What I didn't realize and Sandy surmised was that there was more than one murderer...The man personally responsible for orchestrating all of the murders was Peter Mack, also known as the Raven, with the help of his right hand man, Teddy Whyler, owner of Starlight, Limited. I'm relieved the jury spent only a little time finding Peter guilty of first degree murder for the death of Sandy Forrester."

She brushed the strand of hair out of her eyes, faced the mountains, and breathed in the crisp air. Thankfully, the air was at a level green today, instead of yesterday's red.

Although she longed to get out of there, the reporter was relentless. "How about the involvement of Sissy Tram, an associate in your new firm, Gregory, Cane, and Mack?"

"The firm name is no longer Gregory, Cane, and Mack, but is now Gregory, Cane, and Bailey," Victoria said with a smile. "Sissy and Teddy were found guilty for the kidnapping of Brian Gregory, and charges will be brought for Teddy's involvement in the Raven murders. He was after all the high priest and accomplice in the murders."

"Does it bother you that Sissy Tram, your associate, was given leniency for a deal she cut for her testimony?"

"Not at all. And, by the way, she's a former associate and she may not be an attorney for long. Her license to practice law has been suspended pending an investigation."

"Thank you, Ms. Bailey." The reporter turned full face to the camera with the courthouse in the background.

As Victoria slowly continued down the stairs, she heard the reporter say, "Not only do we have closure on the Raven murders so we can all breathe a sigh of relief, but the case against Mr. Peter Mack is rich in Colorado history dating back to the turn of the twentieth century. You might even consider it similar to the legendary

Hatfield and McCoy feud with one exception; one of the parties didn't even know the feud was ongoing."

The reporter's summary was interrupted when Brian and Elizabeth left the building. Victoria turned around and watched the reporter shove the microphone into Brian's face. "Ah, Mr. Gregory, may we please have a word with you?"

Victoria admired Brian's patience. "Sure."

"Mr. Gregory, we have all been following this case very closely. You were partners with a serial killer responsible for taking the life of your associate, and you were kidnapped and drugged at his behest. Amazingly, he did it to take what was in a Swiss bank account belonging to your family. Your grandfather, Alexander Gregory, opened this account with strict instructions; only you could open it. What was in that account?"

Brian smiled with a glint in his eyes. "I haven't opened it yet."

"Aren't you curious about what you might find inside?"

"Right now, I only have one thing on my mind, and that is focusing on my lovely bride and helping her do the final touches for the grand opening of Evergreen Pooch Paradise next week. We hope you'll join us."

"I wouldn't miss it for the world."

Victoria took a few more steps down, then stopped, and turned at the sound of her name. "Victoria, wait up!" Elizabeth called. "Why are you just running off like that?"

"I thought you and Brian needed time alone after this ordeal, and didn't want you to feel that you had to include me."

"Nonsense." Elizabeth gave her a hug and turned to

Brian.

Brian reached inside his suit jacket pocket and removed a folded piece of paper. "By the way, a mutual friend asked me to give this to you."

She opened the note in her hand. "Meet me at the coffee shop on the corner. D."

"Do you want to join us for lunch?" Elizabeth asked.

"No." Victoria smiled. "I've got plans. See you guys later." Her smile never left as she briskly made her way to the coffee shop.

She stopped abruptly at the door, took a deep breath, and entered. She let her eyes adjust to the dim light and found him sitting at a booth in the corner. He waved, and she made her way between the tables. He stood and gave her a hug and kiss on the cheek.

"I wanted to see you before I leave." David held out a chair for her.

"That's good." She sat across and viewed him with new eyes and a new heart. She looked at him with the warmth and love that close friends would share, an agape love.

She looked down at her hands resting in her lap. "You and I had something very special. At one time I thought it was a once in a lifetime thing." She looked up. "Until Christian."

"God works in mysterious ways. I've had a heavy heart myself because of the immature way I handled the revelation of God's calling on my life. I just wanted to say I'm so sorry I put you through years of anger."

"Apology accepted. I forgave you back in Eustis Park, you know, when I realized that you, Father David, are where you belong. You are doing what you are intended to do. I don't regret anything, not even the anger. Sometimes anger is a good thing. Jesus got angry and overturned the tables in the temple area. It's when anger festers and turns inward that it creates hardships. That's what I did wrong, and that was my choice not yours. I felt rejected and didn't handle it properly. I blamed all men for how wrongly I perceived I was treated."

She tipped her head and gave him that familiar look. "You know, what we shared was special. I have wonderful memories, and it helped shape who I am today. Professionally, I believe I am doing what God wants me to do as well. Personally, I now understand what Elizabeth tried to tell me. The love I have for Christian is different from what I shared with you. No offense, but your brother is amazing in more ways than one. We both felt something the first time we met in Hammes Bookstore. You and I were never meant to be together...I just never saw it."

"I agree. You are in your element."

"Yeah, well, I remember that story of Jonah in the belly of the whale. He could have gone to Nineveh when God asked him to go the easy way. But no, he didn't want to go and ran. But you already know what I have just come to know."

"And that is?"

"That God has plans for each of us. Eventually we will follow God's will even if we have to get there the hard way, like Jonah. God wanted him to be a missionary to the Ninevites and God brought him there the hard way, in the belly of the whale. Ultimately, Jonah did as God intended. I may have gotten to where I am today the hard way, but I believe I also am doing what God wants me to do. We know what your calling is, but what are your plans?"

"Although I work with the dark sacrament, it's Jesus who is the exorcist; he will use me as his instrument. The Mother Church has asked me to work in that field and train others. It's a dark world and people need the light. One of my first assignments is Elizabeth's building. The sub-basement has been totally gutted. I am performing an exorcism of the entire building."

"I thought just people could be exorcised."

"The Ritual deals with exorcism of people and blessing of places, but in certain circumstances, like this one, I like to do more than bless the place. There are about ten prayers in the Ritual that ask the Lord to protect places from evil influences. I'll use a few of these prayers and modify the first part of the initial exorcism of individuals so that it addresses a building."

"How does that work? Do you just do it at the entrance of the building?"

"No. I'll exorcise every room just as if it were a regular house blessing. Finally, I'll celebrate a mass there."

"Let me know when you have that mass. Christian and I'll be there for it."

"I'd like that."

"I understand now that this is your calling and all, but after what we went through, have you had second thoughts?"

"Not really. It is frightening, but, as you discovered, when God calls you to do something, you can go the easy way or the hard way. Always remember, with God all things are possible."

"Amen to that, brother."

"Speaking of brothers, when are you and Christian going on that honeymoon?"

"No plans yet. He's been out of the country finishing up a case."

"What are you doing tonight?"

"I was just planning on having a quiet evening."

The bells on the cafe's door chimed and Victoria looked up. Christian stood there with that crooked smile of his. "Hello, beautiful!" He crossed the room and pulled her to her feet and kissed her. She tasted mint and felt a sense of purpose.

David cleared his throat.

Christian released his bride and gave his brother an embrace. "Good to see you, bro, and thanks."

Perplexed over the glance the brothers shared she looked at her husband questioning. With a sparkle in his eye, he picked her up and headed for the door. Over his shoulder he said, "We'll call you, David, when we get back from our honeymoon!"

Letter to the Reader

I hope you enjoyed *Hidden Bloodlines*. The modern characters in this story are fictitious. Any resemblance to someone you may know, or have heard of, is purely coincidental. However, some of the historical characters actually lived, and others reflect historical characters under fictitious names. The stories surrounding the historic characters are part of Estes Park's history and folklore. The hermit is another historical character who also spent time in the area; however, he did not reside within the ridges adjacent to the hotel property. To my knowledge, there are no rooms and tunnels within this ridge. Elizabeth's poster dog is real. He was my family dog adopted from Poodle Rescue. Although the Horse Whisperer is an entirely fictitious character, the Ute Indians were a tribe native to the area. Their medicine men actually participated in vision quests.

The retreat in Poland, established to train exorcists, does in fact exist. The Ritual referenced in this book was used by Catholic priests in the performance of exorcisms. The forms of demonic possession, demonstrated by the character Jimmy, are based on documented cases.

The Chapel on the Rock at St. Malo's, more traditionally known as Saint Catherine of Siena's Chapel, exists and has been visited by many dignitaries, including Pope John Paul II.

Although Eustis Park and the Preston Hotel are fictitious places, the Preston Hotel is inspired by the historic Stanley Hotel, registered as the second most haunted hotel in the country, and is located in Estes

Park, Colorado. Although I have stayed in the hotel many times, I have not seen any ghosts...yet.

A word about the author…

Karen Van Den Heuvel's diverse experiences as an attorney, certified civil mediator, registered dietician, teacher, speaker, and published author with more than twenty years' experience in the corporate, government, and private sectors have fueled her desire to help people live fuller, richer lives. She lives with her husband in Colorado.